Dear Reader,

There's a place where life moves a little slower, where a neighborly smile and a friendly hello can still be heard. Where news of a wedding or a baby on the way is a reason to celebrate—and gossip travels faster than a telegram! Where hope lives in the heart, and love's promises last a lifetime.

The year is 1874, and the place is Harmony, Kansas . . .

A TOWN CALLED HARMONY

PASSING FANCY

Suzanna Lind's an expert at farming—and comes to help out her new neighbor, a stuffy Englishman who doesn't know a bushel from a billy goat . . .

Edward Winchester came to Harmony to make his fortune on the Double B farm—and finds it's much harder than it seems in his farming manuals . . .

Reluctantly hiring Zan to show him the ropes, Edward is galled when this sassy tomboy—in a ponytail and men's dungarees, no less—snaps that he'll never be a success at farming. He snaps back that she could never be a real lady like the lovely ladies back home. Zan sets out to prove that she can be a perfect lady—right down to delicate manners and a frilly dress—at the upcoming prairie ball. But underneath their war of words, a growing attraction will soon reveal the true gentleman and lady in each of them . . .

Turn the page to meet
the folks of Harmony, Kansas . . .

Welcome to A TOWN CALLED HARMONY . . .

MAISIE HASTINGS & MINNIE PARKER, propri-etors of the boardinghouse . . . These lively ladies, twins who are both widowed, are competitive to a fault—Who bakes the lightest biscuits? Whose husband was worse? Who can say the most elo-quent and (to their boarders' chagrin) the longest grace? And who is the better matchmaker? They'll do almost anything to outdo each other—and abso-lutely everything to bring loving hearts together!

JAKE SUTHERLAND, the blacksmith . . . Amidst the workings of his livery stable, he feels right at home. But when it comes to talking to a lady, Jake is awkward, tongue-tied . . . and positively timid!

JANE CARSON, the dressmaker . . . She wanted to be a doctor like her grandfather. But the eccentric old man decided that wasn't a ladylike career—and bought her a dress shop. Jane named it in his honor: You Sew and Sew. She can sew anything, but she'd rather stitch a wound than a hem.

ALEXANDER EVANS, the newspaperman . . . He runs *The Harmony Sentinel* with his daugh-ter Samantha, an outspoken, college-educated columnist and certainly Harmony's most fash-ionable lady. Once, she imagined a sophisticated doctor would be her perfect match—until smooth-talking saloonkeep Cord Spencer worked his way into her heart.

JAMES AND LILLIAN TAYLOR, *owners of the mercantile and post office* . . . With their six children, they're Harmony's wealthiest and most prolific family. It was Lillie, as a member of the Beautification Committee, who acquired the brightly colored paints that brightened the town.

"LUSCIOUS" LOTTIE McGEE, *owner of the First Resort* . . . Lottie's girls sing and dance and even entertain upstairs . . . but Lottie herself is the main attraction at her enticing saloon. And when it comes to taking care of her own cousin, this enticing madam is all maternal instinct.

CORD SPENCER, *owner of the Last Resort* . . . Things sometimes get out of hand at Spencer's rowdy tavern, but he's mostly a good-natured scoundrel who doesn't mean any harm. And when push comes to shove, he'd be the first to put his life on the line for a friend.

SHERIFF TRAVIS MILLER, *the lawman* . . . The townsfolk don't always like the way he bends the law a bit when the saloons need a little straightening up. But Travis Miller listens to only one thing when it comes to deciding on the law: his conscience.

ZEKE GALLAGHER, *the barber and the dentist* . . . When he doesn't have his nose in a dime western, the white-whiskered, blue-eyed Zeke is probably making up stories of his own—*or* flirting with the ladies. But not all his tales are just talk—once he really *was* a notorious gunfighter . . .

CHAPTER

1

This was supposed to be a dream come true. This parched, scrawny, useless crop was supposed to be the thing that would make possible the return of all that he valued in life. Edward Farquhar Winchester, third son of a belted earl, squatted down and scooped up a handful of Kansas dirt. He broke the clod with his fingers. His dreams blew away in the wind, one with the swirling dust.

He tried to laugh. Even to his own ears, the bitter sound seemed more like a sob. What was left to him now? Go back to England, to face the ill-concealed sneers of his friends and family, or to sense behind their hearty condolences the panicky urge to cast out the failure before the taint spread?

Or he could vanish into the sheer size of this ghastly, bloody country. Other men had found fortunes in the Colorado gold strike. Perhaps he, too, would be lucky. But no, he admitted, hanging his head, luck had never been a whore for him.

He heard someone coming through the field whistling. Hurriedly he blinked away the moisture from his eyes as he rose. When Suzanna Lind appeared at the end of the row, he'd once more assumed a properly impassive mask, as befit a gentleman. Though tigers tear out my vitals, he thought proudly, I can still keep to the Code.

"Miss Lind, is it not?"

"Hiya, Your Worship!"

His cool gray eyes flicked over her. Why in heaven's name the girl didn't get herself some decent clothes . . . at least she wasn't wearing pants. He still recalled with what stunned amazement he'd first seen her in those! Today she wore what was obviously a man's shirt tucked untidily into a much too short skirt, which revealed the heavy boots, also a man's, at the ends of her long thin legs.

"What may I do for you, Miss Lind?"

"The shoe's sort of on the other foot, Your Majesty. It's what I've come to do for you."

"I fail to understand you."

Imitating him without knowing it, Zan Lind squatted down to take up a handful of soil. Unlike Edward, however, she stirred it around with her fingers, sniffed at it, and seemed all but ready to taste it. Then she brushed off her hands and squinted up at him. "Your uncle Fred's hired me to come help you out with this place."

"I beg your pardon?"

"Golly, which word didn't you get?"

When the Englishmen had first come to Harmony, Zan had silently agreed with the other girls when they'd declared Edward Winchester to be "cuter than a bug's ear." Public opinion had shifted some toward him, as soon as he'd begun swaggering around with his high and mighty bearing. Now the girls all thought he looked as if he were always biting on a lemon.

Zan knew they'd have a hearty laugh at her if she admitted she still thought he was a fine-looking man—she being supposed to think men were less interesting than cattle, which, as a rule, they were. Nevertheless, Edward now looked as if he'd bitten the biggest lemon ever grown.

"I do not mean . . . I am merely surprised that my uncle should take such a step without consulting me."

"You'll have to talk to him about that. I've agreed to work for the pair of you, and I mean to keep my word. Looks like you could use the help," she said, rising and nodding at the stunted yellow stalks that surrounded them.

"It's too good of you, Miss Lind. But I couldn't possibly permit you to neglect your own farm. Thank you for coming. Good day." He bowed and walked away.

Zan kept pace with him. He was taller than she, topping her by a good two inches, and had longer legs. But he walked so stiffly that she had no trouble keeping up.

"I'm not neglecting a thing," she said, sticking her hands into the pockets she had slashed into the skirt. "Our crops are looking fine, and Pa said I could take this chance to earn a little something of my own. He's been giving me a share of what we make, but twenty dollars cash money is too good to pass up. And then Fred promised me a ten percent share of this year's harvest, if you wind up having anything to bring in."

"You can keep the payment," Edward said. "But I believe we shall dispense with your services."

"I can't take money I haven't done anything for," she protested. He walked on as if she hadn't spoken.

They reached the yard of the Double B. For two bachelors the Englishmen kept the yard well, though there were no flowers or other female touches that made the Lind farm seem so homelike. The chickens looked healthy, scratching vigorously within their pen, the rooster striding about as stately in manner as Edward himself. The barn stood facing the house, its sloping roof only half-covered. As she would have heard about it if he'd hired anybody to finish the shingles, Zan realized that Edward was most likely doing all the work himself.

After gaping a moment at this monument to his stubbornness, Zan hurried after Edward. He'd already gone into the white clapboard house. Crossing the uneven floor of the wraparound porch, Zan marveled at how much the two men had accomplished in the short time they'd lived in Harmony. The Double B had originally belonged to the Nevelsons. They'd sunk a lot of cash into the farm before pulling out during the '72 drought. Since then, the place had been going to pot.

"Uncle! Miss Lind is here with some ridiculous story!"

Zan could hear the low, chuckling tones of the older Mr. Winchester. He sounded as if he were soothing his nephew. Figuring she'd better get in on this conversation, she pushed the door open.

"Golly Moses!"

The rumors she'd heard were true. Billy Taylor, who made occasional deliveries out here for his father at the Mercantile, had described the inside of the house as being "prettier than an upstairs bedroom at the First Resort," only to be thrashed by his mother for knowing anything about the cathouse. Zan didn't need to know about Luscious Lottie's decorating to know this was the most elegant room she'd ever seen.

A chandelier, all sparkling and trembling with crystals, hung above a round oaken table. A tea set, edged in gold, sat in the center of the table. The rug under the table was rose, green, and gold, each flower deeply carved into the pile. A gold-framed mirror bigger than a pier glass hung on one wall above an ornately carved sideboard, all alive with silver and shining goblets. Gazing around in wonder, Zan could overlook that the ceiling and walls were naked plaster and the floor rough-hewn planks with nothing under it but sod.

Feeling as clumsy as a waltzing ox, Zan tiptoed past the treasures on either side. Above her head the chandelier rang faintly with fairy laughter. The men's voice were coming from the back of the house.

"I made very careful inquiries before hiring this young lady. Certainly, a man would be preferable. However, 'Earth has swallowed all my hopes but she, She is the hopeful lady of my earth.' *Romeo and Juliet*."

"All the same, you should have consulted me, Uncle. I know the crop doesn't look good—"

"Dreadful's more like it."

"Very well, dreadful. But how can she help?"

Pat on his words, Zan entered the kitchen. "I can't. Not with that mess you've grown. But I do know what to do about it."

"Indeed?"

She stood up a little taller. No man could fluster her with a single raised eyebrow. "Yes, sir. We're going to plow it all under and plant sorghum."

"What is that when it is at home?" Fred asked, sitting down heavily after rising on her entrance.

Finding it easier to talk to the open face of the older man, Zan said, "It's what we make molasses out of. It's about right for us, 'cause you can put it in even this late in the year."

"And why," Edward asked, still sneering, "should *I* bother?"

"Because the squeezings are selling for ninety cents a gallon, since the price of sugar's gone so high this year already. If everything goes just right, we'll get eighty gallons to the acre, maybe more."

"Sounds just the ticket," Fred said, glancing up at his nephew.

"You say the . . . the 'squeezings' are selling for this price. I assume this desirable product does not merely gush forth from the ground. How does one obtain it?"

At least he was sounding less like something that had been frozen for a thousand years. "You've got to mill it."

"With what, pray tell?"

"With a mill, of course. You get these big iron rollers to crush . . ."

"Therefore, I must lay out capital for this venture?"

"I'll be happy. . . ." Fred began, but his nephew silenced him with a glance.

Zan said, "You don't have to buy a thing. The mill's got some rollers that have been lying out in the grass since the end of the war, practically. The molasses pan is tied up by the river. The Taylor kids have been using it for a boat since Hector was a pup."

"A boat?"

"Sure, it's big enough. And since it's mostly wood, it floats just fine. So all we've got to do is get the equipment cleaned up and work a deal with the Taylors to use the mill. We can swing it so they'll be happy to get some money at a time of year when everybody else is finished with grinding their corn and wheat."

"Well, you've got every detail worked out, Miss Lind. I'm impressed," Fred said brightly, his jovial gray eyes beaming. In shape and color they were practically the same as Ed's, but lost in a fine maze of wrinkles. When he smiled, they were nearly swallowed up. Zan wondered what Ed would look like if he ever let go and grinned. It seemed her imagination couldn't stretch that far.

She knew that he wouldn't be nearly as easy to convince as Fred. "There must be a flaw," he said. "Otherwise, every person in Harmony, if not Kansas, would be putting in sorghum. Are you planning to tell us what the drawbacks are, Miss Lind? Or shall they simply be a delightful surprise?"

"Most folks put in a patch of molasses cane for their own use. Drought can't hurt it like corn. It just kind of curls up and waits for rain."

"You seem very well informed. Your father planted corn and timothy this year, did he not?"

"Yes, he did." She should have known he'd pick that up. Some folks thought his eminence was stupid, because he wanted to farm Kansas according to the books he'd brought along from England. Well, she thought, maybe he isn't too bright when it comes to farming, but no man with eyes like a pair of sod-augers could be all dumb.

"If this sorghum is all you say, why didn't he plant it?" Edward demanded a second time.

"It can be kind of hard of the land. That's why folks didn't keep on growing it as much once the war boom in it passed. And if a frost hits early, you can lose a lot of your yield. But since your land can't even support corn right now, a course of sorghum won't do too much harm. Then, next year, we can rotate in some beans or clover."

"So you are planning to continue this arrangement next year. At the same price, no doubt. How convenient for you."

Zan prided herself on keeping her temper. As one of a family of five children, it didn't do any good to be flying off the handle at every little thing. But Ed Winchester could flay the hide off an elephant using only his voice.

"Look here, Your Worshipfulness, I'm not trying to put anything over on you. I got just as much interest in making this fly as you do. But if you don't want my help, then I'll scoot on out of here."

"Come now." Fred glanced anxiously between them. " 'Forget, forgive, conclude and be agreed.' *Richard the Second*. Edward, Miss Lind is right."

Zan smiled at the portly gentleman. "You know, you're almost as good as a play."

"Thank you, my dear," he said, half-bowing in his chair. "You are obviously a lady of vast intelligence and perspicacity."

More confident, Zan gave Edward a straight look. "It's your land, Mr. Winchester. Sorghum's the best thing I can recommend to you. But if you want to keep on trying with your corn, well, I'm hired for the summer. You tell me what to do, and I'll be here bright and early every morning to do it."

"*Mister* Winchester?" he asked, that eyebrow leaping up again. Somehow, though, this time it didn't seem insulting, but almost like a smile. "I'd become rather used to 'Your Majesty.' "

"You're the boss. I'll try to be respectful. 'Course, I don't expect it to be easy."

Edward bit his lip and frowned. Without another word he left the kitchen. Zan would have followed him, determined to get a clear answer, if Fred had not caught her hand.

"Give him a little time," he said. "He'll want to check your facts before he decides."

"That mean he doesn't trust my word?"

"Let us say, rather, that he prefers to find his own counsel."

"I guess I know what that's like. My mother says I mull things over longer than anyone she knows, and when I've made up my mind, a river of advice can't change it."

Frederick Winchester, without youth or beauty, had endeared himself to the folks in Harmony with his joviality. No corn-shucking or spelling bee seemed to be complete now without his being there, usually in the front row. Unlike his nephew, Fred—as he was universally known— seemed to have grown a true affection for America and Americans.

Zan had even heard a tale that Miss Maisie and Miss Minnie of the boardinghouse were switching their interest from the uncatchable Zeke Gallagher to newer prey. Maybe Fred's love for America had a single source, though, Zan wondered, how could a man choose his favorite among two peas or which was his favorite shoe, left or right? That was what it would be like choosing between the middle-aged twins.

After a moment's silence, Fred excused himself and went out the back door, closing it noiselessly behind him. Zan glanced around the kitchen. Here were no fancy touches, except for the dishes which matched the tea set in the other room. The stoked stove gave off a slight, reminding heat, accompanied by the smell of warm polish.

Everything was quiet, except for the distant hum of crickets. She might have been alone in the house or in the universe. Zan fell into her nervous habit, brushing her lips restlessly with the pointed end of her long blond braid. She just had to get this job, come hell or high water. What was Ed doing all this time?

"Where's my uncle?"

She jumped, never expecting the citified Ed to walk so quietly. "Out back, I guess. You know . . ."

The unthinkable happened. Ed actually came close to smiling or at least refrained from sneering. "I'm most grateful for your suggestion, Miss Lind. Porterfield and Thierry both agree that sorghum is a viable crop under these conditions. And you were quite right about the drought resistance."

"I've never met Mr. Porterfield or that other feller. Are they new in town? They sound like they know what's what."

"They are eminent authors; not from Harmony. As a matter of fact, I believe Thierry died some years ago."

"Sorry to hear it. Do I get the job?"

His smile, if such it could be called, faded. "I'm afraid it simply wouldn't do, Miss Lind. I shall, however, be more than happy to pay you twenty dollars, as agreed, for your excellent advice." He held out the money, a broad-milled coin that flashed in the sunlight.

Zan didn't glance at it. "I didn't agree to take money for advice. It's free as the air, or ought to be. What I want is what your uncle promised me. Twenty dollars, a job, and ten percent. Nothing more, or less."

"Come now. You must see that would be hardly suitable. Even now . . . perhaps we should step out-of-doors."

"Why?"

"A young lady alone in a house with a single man might . . . Surely you know how gossip spreads?"

"You and me?" She laughed, shaking her head. "Nobody ever gossips about me. I've always done pretty much what I pleased. Oh, Mother keeps me decent or I'd never be caught in a skirt, but I plow, I plant, I spread manure . . ."

"Fertilizer, if you please."

"Golly, you sound like an old maid, Your . . . Mr. Winchester. Nobody ever says anything about me. Why should they? There's a lot prettier gals in town to shake fingers at."

"Nevertheless, I believe a lady should adorn a home, not labor to support it." He sounded, she thought, about seventy-five years old and bitter with the years.

"Most of the ladies around town have to do both. I would, too, but I only know how to do one thing—farm. And I've just got to have this job!"

"Why? It would be better to stay at home as a good girl should and sew for your hope chest. Some day, I feel confident, a fine young man will come along and—"

"Mr. Winchester, that's the whole problem. There is a fine young man, but I don't want to get married."

All the way home Zan kicked herself for her foolishness. Ed Winchester hadn't cared one jot for her trials. She'd been a dunce even to bring Quintus into the discussion. If Fred hadn't already been on her side, the story she told would have softened his heart like butter at noonday. Hard-hearted Ed hadn't batted an eye, only shaking his head and repeating his turndown.

And her danged pride hadn't even let her accept the twenty dollars he kept pushing at her. She could have used it, too. Every sunset put her dream farther out of reach. There had to be another way to raise a hundred and fifty dollars by September 15. But what? Fred's offer had seemed like a miracle. She should have known His Lordship would play the devil with it.

As she had all her life, Zan turned toward the large barn at the back of the Lind farm. The sight of the cows' fat red backs, the contented *slurp-crunch* of chewing, and the occasional meeting of a mild bovine eye seemed solace for any ill. The high rafters and long aisle, blurred by a thin dusty haze, seemed more hallowed to her than Harmony's tiny Methodist church.

She'd been chief acolyte from the time she was old enough to clump along in the miniature boots her father had crafted just for her. Faith, her older sister, had been her mother's daughter and could cook and sew like a dream. These talents were most useful now that Faith had married Kincaid Hutton and together with him had decided to open a hotel.

Zan had lain awake countless nights, wondering to what use she could be put, trained by a loving father to be as good a farmer as he was himself. Ten years had passed after her before the first boy, Ben, had come to the Lind farm. Now eight, he showed signs of being as outstanding a farmer as his father. Suddenly, it seemed almost overnight, people were looking differently at Zan, expecting her to become a usual girl, silly, vain, and on the catch for any single man still breathing.

"Oh, Papa," she said, sitting down on a stump behind the barn. "Why couldn't I have been born a Ben?"

"And what is the matter with a Zan?" he asked, turning over a scythe in his hands. The sleeves of his rough canvas shirt were rolled back, showing his thick, reddened forearms.

Like her own, his eyes were changeable. Right now, as he glanced at her sharply, they were as blue as fallen pieces of sky. "The young English—he wouldn't take you on?"

"No. I told him my idea for sorghum and he offered to pay for that, but he wouldn't even think about something permanent. What am I going to do?"

"When Quintus comes, you will forget about the Beakman place, or buy it together. Yes, you wait till he comes and I'll give you the money to buy. A wedding present."

What was the use in arguing? He had his heart set on her marrying the son of his old playfellow from Sweden. If Faith hadn't fallen head over heels for Kincaid Hutton, and married him out of hand, Zan knew she wouldn't have even been considered for Quintus Widstrand's bride. Like every other man for miles, he would have seen Zan as a friend, and Faith as the woman of his dreams. But Faith was indisputably married, and almost indecently happy with her husband and young stepdaughter, Amanda. Now it was Zan's turn.

She stood up. "I better get after those watermelons before the caterpillars eat 'em all."

"You should help your mother in the house," her father said, beginning to strip the steel along the curved blade. He did not look her way. "Ben and Gary can pick off the bugs."

Her hands shoved in her empty pockets, Zan kicked a rock across the yard ahead of her as she walked. She'd wrung her brains dry trying to come up with a way to raise that money. Even if every fruit and vegetable in the garden, every bit of comb in the hives, had been hers to sell, she knew she'd still come up short. Thinking about spending the rest of her life in a kitchen only hardened her determination.

She didn't know how, but Ed Winchester would be convinced that he needed her help, if she had to use this rock to help make up his mind.

CHAPTER

2

Up and dressed long before the sun had ventured even a single beam over the horizon, Zan crept down the back stairs, her shoes in her hand. A low-burning lamp, always left alight in the kitchen, guided her down the sharply sloping, narrow steps. The family dog lying across a rag rug at the bottom of the stairs lifted his head and tentatively thumped his long tail.

"You want to go out, Gulbrun?" she whispered.

She opened the back door, but the dog only looked out at the darkness before yawning, curling his black tongue. Then he got up, padding after her on large, silent feet, his tawny back sleek in the lamplight. At least once an unexpected traveler had asked the Linds to call off their lion.

Gulbrun sat beside her, eyeing the cold biscuit, split with molasses, that she wolfed down for her breakfast. When she'd finished, she held out her hand, and he licked the sweetness from her fingers. "Mother will feed you when she wakes up," Zan reassured the dog. "Go back to sleep."

From behind her, her mother's soft voice called, "Zan? Is that you?"

"I hope I didn't wake you. . . ."

"What are you doing up so early?" Mrs. Lind came into the large open room, a print wrapper around her comfortable body and her still-blond hair hanging in two long braids. She looked about seventeen as she peered into the lighted room, blinking.

Zan scrambled leggily down from the edge of the table. "I thought I'd get an early start at the Double B."

"Oh, I see." Probably her mother did understand completely. Though Zan was not as close to her mother as Faith was, she had no doubts of her mother's sympathy or affection. "I won't expect you for noontime, then. What about breakfast?"

"I've had a biscuit; that'll hold me."

"You must eat more than that. With two men cooking, goodness knows what you'll get later. I'll fry you some bread and an egg."

"No, Mother, really. . . ."

"Sit!"

Both Zan and Gulbrun sat, the dog grinning as widely as the girl. Her mother may not have come up to her shoulder, but Zan knew who was boss in this kitchen. In a few minutes her mother had roused the old black cookstove, and delicious smells began to waft through the air. Zan realized how hungry she really was.

"Now, eat," Mrs. Lind said, sliding a plate in front of her daughter. She watched while Zan cut the first bite. "Your father said he won't be using the mule team today."

"No?" Zan said, her concentration fixed on the food before her. Then something odd in her mother's tone penetrated her absorption. If she didn't know better, she would have thought her mother looked and sounded almost . . . shifty. "Oh? What about the harrow?"

"It seems to me that if he doesn't need the team, he

won't be using the harrow, unless he wants Gary and Ben to pull it."

"Well, he wants them to do everything else," Zan muttered.

Her mother rested her work-worn hand on her daughter's shoulder. "Hurry up and finish your breakfast. You have much to do today."

The mules, Hank and Herman, didn't seem to mind the dark. They wore their oversize harness with an air of pride that a purebred Percheron couldn't beat. Zan drove them easily out of the yard and down the lane. However, when she tried to steer them to the left, to head for the Double B, they paid no attention, turning toward the right and their own fields.

"Come on, fellers—this way!" she called, giving a firm signal on the reins. The mules stopped dead. She could almost hear them thinking critical thoughts of her.

"Well, then, if you won't, you won't." Leaving the reins slack, she jumped down and started off on foot. After a few minutes she could hear the jingle of their harness as they followed her. She grinned at their curiosity, but didn't look back, as that would only make them conceited.

" 'Morning, Your . . . oh, it's you, Fred," she said as she walked onto the Double B in the pink light of dawn.

"Ah, Suzanna! 'The hunt is up, the morn is bright and gay, the fields are fragrant, and the woods are green.' *Titus Andronicus*."

"I guess they are at that. Where's . . . ?" She glanced around their yard. "Isn't Ed up yet?"

"He's gone out to plow the field with the oxen. Don't look so surprised. My nephew isn't as indolent as you might think from his manner. Quite the opposite."

"I didn't think he was." But she had suspected he was lazy. Even now, she wasn't sure he didn't go plowing so early just to show her up. "Which field has he gone to?"

Fred lifted his arm to point. His hand hung limply as he stared off to where the mules clumped into the yard. "What the . . ." He swallowed his oath.

Zan merely smiled at him. "Where'd you say he was?"

Now that the mules had come so far, she could again drive them. They weren't about to walk all the way home without her. Ed, at the far end of the field, had completed the first leg of a "round." Before he turned his heavy-headed animals, Zan had released the lift on the harrow and walked her team into the cornfield. "Gee up!"

The sickly corn, hardly more than weeds, fell down beneath the spinning disks. Chopped and mulched, the yellow stalks lay scattered behind her, a thin layer of dirt unevenly mixed among them. She'd make a second pass later, to further mix in the dead matter. Right now she kept her eyes on the mark she'd set in the distance. It would be a disgrace to drive a crooked row.

Zan almost laughed aloud when she passed Ed. His surprise seemed to jump out at her. Though she didn't do more than flick a glance in his direction, it was enough. Obviously he thought they'd settled everything yesterday. He didn't know her, not yet.

She heard him call a halt to his team. Laughing a little now, she encouraged her mules to walk on. Ed caught up in a moment, and she forced her face to be solemn. A giggle, though, capered in her voice.

"What are you doing?" he called, jogging along beside.

"What does it look like to you?"

"It looks like . . . Stop! I can't talk to you like this!"

Before she knew it, he'd leaped up onto the jiggling board and gave a solid yank to the reins. Hank and Herman stopped, turning a reproachful glance over their narrow shoulders. "It looks like an arrant piece of knavery," Ed said.

"Which play is that from?"

"*Henry* . . . never mind. When I ask what you are doing here, Miss Lind, I don't wish to know the occupation you are engaged upon. I want to know why you have disregarded my wishes as to your employment."

"I reckoned you just didn't mean it."

"Didn't . . ." At a loss, he pushed back his store-bought hat and seemed to search the sky for inspiration.

Zan had a moment to study him. As was usual, he wore a white linen shirt with a black satin-backed vest over it and well-tailored gray flannel trousers. She was used to trousers made of duck and shirts still advertising the flour that had originally worn the cloth. The only man in town who dressed even half as fine was Cord Spencer, who ran the Last Resort and was all but a professional gambler.

Looking up at Ed, balancing easily above her on the narrow board, Zan felt a strange clutch in the area of her stomach. She hadn't felt anything like it since the night she nearly fell down the well in the dark.

"I meant it," he said. "I don't need your help."

"Why not use me, since I'm here?"

"You're a female. Young ladies shouldn't . . ." He waved his hand over the field. "They don't do things like this."

"Why not?"

"Because that's the way it is."

"Maybe in England, though I feel awful sorry for 'em if it's true. What do they do all day if they don't work?"

How to explain the gentility and grace of a breed of women half a world away? And not merely far off in distance, Edward thought, but certainly beyond the understanding of a girl who seemed half-wild, despite her respectable parents. Even now, Zan Lind met his eyes, challenged his opinions, and doubted his masculine authority, things the proper young English girls of his acquaintance would never dare do.

"They shop," he said inadequately and watched the laughter bring a fresh sparkle into her blue-gray eyes beneath the brim of her shapeless straw hat. "And play their pianos, and take tea at one another's homes, and go to museums. Then at night they dress to attend balls where they dance with many different gentlemen. They are always ladylike."

"Sounds danged dull to me! Don't any of 'em ever want to whoop and holler? Seems sometimes I just get crazy and want to gallop off to the end of the world. But I guess English girls don't get to ride much."

"Actually, they are some of the most accomplished horsewomen in the world. There's a place in London called the Rotten Row where they ride every day in beautiful habits." He could close his eyes and almost imagine himself back there, in the cool fragrance of Hyde Park, far from the desolation of Kansas. Why, they boasted if one of their trees had a bole more than a foot around, hardly a sapling on his father's estate.

Her voice broke his reverie. "Rotten Row? You English are sure strange."

"It's a corruption of *Route de Roi*. The king used to ride there."

"Must be a corruption, if it's rotten. Well, the day's dragging on, Mr. Winchester. Guess we'd best get to it."

"Didn't you hear what I said?"

She had taken a crick in the neck from looking up at him. Now she gazed ahead, looking for her mark. "Sure. I can even understand what you mean. But I'm not English—I'm American! The only tea party I care about's the one that was in Boston Harbor a while back. So I'll tell you what . . ."

"I don't care to hear it. . . ."

"If I can outwork you today, I get to stay on. If you outdo me, why, I'll put on an apron and never look farther than my own kitchen door. Can't say any fairer than that!"

18

"Such a competition is utterly out of the question."

"What's the matter? Think I'm going to beat you? I promise not to tell anybody if I do, though some folks'll be mighty sore if I keep it to myself."

"I'm not concerned with the opinion of anyone in Harmony."

"If you wanted, we could have half the town out to watch us work. They purely love that kind of contest, just like that spelling bee your uncle lost. I just know Miss Maisie and Miss Minnie would come farther than this to watch me wallop you."

"That won't be necessary. And Uncle didn't lose that match; your own sister declared it a stalemate."

Zan shrugged. "Have it your own way."

She saw his well-cut lips tighten. "What rules shall we abide by?"

In the end they brought Fred out to be the judge. He sat on a stump between two fields of more or less equal size. Zan conceded the field that Ed had already begun, apparently giving him a bit of an edge. He glared at her so fiercely that she didn't feel too bad about cheating him. She knew that it was harder to continue to plow straight when the driver had to match what was already laid.

When Fred stood up and brandished a white handkerchief, Zan chirruped to the mules. They didn't move. Fighting down her excitement, she cajoled them with a singsong flattery. "Oh, Hank's the best-looking mule for miles, for miles. No other mule can beat him; he wins all the trials. And no mule's smarter than Herman. If I had to pick another one, I'd sooner choose a merman."

The long ears twitched back, but not one hoof moved. "Come on, my darlings. You're not going to let a couple of stupid oxen, driven by a gol-durned blue blood get ahead of us?"

She heard them sigh, whickering out their lips. After a long glance, in which they seemed to exchange some weighty philosophy, they agreed to pull the harrow.

The sun had mounted high into the blue enameled sky by the time she'd finished half the field. There wasn't much breeze. As the sweat rolled down inside her blouse, Zan wished she could hike up her skirt to her knees as she did when plowing at home. If it hadn't been for Fred, she would have done it.

But after the lecture she'd gotten from Ed, she didn't care to have the older man fall down in a dead faint at so unladylike an action. She imagined English girls never got too warm. They probably had ice-cold springwater in their veins.

At the end of a round she wasted a second to stand up, trying to get a glimpse of the other field. Ed's back was still straight as a railroad tie. If he felt the heat, he didn't show it. "More ice water," she grumbled.

At noon, as agreed, they stopped to feed and water the animals. Fred came out to talk to her. He carried, on a silver tray that flashed in the sunlight, a cut-glass pitcher of lemonade and two stemmed glasses.

"I don't know why Edward is being so disagreeable," he said, pouring out. "I'm blessed if I see any difference between this field and his work."

"I'm no lady," Zan said, drinking deeply from the glass he'd given her. It might be elegant, but it didn't hold very much.

"Oh, don't say that, my dear. More?"

"Yes, please."

While he poured, she wiped the sweat from her brow with her sleeve and put her hat on again. "Sun's a might strong for June," she said after drinking.

"The weather is the most difficult thing to adjust to," Fred said, looking over at his nephew. "I shouldn't wonder if half his bad temper comes from it."

"Don't you have summer in England, either?"

"Not like in America. Even one ninety-degree day in England is such a rarity that some unfortunate persons might perish from such extreme heat. However, usually the temperature is most mild if uncertain—we might have a week of forty-degree days in the midst of July and rain with monotonous regularity."

"Can't quarrel with rain. We could do with some of that here. At least you must be all right with our winters, if it's that cold there anyway."

"Actually, the winters tend to be mild. A single snowstorm such as we experienced in April would have brought Britain to a standstill, except perhaps in the absolute farthest north. But as the Bard says . . ."

Zan wasn't listening. She'd seen Ed leave his cattle and come striding across the fields toward them. When he was within earshot, he said forcefully, "Are you entirely ready to go on? Or shall we call off this farce now?"

She gave the goblet back to Fred. "Here, give him some of that lemon juice. Maybe it'll sweeten him up."

By the time the sun had begun to set, deep marks from the reins crisscrossed Zan's hands, and her fingers were nearly numb. Her shoulders ached as though she'd been lifting hundred-pound grain sacks. She was so stiff that rising from her seat to glance over into Ed's field nearly overset her.

What she saw, however, made her strength return. He was rounding off to come straight back down the field, the last leg he'd have to make before finishing. She herself had just made that last turn.

"What do you say, boys? You got enough left to beat 'em?"

The mules charged ahead as if they'd only been waiting for her to ask. Zan couldn't help but let out a whoop as the wind from her increased speed snatched the hat from her head. Glancing at Ed to see how he took this challenge, she was stunned to see him plodding on, with no more concern than if she lagged ten furrows behind.

Well, if that was how he was going to be, she'd show him it didn't mean anything to her, either. With obvious unconcern, she took the mules up to the house, to walk them cool and to give them water. When Ed showed up, she had just splashed a dipper over herself.

Shaking off the droplets, she turned to him. "Want some?"

"Thank you. I'll wait till the mules are done."

"Suit yourself."

Zan opened the two top buttons on her shirt and patted the exposed skin with her wet hand. The slight breath of moving evening air cooled her off instantly. "Wasn't it hot today? Like to scorch the hide off old Nick."

The streaky evening light showed him standing as rigid as a pole. She gave a mental shrug. "That's enough, boys. Don't want to swell up," she said, pushing the mules' noses away from the water. "I'll leave the harrow for tomorrow. No reason to drag it all the way home and back again."

Ed brought forward his team to drink from the tank. He rested his hand on one ox's massive neck. "It was wrong of me to work them so hard," he said, almost to himself. "One can hardly expect them to win over lighter animals."

"Father says that oxen are only good for breaking the prairie. After his first season here, he got rid of his."

She noticed that he was absently scratching behind the long ear under the horn. The huge beast lifted his muzzle from the water and seemed to close his eyes, as though in pleasure. "A poor return for their service."

"Oh, they were sold to a man who drove 'em East, to sell

to new settlers. We didn't have any more use for 'em."

"Every creature deserves to have the yoke lifted sometimes."

"I guess." She didn't know how to answer. An animal had to be useful, or what was the point of feeding it? Even the cats had to catch mice in the barn, and the dogs must keep watch.

"Speaking of work," she said. "What time do you want me here tomorrow?"

"Not before eight, if you please."

Secretly pleased that he'd given in, even if she'd had to beat him to win her point, she could still protest, "Eight? Half the day'll be wasted!"

"Nevertheless . . ." He began to walk away. The oxen turned with him and headed for the fenced pasture.

Leaving the mules, Zan caught up with him as he opened the gate. "I figured on being here before dawn, like this morning. We've got to use every hour if we're to get the manure spread and a second pass with the harrows. And we only did two fields today. It's going to take the better part of the week as it is, and if I don't even get here till eight . . ."

"I understand your point of view. All the same, kindly don't arrive before eight o'clock in the morning."

"Why, for gosh' sake? Are you planning to sleep in? Can't do that and make a farmer."

He was little better than a shadow, but she could feel his disapproval as he drew himself up. "Miss Lind, am I or am I not your employer?"

"You are, if you're going to keep our bargain."

"Very well. Be so good as to follow my instructions without arguing, or I shall be forced to discharge you from my service."

He stalked away toward the house, leaving Zan gaping after him. As he stepped onto the porch, Uncle Fred opened the door. "Come in, you two. I've made supper for you."

Zan realized she was as hollow as an old tree. Maybe hunger explained Ed's cantankerousness. In which case, she reflected, hurrying across the yard, he must be hungrier than a bear in spring every live-long day of the year.

Taking off her hat as she went in, she grinned at the sight of all the food on the table. With an amazed glance at her host, she asked, "You did all this?"

"I'm accounted an excellent chef," Fred said, relieving her of her hat. "And, of course, there is no one else to cook. Certainly, Edward can scarcely boil water."

"But all this . . . ?" Covering the freshly linened table were a platter of ham slices, a silver sauceboat filled with brilliant red sauce with cherries poking out like stones in a current, a loaf of bread still steaming from the oven, a large bowl of fresh peas gleaming with butter, and at least two kinds of pie.

"We may be a bachelor household," Fred said, "but that is no reason not to have some of the trappings of civilization. Good, simple food and a few minor luxuries make for a contented life."

"Most bachelors live on beans and what their lady-friends bring 'em."

"To be perfectly honest, the pies are the contributions of Mrs. Hastings and Mrs. Parker."

Zan gave a low whistle. "Poor Zeke Gallagher must be sleeping hungry tonight."

The older man's eyes twinkled in the candlelight. "I fear so, Miss Lind, I fear so. May I pour you out some cider?"

"Sure," she said hesitantly, unable to see a jug anywhere.

Fred picked up a glittering crystal decanter and poured some of the amber liquid into a matching goblet. As Zan reached for it, she saw as though for the first time her dirty, broken nails. "Uh," she said, curling her fingers inward to

24

hide them. "Is there some place I can wash up?"

In Fred's room the washstand was similar to her own at home, of roughly cobbled wood with a tiny, smeary mirror. But the combs and brushes Fred offered for her use were backed with silver and the washbasin of fine china. Painted at the bottom of the bowl was a decorated shield supported by some queer-looking animals. They looked like Gulbrun, only with wings and a beak where the muzzle should be.

Even after scrubbing the back of her neck and digging out the grunge from beneath her nails, Zan didn't feel much better. And she knew she must smell of sweat and dust. Though her mother insisted on clean hands and faces before meals, Zan had never thought to change a shirt that dust rose from in little puffs at every motion, nor to scrub scratched arms and legs. She did her best with her hair, ruthlessly wetting down the wispy tendrils that always sought for freedom.

When she returned, the two Englishmen were standing by the sideboard, filled goblets in their hands. Some instinct told her they'd been talking about her. Fred handed her a glass. "A toast to our new venture!"

Zan raised the glass to her lips and stopped, staring at Ed. "Golly! You're baked!"

Above the crisp collar of a clean shirt and the black band of his tie, his face and neck were as red as a freshly painted barn. His gray eyes seemed extra bright gazing out from his scoured skin. A band of white crossed his forehead where his hat had offered some protection from the fierce rays of the sun.

"Never mind, Miss Lind. My uncle has offered a toast." He raised the glass, and she saw that his hands were also sunburned. Moreover, a large blister had arisen between his thumb and forefinger.

Zan well remembered the countless times the reins had left similar marks on her own hands, before they'd toughened up.

Maybe no beau would ever admire and caress the smooth whiteness of her fingers, but she could plow with the best of them.

Absently she drank. "I'm real lucky. I almost never get sunburned. But the couple times I have, it sure hurt. If you want to loosen up your collar, never mind me."

"On the contrary, I am perfectly comfortable."

"Danged if I'd wear a claw-hammer coat and boiled shirt after working all day."

Fred said, "If you did, Miss Lind, I'm certain you couldn't look half as charming as you do tonight. Shall we dine?"

It wasn't too difficult to tell, his denials aside, that Ed suffered agonies every time he moved. Zan admitted that part of the reason for his grimaces might have been her conversation. Fred had really seemed to want to know about her plans for the dressing of the fields.

Only on the walk home, the mules following her patiently back to their own stalls, did Zan realize that the older man might have just been polite. Maybe he didn't really want to hear about horse manure versus cow.

The mules were soon brushed and bedded for the night. She went in to the house to let her parents know she was back safely. Her father had already gone up to sleep, as had the younger children.

"They asked me to stay for supper, Mother. You don't need to worry I won't get fed. Fred's a humdinger of a cook."

"You call him Fred? That is not suitable."

"Everybody else calls him that. And if I call 'em both Mr. Winchester, I won't know who I mean."

"That is true. I'll ask your father in the morning what he thinks is right." She lifted up on tiptoe to kiss her tall daughter's cheek and wrinkled her nose. "You take a bath before you sleep, Suzanna."

"In the morning, Mother."

"Now. There's plenty of hot water in the reservoir. And use the yellow soap. It is not good for a young lady to smell like a mule."

Zan agreed, less reluctantly than she might have. The irritating prickle of dried sweat and dust seemed harder to bear tonight than at other times. She didn't, however, put in all the hot water her mother would have insisted on. There didn't seem a need to get parboiled, coming up red as a new potato or Ed Winchester.

After her bath, sitting on her bed in her nightgown while she brushed out her floating hair, she found thoughts of him in her head. Before supper was over, the full color in his face had come up. He resembled nothing so much as the setting sun.

She'd tried to interest him in her mother's remedy for sunburn, but he'd continued to deny that he felt any pain. Zan put out the lamp and tried to sleep, but it wasn't any good. Before her sister had moved out to take the school, a move that had led to her marriage, Zan would listen to Faith's deep breathing until she herself fell asleep.

Now, all alone in the small room with the sharp-pitched ceiling, she had no such company to lull her to sleep. And every time she closed her eyes, she could still see poor Ed.

She tossed the crazy quilt aside and swung her legs out of bed. Feeling in the dark, she slipped on a clean shirt and skirt over her plain white nightdress. "Mother'd never begrudge one pail of milk," she told herself in a whisper. "She'd be offering it with both hands, if I told her what I wanted it for."

27   .

CHAPTER
3

At night the open, smiling landscape seemed as mysterious as the white space in the middle of maps marking the unexplored and the unexplained. The moon dripped just enough light to make the shadows even darker, not enough to illuminate the small rustlings of secretive creatures in the tall grass.

Zan staggered along, throwing her left arm out to balance the weight of the full pail. Some splashed against her skirt and she told herself again to slow down. She was as stupidly awkward as if milking the cows hadn't been one of her favorite chores for years. But the thought of Ed lying in pain from his sunburn sent her hurrying onward.

At the side of the house a light glimmered through the shutter. It wasn't where she'd washed up earlier, so she figured it had to be Ed's room. She'd just poke her head in and tell him what to do. Wouldn't take more than ten minutes, she figured, even if he was as set against home remedies as he was against everything else here.

"Yoo-hoo?" she yodeled softly, pushing open the front door, surprised to find it unlocked. She'd always heard that city folks locked up tighter than a drum to protect their valuables. Maybe these Englishmen had so many fine things they didn't care if someone walked off with them. She wondered if the silver and china she'd eaten from tonight were even their best.

That would explain why Fred hadn't seemed to mind when she'd broken that glass. Who knew it would tip over so easy? Of course, Ed had scowled as black as a thundercloud set down at a table, but that didn't bother her. A girl couldn't go letting some man get the better of her with just a crossways look or she'd have no self-respect left.

She crossed the fancy rug with extra care, wishing she'd gone in the back door. A thin ribbon of light spilled onto the hall floor from the side. Zan set down the pail, tapped, and opened the bedroom door. "It's me, Mr. Winchester. You decent?"

"What the deuce?" A frantic splashing and trickling took place as Ed shot to his feet in the bathtub. Zan had a single, teasing glance at his naked body before he wrapped the white towel around his midsection.

"Miss Lind! What the . . . what are you doing here?"

"I brought you something for your sunburn." Her face burned as hotly as if she were the one who'd been in the sun too long. Try as she might, she couldn't keep her gaze from traveling over him from top to bottom.

"Be so good as to shut your eyes."

She obeyed. His image did not obligingly go away. He was lean and long, with more strength showing in his chest and arms than she would have thought only seeing him in clothes. Except for the red of his face, throat, and arms, his skin wasn't tanned. He looked clean, not just from being in the tub, but as though the soil of Kansas hadn't yet entered into his soul to come out through his pores.

Hearing slurping sounds as he stepped out of the tin tub,

she stole another fast peek. Yes, she'd seen a furze of hair on his chest, as dark as that on his head where only certain lights brought out the auburn gleams.

He reached for his shirt, lying across the end of the rough-hewn bed, and the towel slipped, showing a flash of haunch. As quickly as he grabbed for the descending material, he shot her a glance. Zan snapped her eyes closed.

"You want this, or not? My mother swears by it, and with five blond children she ought to know."

"What is it?"

She heard the bed creak as he sat down on it, obviously to pull on his trousers. "It's milk."

"Milk?"

"Yes, milk. You know, from cows?"

"I didn't think it came from a male ostrich."

"Shouldn't think so. Can I open my eyes now?"

"Not yet. Let me find my shoes."

"Shoes?" She opened her eyes. "Bare toes don't ruffle me. I even saw somebody's ankle once."

"Did you swoon? Never mind." Ed threaded his belt through buckle and tongue. He wore only shirt and pants, the linen shirt clinging to his still damp body. "Miss Lind, it's most irregular your being here at this hour."

"Why don't you wear suspenders like everybody else?"

"Suspenders? Oh, braces. I used to, but they were taken away from me at Eton. They make admirable catapults. By the time they were returned, I had grown quite accustomed to belts."

"What's Eton?"

"A school for boys." He ran his hand through his hair, still gleaming wet. Then he took the stiff collar from the dresser beside his bed and fastened it around his neck, the high points forcing his head up. Even his tone became stiffer, more clipped and formal.

"Now, Miss Lind, as I was saying . . . it's very good of you to come to succor me in my hour of pain, but truthfully, it's not so very bad."

"Looks pretty raw to me."

"Appearances often deceive."

She gave him a half smile. "Tell you what . . . I'll leave this pail and tell you what to do. If you don't need it, well, there'll be plenty of milk for your morning coffee."

"It's really not necessary."

"Can you make a fist?" She nodded at his glowing hands. "Can you make a fist and not make a face?"

"Certainly." He held out one hand and slowly closed the fingers. Zan could see the tight skin stretch over his knuckles. His face remained impassive, as though he felt nothing. He seemed to look blankly inward, though Zan could feel the effort he exerted.

"There!" he said, opening his hand. Yet not all his self-control could keep a ghost of relief from his voice.

Zan let her own voice show what she thought of his foolish bravery. "Next you'll be telling me that sharp collar doesn't feel like a rusty knife against the back of your neck."

"A gentleman's attire is always comfortable."

"Sure it is. You got a handkerchief?"

He brought one out from his pocket, a delicate drift of linen as fine as a woman's. Zan crossed over to take it from his hand and paused, her fingers an inch away. "You ever have the feeling that you've done something before?" she asked slowly.

"Yes, every one has. Do you feel that way now?"

"It's peculiar, but the tub, you on the bed, even that water on the floor . . ." She met his gray eyes. "You must think I sound like a crazy woman."

"Not at all." Ed pressed the handkerchief into her hand. "I have often had that sensation since coming to Kansas.

Perhaps because each day is so like any other day."

"You really feel that way? Seems like every day is different to me. Sure, the chores are the same and meals, mostly, 'cept like tonight . . . I never ate off such fine china plates before. Other than those things, though, every time the sun gets up seems like something new is happening."

"I envy you your enthusiasm," he said dryly.

Zan realized she'd been talking a blue streak. "Just listen to me, gabbling on. Let me show you what to do with this milk."

As soon as she lifted the bucket again, Ed came to take it from her, his warm hand wrapping over hers. "Allow me."

"What for? I've carried it this far. Another three feet won't break my arm. You sit down again. And you better take off your shirt so it doesn't get wet. Any more wet, that is." A trickle of water ran from the short hair on his neck to wrap under his collar. Zan's fingers twitched, and she found it surprisingly difficult not to reach out to trace the same path.

"I couldn't possibly. Are you supposed to apply the milk to the painful areas?"

"That's right," she said, smiling at his good sense as she put down the bucket beside the bed. "It takes the heat right out. Let me show you."

"It's not necessary." He hadn't moved away to seat himself. He stood right beside her, taller than she was by an inch or two.

Zan couldn't seem to look away from him. The feeling of doing all this before was back and stronger. Only . . . something didn't fit. She didn't know what was missing, except that a puzzling disappointment filled her.

"I think you'd better go," he said sternly.

"You still worrying about what people will say?"

"I am."

She tried to laugh, but it got stuck in her throat, leaving her a little hoarse. "I told you, there's no need. I'm too plain and skinny, and it's not as if you've got some kind of reputation as a wild man with the ladies."

"Plain?" he repeated, a frown between his dark brows. "My entire concern, Miss Lind, centers around the indisputable fact that you are exceedingly lovely."

Now she could laugh, and did, incredulously. "Oh, come on! That's the funniest thing you've said yet!"

The frown did not pass from his face. If anything, it carved more deeply into his brow. Ed stepped up closer to her, cupping her face in his hot hands. "Impossibly lovely," he murmured.

Zan stared up at his gray eyes, absently noticing the faintest ring of light brown around his pupils. She held as rigid as a frightened bird, though it was not fear that made her heart beat so fast it thrummed in her throat. For the first time, she saw desire in a man's eyes, and felt her own.

Ed took his hands away and drew a shaky breath. "Perhaps I have simply not yet made a reputation," he said, squaring his shoulders. "You'd better go, before we both develop one."

"Uh, yeah," she said dimly. Stepping back, she kicked over the bucket. The white liquid splashed out, inundating the floor like paint.

"Sweet mercy!" Zan dropped to her knees at once, snatching the bucket upright and mopping fruitlessly with his handkerchief. "Something about this house sure makes a girl clumsy!"

"Never mind, never mind," he said, on the floor beside her, his towel in his hand. "It doesn't matter in the least."

"Try to do some good for somebody," she said, "and see where it gets you."

"This is useless." He rose easily from his knees. "I'll bring in the mop. Please get up, Miss Lind." He put down a hand to pull her up.

Maybe he was too strong and pulled too hard, or her feet slipped in the milk as she came up too fast. For whatever reason, in an instant, they were reeling backward across the wet and uneven floorboards, flailing for balance in each other's arms. Ed landed against the wall, shaking down a fine dust from the ceiling.

His lips slanted over hers, searching. Shocked, Zan didn't move, couldn't breathe, locked against him from breast to thighs. Then, her hands tightening when he would have moved away, she kissed him back with hungry innocence.

From down the hall, Fred called, "Are you all right, Edward? I thought I heard a bang."

They broke apart, both breathing as hard as though they'd run lickety-split from Harmony to the Double B. Ed recovered first. "I dropped the basin, Uncle. That's all. Sorry to disturb you."

"Not at all, my boy. Good night!"

"Good night." He pushed away from the wall, gazing at Zan with examining eyes. "Do you see now why it is unwise to be alone with a man, especially in his room and after dark?"

"I hope you're not saying you kissed me only to prove your point? I'll be awful angry if you do." She shook back her hair, and tugged her blouse around from the skewed waist of her skirt.

"No, I would never do such a thing. This was . . . spontaneous. Yet I hope also that it served some purpose."

"Well, thank you."

"Thank . . . for what, Miss Lind?"

"Golly, the least you can do now is call me Zan! And the thanks is for kissing me. I've never been kissed by a grown man before, 'cept as a forfeit at a party. Everybody figures it's kind of a punishment, I guess."

"You can't tell me Cord Spencer never . . . and I thought he was a man with taste."

"Cord? He never had a second glance to spare from Samantha. Besides, I'd never even think about taking up with a gambling man like she did. If I ever marry . . . which I don't say I will seeing as it takes two . . . it'll be to somebody solid." Zan forced herself to meet his eyes. "Somebody who can help me get what I want."

"What do you want? Other than not to be married to this boy from Sweden."

For once he seemed less distant. Maybe it was the kiss that made him look at her without curling his lip. "I want to buy my own place. There's a farm down by the Smoky Hill River. The timber's been cut pretty far back by this time, wood being so scarce, but there's water and the ground's good. Barn's too big, but better too big than too small, and the house is okay. And what I want is . . . You promise not to laugh?"

He nodded gravely.

"I want to plant an orchard. Apples, plums, peaches, whatever will grow. There could be a second Eden there, you know? I want to be able to go outside and pluck my breakfast right off the tree."

"Why should I laugh at that?"

"Everyone else thinks it's foolish. There's been a million fruit trees planted out here in Kansas and not one in ten ever put out a bud. Between the heat, the droughts, and the locusts . . ." She shrugged, hanging her head.

He touched her chin lightly with his fingertips, drawing her head up. "You're talking to a man who lives a foolish dream," he said, his eyes kind. "I'm not about to laugh at a fellow lunatic."

Zan went home carrying a light heart. Ed Winchester would be easy to work with now that he showed himself human. Even if he hadn't kissed her, she could tell he was getting used to the idea of having her around.

As for that kiss . . . Zan stopped in the middle of the road, her fingers pressed to her lips. For that one instant, when he had brought his head down, she had felt as dainty and cuddly as her sister, Faith. It hadn't lasted, of course. She could no more hide her strength than conceal a watermelon under a thimble.

She could be sure, she thought, walking on, that Ed wouldn't be taking any advantage. Most likely, he'd been wondering about her in the same way she'd wondered about him. Now that curiosity was satisfied, she could be sure there'd be no more.

Only after she finally went to bed, lying with her arms crossed behind her head in the dark, did she admit that maybe some of her curiosity persisted.

"Morning, Ed!" she called, jumping down from the wagon. "Hey, you look a whole bunch better. Did you use some milk of your own?"

"I thought we came to an understanding that you were not to arrive for work before eight o'clock."

"Isn't it eight?" Squinting up at the sun, newly risen, she shook her head. "Sorry, but I don't carry a watch. But I'll make a real effort to get here late from now on. You taking your team out?"

"I am." A little breeze swirled along the ground. A look of distress crossed his brow as a whiff of what she had in the wagon reached him. "What is that . . . aroma?"

"Best quality cow ma . . . fertilizer." Free and easy in her dungarees, she hopped up on the wheel to gaze with pride at the dark mound in the wagon bed. "Father's done his spreading out for a while. It was just piling up, so he didn't mind sending you a wagonload. There's plenty more when we want it."

Ed stepped upwind kind of quickly. "That's very good of Mr. Lind."

"Oh, Father can be right generous. And this is quality, too. I dug it from the middle of the pile, so it's good and rotten."

"You dug it?"

"Sure. The boys are too little still to handle the shovel, and Father has too much else to do. Now, what I figured we'd do is . . . you plow that back field, and I'll go along and dress the fields we did yesterday."

"Absolutely not!"

"What's the matter?"

His face grew redder, though Zan couldn't tell if it was with anger or sunburn. "You will plow and I will spread this fertilizer."

"You can't. You don't know how much to use. Too much and the yield will suffer. Sorghum doesn't like too rich a soil."

"Then you'll tell me how much. No lady should ever have to deal with . . . She shouldn't even know the word!"

"We're not back to that again! It's like I said, Ed—"

"If you're going to call me something other than Your Lordship," he interrupted, "at least make it Edward. I abominate nicknames."

"Should I call you Your Lordship? It'll be hard, but if it's the right thing—"

"No. Edward will suffice. Now, Miss Lind, as I was saying—"

"If I call you Edward, you've got to call me Zan. It's a nickname, all right, but only my folks call me Suzanna and then only when they're mad at me."

"Suzanna is much more dignified."

"Maybe it would be, if I hadn't bit the last person who called me that. Course, I was only two." She peered at

37

him to see if he believed her. "They say he still shows the scar."

He stared at her. Somehow, Zan knew he remembered her visit last night. She wasn't used to looking at someone and knowing what they were thinking. It unnerved her. Stammering, she said, "Did . . . did the milk work?"

"The milk? Oh, yes. I tried your home remedy with what was left."

"That was the only spilled milk I ever saw that didn't get cried over." She meant it as a joke, but somehow her words only made the memory of his kiss more vivid. Bad enough that she should know what he was thinking; to have him know her thoughts was almost unbearable.

"We'd better get to work," she said hesitantly. "We're burning daylight."

"I absolutely refuse to allow you to work with that stuff on my property. It's indecent!"

"Oh, for crying . . . Listen, don't think of me as a girl, okay? Think of me as a hired hand."

"Impossible!"

"And don't talk pretty to me. I don't like it." She hauled herself up into the driver's seat. "I'll see you at noon."

When the break came, however, he'd not returned to the yard. Zan escorted the mules in, turning them out in the pasture, and leaving the wagon in the second field. Her arms ached from sprinkling the manure thinly over the chopped cornstalks. After she ate, she'd hitch Hank and Herman up to the harrow again and turn the mixture over.

Fred hailed her as she walked toward the house. His fringe of gray hair was rumpled, and there was a streak of flour on one of his plump cheeks. "I imagine you're famished."

"I am a might peckish, but I better put myself under the pump first. I believe I don't smell exactly civilized." She knew she had a streak of something worse than flour clinging to her face from when she'd readjusted the bandanna she wore over her nose and mouth.

"My dear Miss Zan, I am confident you would always be fragrant 'with sweet musk roses and with eglantine.' *A Midsummer Night's Dream,* Act Two, I believe."

"I'd take that bet, Fred, but it's tough to collect money from a man passed out on the floor. I'll go and wash up."

Zan pulled the red bandanna from around her neck and removed the other one that protected her pinned-up hair. Even with well-rotted stuff like she was using, the dust raised by shoveling got into every pore. Her eyes itched and she'd been sneezing like a fiend for the last hour.

Pumping up the cold, fresh water, she put her head under the first gush, not caring if her shirt got soaked. Made of the same material as the two bright red bandannas, it would dry as quickly in the sunlight. Even as she paddled the water from her face, she knew it would take more than a dousing to make her fit company at table.

Rapping on the back door, she said as much to Fred. "So, if you don't mind, I'll take my meal out-of-doors."

"Nonsense, my dear. . . . Well, I shall concede the point. Wait a moment, and I will collect a basket for you."

"Is Ed . . . Edward back yet?" she called through the opening as she leaned against the wall to wait.

"No, not yet. Actually, you know, I don't expect him. I took him some water for the stock about an hour ago. He is kinder to his creatures than to himself."

"Go ahead and put some food for him in there, too. I'll carry it on up to him."

Above her, the sun seemed stronger when she didn't have anything but a walk to occupy her thoughts. Spreading manure was more of a thinking task than some hardheaded men might imagine. She wondered if he'd rag on her again about what a woman was supposed to be like.

Zan began to walk faster, the dirt puffing up before her boots, admitting to herself that she almost liked hearing him get so excited about something. At least it made a change, almost as great as what she'd felt last night, when he'd seized her in his arms.

CHAPTER

4

The oxen stood patiently in the center of the half-plowed field, still yoked to the plow. Zan could see no sign of Edward. She hallooed for him. Suddenly the right-hand ox seemed to sprout a second head as Edward stood up and waved a hand lackadaisically.

Zan hurried up, rehearsing mentally what she'd say. Something quick about wanting to be sure he kept his strength up so she'd collect her ten percent. That should rile him.

But his worried expression kept her from speaking heartless words.

"Look at this! I can't believe I was so careless!"

Zan looked where he pointed. She saw only a small raw wound, created on the neck of the ox by the rubbing of the wooden yoke. "Oh, that's not anything," she said reassuringly. "They get those all the time. Dab a little tar on it to keep the flies off, and he'll be good as new."

"No, I've been working them too hard. All the plowing to put the corn in, and now this. I'll unhitch them and take them back to pasture."

"That's crazy! What about the plowing you've still got to

41

do? Time's wasting, you know. We don't have all summer to get this crop in."

"It can wait over one more day."

"I'll remind you of that when the first killing frost hits and we lose everything!"

Edward paid no attention, working free the pegs that kept the yoke on the oxen. "It's a matter of principle," he said, as though to himself. With a grunt he lifted the heavy yoke. "Walk on, Buck. Walk on, Bright."

Exasperated, Zan put down her basket to lift from the other side. The huge steers, each weighing perhaps fifteen hundred pounds, walked out from beneath the wooden bar as obediently as a pair of dogs. Letting the bar fall to the ground, Zan said, "I suppose now you'll be getting 'em a couple of goose-down pillows and a handful of penny candy?"

"On the contrary, a bag of good feed and fresh water. Then a dab of ointment, as you say, to keep off the flies. I don't want this wound to become infected."

"Do what you want," she said, washing her hands of the business. "I'm going to eat my lunch!"

Zan snatched up her basket and stalked off. An old cotton-wood served as part of the marked limit of the Double B's property. There'd be a little shade under its spreading branches, though the sun stood nearly straight overhead.

She'd nearly reached its leafy coolness when she remembered she had Edward's lunch in this basket as well as her own. Let him get something else from Fred, she told herself, though she guessed he wouldn't. A wicked voice answered that if he hadn't enough sense to eat when he was hungry, then God help him.

Heaving a sigh, Zan turned around to head back toward the yard and farmhouse. She'd said she'd bring him something to eat and come hell or high water, that was what she would do. However, she'd not promised to sit with him while they ate.

All the same, she couldn't but think how pleasant it would have been to sit under that cottonwood together.

As she came up to the barn, she heard singing, or rather humming, since she couldn't distinguish any words. It was Edward's voice, though. Deep, agreeable, and soothing, the sound told of his contentment.

Zan put her hand on the framed opening and bent slightly forward to peer inside the barn. Sunlight sifted through the unshingled rafters, leaving some areas dark and others brilliantly lit. One such beam brought out the rich red undercoat of one massive ox. His muzzle buried in a feed bag, his large eyes were closed and he seemed to sway his weight from side to side. Zan almost expected to hear low bovine purring.

Edward worked a currying brush over the wall-like sides, reaching out to brush the humped back. He carried on a tuneless song, stopping sometimes to inquire whether Buck was enjoying the treatment. "You'll have a restful holiday today. Tomorrow we'll gallop through the plowing before you can say 'Jack Robinson.' "

Zan began to withdraw slowly, knowing how much Edward would hate to be surprised in this softened mood. Some lonely old maids held earnest conversations with their dogs or their tabby cats. But she'd never seen a man talk to a steer like he expected an answer.

Pretending to have just come up, Zan yoo-hooed him for all she was worth. "Now that you're done for the day," she said, entering the barn, "I guess you'll have time for a bite to eat. We can stop down by the river on the way into town."

"Town?" He finished off the ox's shaggy forehead and then hung the curry brush on a nail. "I haven't any intention of going to town. Having to cease plowing for the day is not a sufficient reason to shirk the other tasks that await my attention. This roof, for instance," he said, glancing upward. "I shall take this time to finish it."

"You'll take this time to talk to Mr. Taylor, if you're smart. Or maybe you're forgetting that we'll need his mill to make our molasses."

Obviously he had. "Of course," he said, recovering. "Mr. Taylor would be justified in refusing our business if he hears from another source that we rely too much on his good-will."

"Huh? I mean you better tell him before someone else does. He's a nice man, Mr. Taylor, but he'd be right to feel slighted if we let it get around we want to use his mill and we never asked him first."

"That's what I said."

"You did? When?"

Once again he ever so slightly relaxed his face from its usual frowning lines. Zan thought of this expression as a smile, if not much of a one. She wondered if he had bad teeth, which would explain why he never showed them. But no, there'd been no foul smell or taste when they'd kissed. She was glad of the uneven light inside the barn that hid her blush.

"We ought to get moving," she said. "I'm hungry."

His restraining hand on her arm made her heart thud in a funny rhythm. She looked slowly up at him. "I don't see why you need to go to town," he said, his gray eyes all but black in the gloom. "I believe you were engaged in spreading fertilizer."

His aristocratic nose twitched and he released her. "I can tell you have been."

"I washed up," she said, stung. "'Sides, folks in Harmony are used to this smell. It doesn't trouble anybody, 'cept those who are bound and determined to be troubled."

"If that's a slight directed at me . . ."

Zan paid no attention. "You know, it may sound kind of funny, but I don't mind the smell of manure. What good is a pretty smell to anyone? You can't eat a flower, and toilet water wouldn't keep a weed alive. But manure . . . spread it around and jump back! 'Cause it makes things happen."

"So you haven't any use for aesthetics?"

"As-what?"

"Beauty for beauty's sake."

She glanced at him, her mouth set. After a moment she said, "All my life I've heard that beauty is as beauty does. I guess folks meant to be comforting, and to keep me from being envious, which is a sin."

She supposed it must sound as if she were hoping for a repeat of his compliments of last night. But she'd meant what she said about disliking pretty speeches. Besides, she thought, even if I believed him, his opinion about my looks isn't going to change everybody else's.

He said, "I can understand your feelings on the subject, Zan. But you'll allow me, I hope, to prefer perfume."

While Edward washed up, Zan leaned against the wall, the basket at her feet. He laid his jacket and hat across a barrel head and daintily turned back his shirtsleeves. However, when he splashed in the water, he made as big a mess as any other man.

The back door slammed and Fred came out with a towel for his nephew. Zan slapped a quick hand over her mouth to keep from laughing. The bald-headed man wore a blue calico apron, his trouser legs showing under the flap.

She couldn't tell if Edward reacted to the comical sight as he buried his face in the towel. Maybe he was used to it. When he emerged, he said, "Thank you. Zan and I are going into town to talk to Mr. Taylor about using the mill at harvest-time. Would you care to accompany us?"

"Ah, no, my boy. I'm too fly a bird to be caught by that ruse. 'Two's company; three's none.' "

"Not up to Shakespeare's usual standards, Uncle?"

"I don't believe that morsel is his, but true none the less."

"Not in this instance." He looked toward her. "Zan, would you mind if Uncle Frederick accompanied us into Harmony?"

The older gentleman's smile was wiped away and then slowly regrew. "Oh, I didn't see you there, my dear."

"You're welcome to come along if you want. But you'll have to put more food in this basket. I could eat a wolf, raw."

"You haven't eaten yet?"

"Zan fancied to stop by the river," Edward said. "I have no objection to the plan."

"Why should you, my boy? Why should you? A charming notion. But, alas, if you are going to walk, you must exempt me. My old war wound, you know, seems to be acting up a tad." Fred's smile was now wide enough to show most of his straight, white teeth. Zan wondered how many were store-bought.

As he walked up the wooden steps, he leaned heavily on his right leg, keeping it straight. "Funny thing, it'll be right as rain one minute; useless the next."

"Which war would this be, sir?" Edward asked. "Agincourt?"

"No, sir," Fred said, with a nod toward Zan. "Waterloo."

As they walked out together, Edward taking the basket from her, Zan said, "The pair of you sure talk funny. Danged if I can make out what you're getting at half the time."

"You are not the first to make such a comment on Uncle Frederick. My own father has been known to request a translator. Fortunately, Frederick's wife—"

"Wife? Was he married?"

"Yes, as a young man. I never met my aunt May. They say it was a *mésalliance*. Yet, by all I ever heard, she must have been charming. She won them all over when they would have driven her out. She died regrettably young."

"What's a mis-alliance?"

"Uncle Frederick is the son of an earl, as I am. She was but the daughter of a yeoman farmer. In other words, her father farmed some land that was owned by my grandfather. Uncle should never have married so far beneath his own station. There was quite some to-do about it at the time. They even threatened to disown the pair. When May died, however, I believe only Uncle Frederick himself was more disconsolate than was Grandmother."

"You make it sound like her big mistake was being a farmer's daughter. Being one myself—"

"England is not at all similar to America. In England everyone knows his place. To move outside one's own circle . . . apparently May's father wasn't any happier about her marriage than Frederick's. I've heard a story of how he came to call on the earl to make his opinion of Uncle Frederick known. It was not complimentary, and I believe he ended by lumping all the nobility into a fraternity of wastrels. Grandfather very nearly had an apoplexy on the spot."

Zan walked on beside him, digesting this story. She wondered if it were somehow aimed at her. Edward might be taking this way of telling her that his kiss didn't mean marriage. Not that she had treasured any thoughts of it.

"I wouldn't have done it," she said finally. "Seems kind of selfish, if you know what I mean, to cause your family a lot of heart-burning over wanting to marry somebody they don't like. But then, I've noticed folks in love don't ever think of anybody but themselves."

"Yet, I think you said your father wants you to marry this . . . what was his name?"

"Quintus. That's different. It's not like I'm turning him down 'cause I'm crazy for somebody else. I don't want to marry anyone, not even the King of England." There, she thought, that should set your mind at ease, Your Lordship.

"We don't have a king these days. We don't even have a prince consort anymore. Only a lonely queen."

Above them in the open sky a long wild cry sounded. As though it had some power over him, Edward stopped. His head jerked up to scan the sky. "Do you see him?" he asked, his voice nearly a whisper.

Zan looked around cautiously. Did Edward maybe think that Indians still haunted this part of Kansas? "I don't see . . ."

"There!"

His finger stabbed upward. Zan saw only a bird floating in the sky. "It's a hen hawk," she said, slightly disappointed. Judging by his excitement, she had expected Elijah and his fiery chariot at the very least.

"Is that what you call it? I would say it is one of the red-tailed hawks, possibly Krider's." He shaded his eyes with his hand. "Do you see how white it is on the underside? Would you say that is a white-headed bird, as well?"

"Golly, I can't see that good! What difference does it make anyhow?"

Edward brought his attention back to her. "I have always been keenly interested in birds. When I was younger, I used to shoot them and stuff them. But now . . ." He shook his head. "I prefer to just watch. I've made quite a few sketches since I have come to America. You have a wide variety of interesting species over here."

"You mean you found one thing you like? Come on," she urged. "I'm starving."

She led him down the road, the immature corn in rich green rows to either side. Along the verge, wildflowers grew, a profusion of deep blue larkspur and white daisies, mixed with the humble dandelions. A few bees and butterflies worked among the blossoms. Zan half-expected Edward to get down on his hands and knees to study the insects, but apparently it was only birds that interested him.

"It's always a shock to me," he said, "when I see the trees, down where the river flows. The change is so sudden, from field to forest."

"Not exactly a forest, God knows. But it sure rests the eyes. Wait till there hasn't been rain for a couple of weeks. Then the trees by the Smoky are the only green things around."

"I can see why you would prefer your farm to be by the water's edge. Both for irrigation and aesthetics."

"Oh, Beakman's place isn't like this. Most of the timber's been sold off. It's scarce, and gets a good price. 'Specially the hardwoods."

They were among the trees now, broad leaves swaying overhead, dappling them with broken sunlight. Edward could hear the rush of the water from nearby, a miracle in this land of thirsty soil. He followed Zan's slim figure, thinking that seen from behind something could be said for a female in pants. Sternly he quashed the thought.

Trousers were, and so far as he was concerned, would always remain indecent on a woman. For a women to wear such things could be viewed as a blatant usurpation of man's proper authority. Unchecked, who knew where it might lead? A female prime minister, perhaps.

Edward chortled at the outrageous thought. Zan, glancing back, neglected to duck while walking under an extended tree-branch. Her lovely face screwed up as she pressed one hand to the top of her head. "Did you say something?"

"No. Are you all right?"

"Oh, yeah. My father said my head's my hardest part."

"I can believe it." The rest of her would probably be as soft as milk. Her breasts, for instance . . . small but shown to advantage in her red shirt. Edward controlled his stampeding imagination. He knew her by now to be lean and well-muscled, fit as a soldier, not soft anywhere.

As he followed her to the water's edge, he revised his opinion. Her lips had been soft, tentatively moving under his. And no doubt the places never touched by the sun would be pleasing to his questing hands. He wondered what it would be like to make love to a woman who could match a man strength for strength. Would she be as straightforward in bed as in all her other dealings with him? Once he tutored her in the ways of the flesh, no doubt she would be.

"Sit down," she said, in the tone of one who has said a thing several times.

She perched on a twisted root, one hand dipped inside the basket, as she stared up at him. "You got sunstroke or something? Sit down."

The wide peat-colored water slipped by a few feet from where he sat, making its own breeze. Just to his left he could see the wooden bridge that crossed the Smoky Hill. The water did not appear deep to him, though it was swift and broad, yet he remembered hearing how even a rivulet out here could suddenly become a raging hell of water if too much rain fell for the earth to receive.

"Here you go," Zan said, handing him a sandwich. "I think it's some kind of canned meat."

"Macready's Best Potted Ham. We brought quite a few tins of it with us. Uncle Frederick has always been fond of it."

"Eat up. There's another in here for you." She raised both arms above her head and said explosively, "It's awful pretty here, isn't it?"

He averted his eyes from her thrusting breasts. Under his hands was some sort of grass, with tiny blue flowers peering up from under the leaves. Suddenly he knew why he couldn't keep unsuitable thoughts about this most unsuitable girl from his mind. The last time he'd picnicked by a river, it had been the Thames, on an excursion to Hampton Court. There he'd proposed to Nerissa, she of the brunette ringlets and dimpled smile.

She'd flirted with him for weeks, singling him out from among the others who pursued her. When she walked away from the others with him, he'd known it was time to ask. She had agreed, pending her father's approval. But when he'd chastely kissed her, she carried on as though he'd attempted rapine, running to her mother and crying like a madwoman.

"Has that one gone bad?" A sharp voice, louder and far less dulcet than Nerissa's, reached his ears.

Edward started and looked around. Zan leaned back against the tree trunk, one knee up, clasped in her interlinked fingers. "Judging from your face," she said, "you look like you just bit into a worm. That sandwich okay?"

"Yes, there's nothing wrong with it."

"Good. You know, every time Fred does something, I get more and more impressed. There's a couple pieces of pie in here, and they're not crushed a particle. More'n I can do. Here, have a slug of this."

She uncurled and handed him a flask. Tilting his head back, he let the cool tartness of the lemonade flow down his throat, washing away the bitter taste that rose every time he thought of Nerissa.

"Sometimes when the summer gets real bad," Zan said, "my brothers and me come down to the river to swim. We'd have more fun than a pig in a wallow. Faith used to, too, till she got too grand. Maybe you'd like to come along with us, one of these dog days."

"My brothers and I would swim as well in the summer. There's a large ornamental lake on my father's estate. Once, I remember . . ." He looked back at a happier time.

"What?" Golly, Zan thought, I do believe the man's about

to crack a smile. She waited for it, as she sometimes waited for the dawn, with eager anticipation of an ordinary wonder.

He fought it down. "Nothing. Hadn't we better be going on?"

"Hold your horses. I never pass up a piece of pie. Then I might lie down for a nap. The sun sure takes it out of you."

"I'll wake you on my return, then," he said, pushing himself up from the grass.

"What's the all-fired hurry? Five minutes to eat pie, and it's blackberry. Mr. Taylor isn't going anywhere."

"You are the one who is always driving forward, are you not?"

"Least I know the difference between driving hard and driving foolish. There's working time and there's pie-eating time, and this is pie-eating time. You go on, if you've a mind to, and I'll catch up."

She raised the wedge of gold pastry to her lips, using both hands, and nibbled off the point with her white teeth. She closed her eyes in appreciation, giving a little shake of her head. A low "mmmm" of pleasure came from her as she licked the purple juice from her lips.

Edward watched in fascination. He knew when a women was trying to engage a man's attention. She'd give herself away with little sideways glances and obvious disdain. There were none of these signs with Zan. She was simply eating and enjoying a piece of pie. Yet he found her the most erotic sight he'd seen in years . . . no, in a lifetime.

"Sure I can't interest you?" she asked. She took another healthy bite, and the juice dripped down her chin. Before she could raise her arm to rub with her sleeve, he knelt down and wiped the stickiness off. He watched her bright eyes widen as he licked his thumb.

"It is good," he said, holding her gaze.

Zan found she couldn't look away. She still held the pie wedge in the air. Edward grasped her wrist and pulled her hand close to his mouth, taking a bite from the pie. He did something to the underside of her wrist. Her whole arm tingled.

"It's very good," he said, swallowing. Then he took the piece and laid it down on the basket. Leaning forward, he lipped away the purple juice that had run down her chin.

Her breath coming fast, her lips were too dry to form words. Parts of her were cold and others hot and heavy. She trembled as he slowly made his way from her chin to her jaw, scouring with his hot tongue.

Coming to her neck, he nipped the tender side. Zan stiffened, a soft wordless cry breaking from her. She knew it was not a protest, but a demand.

Edward, however, jerked away as though she'd suddenly turned into a snake. "I'm . . . sorry," he said, passing his hand over his brow. "I don't seem to know how to . . ." She saw him straighten up, the haughty expression returning to harden his features.

"Pray accept my apologies, Miss Lind. Between last night and what just occurred, I have been acting the cad. I want to assure you that nothing of this sort will ever happen again."

Zan blinked at him, wanting to tell him she didn't mind all that much. He didn't give her time. Turning from her with a jerk, he walked down to the water's edge.

CHAPTER
5

"No, Pa's not here. He's gone down to the Last Resort," Mary said. She was the second oldest of the Taylor girls and often minded the counter when her parents were out. As she and Zan were the same age, they had been playmates when children. Mrs. Lind had cherished hopes that Mary's gentle ways would rub off on her own, wilder daughter. But dolls and sewing bees couldn't hold much enticement when there were gardens to hoe and crops to reap.

"We'll go 'long and see if we can't find him."

Even in the dim light of the store, Zan could see Mary's scandalized expression. "You shouldn't go *there*. They drink there. Mama says—"

"Thanks, Mary. Give my best to your Mama when you see her. Come on, Edward."

He looked up from a pyramid of tea cans. "Did you receive any Earl Grey in this last shipment, Miss Taylor?"

"No, sir. We've got black and green and China, just like always." Edward nodded and went out. Zan would have followed, if Mary hadn't caught her arm. "He must have asked me about that Earl feller twenty times since he came here. Who is he?"

"I don't know. The name of some kind of tea, I reckon. Can't you order him some next time? Save him from bothering you all the time?"

"You seem mighty particular about His Lordship all of a sudden," Mary said, giving her a sideways glance.

"Who knows? Something's got to sweeten up his temper. Maybe gray tea will do it. I better go."

Crossing Main Street with him, Zan had a horrible suspicion that the next person to do business at the mercantile would hear a wagonload of gossip about her and Edward. If anyone knew the whole of it, there'd be a scandal for sure. She could only be glad nobody knew anything about their sparking. Her fingers still tingled!

She stole a glance at him. His face was set in its usual grim lines. Zan wondered if she'd ever be able to read him, or if he'd be a mystery for the whole summer. For instance, she was dying to know why he'd kissed her. The two times didn't seem to have anything in common, besides her being alone with him. With a flicker of anticipation, she remembered they'd be alone on the walk back as well.

From the pink boardinghouse, finally mellowing into a bearable shade, came twin halloos.

"How-do, Your Lordship!"

"Well, Zan Lind, as I live and breathe!"

"We're for it now," Zan muttered to him.

Edward took off his hat and bowed, one hand over his heart. "Good afternoon, ladies."

"What brings you into town, Your Lordship? Is Fred with you?" Miss Minnie asked.

"Course he's not. Do you see him?" her sister demanded. Giving Zan a squinting look, Maisie said, "Them pants is a down-right scandal. Surprised your mother lets you out of the house like that. But Inga Lind never had a lick of sense."

The only thing to do was nod and smile and pretend she hadn't heard. "They're awful comfortable, though, Miss Maisie. You ought to try a pair."

Minnie cackled. "Huh, she'd look like a walking windmill."

"And you'd look just the same. What's more, you're more likely to pull a fool stunt like that than me. Such a thing at your age."

"How's my age different from yours?" Minnie said crushingly. "What's this I hear about your working for the Winchesters, Zan?"

"Miss Lind has agreed to help me with my farming," Edward said, before Zan could answer.

"What you paying her?" Maisie asked.

Zan smiled like a cat with a free entrance ticket to a dairy barn. "Not enough. Come on, Ed . . . Your Lordship."

But Miss Maisie wasn't through yet. "Guess that means your father's hard up, if he's got to send you out to working."

No matter how Zan replied, whether yes or no, the answer would be all over town in a heartbeat. A sacrifice had to be made. Fortunately, she had one ready made from the mercantile. "We better be getting along to the Last Resort. Got business to see to. Nice talking to you, ladies. . . ."

"You don't mean to say . . ." Minnie pressed her hand to her thin chest. "Edward Winchester, you should be ashamed taking an innocent . . . well, Zan into a den of iniquity!"

A lightning flash seemed to come and go in his gray eyes. "We have a motto about that in England—the royal motto. *Honi soit qui mal y pense*, which in English means—'Evil to him who evil thinks.' "

Maisie gave a sharp cackle. "He's got you there! 'Sides, what could happen to Zan in such a place? A man wants a

56

pretty gal to sit on his lap, not a bag of bones, or that's what your husband used to say."

"Maybe my husband used to say it, but yours practiced what mine preached."

"Come on," Zan murmured quickly. "Let's go."

Walking away, she felt better. Mary could gossip all she wanted. Chances were nobody would listen to her tale of a romance between Edward and herself, not with the wild stories the twins would spread at the drop of a hat.

"Told you there was nothing to worry about," she said. "They wouldn't believe you and me were sparking if they caught us in a haystack with our britches down."

"They are right, however. You are a scandal." But he didn't seem disapproving. If anything, there was a note of admiration in his voice.

"No, I'm not. Miss Lottie's a scandal. Hey there, Miss Lottie!" she called and waved at the plump woman in the tight scarlet dress walking up the other side of the street.

The black-fringed parasol lifted and a ladylike hand languidly summoned Zan to come over. "Back in a minute," Zan said. Deftly avoiding a wagon and team, she skirted sinkholes and muck in the street. After a few minutes' conversation and a handshake, she came back.

When she reached the boardwalk on the other side, it was to find Edward scowling at her. "How do you know . . . *her?*"

"Oh, I've done some work for her before."

"What?"

She couldn't help laughing at his outraged expression. "Couple of weeks ago, after Mr. Sutherland and Abby decided to get hitched up, I did some weeding and whatnot in that rose garden she planted."

"Yes, of course, I don't know what I was thinking."

"Miss Lottie likes the tone it gives to the place. She's just asked me to come back once a week to keep it looking nice."

"You can't possibly."

"Oh, don't worry. I'll work in the evenings after I'm done at your place."

"That's worse! At night would be when the . . . shall we say . . . debaucheries take place."

"De-whateries? If you mean the . . . um . . . entertainment, it sure as shooting doesn't take place in the garden. Too many prickles. 'Sides, I'll be gone by dark and nothing much happens at the First Resort till then anyhow."

"How would you know?"

"Heck, everybody knows that much. You know, I kind of feel sorry for her," Zan said, looking across the street at the woman in the too-tight dress. "What with temperance coming in and folks getting so upright and moral, I don't know how much longer she can hold out. I hear she's been thinking of moving to Dodge. That's where the real money is when it comes to carrying-on."

"Her business dealings shouldn't have any place in your thoughts. I don't wish to scold—"

"But you're going to. Look here, Edward, I'm a business-woman myself, or would like to be. Maybe it's a different business, but that doesn't mean I can't be understanding about another's trouble."

He started walking past the jail to the bright red building that held the Last Resort. "I'll never get used to you," he said, turning in.

One of the drawbacks to traveling with Uncle Frederick was his insistence on finding quaint establishments that to him expressed the true character of a country. If to him the true character had consisted of the finest restaurants and palaces of culture, Edward would have found no quarrel with the older man's explorations. Regrettably, however, Frederick's ideas were culled from sensational fiction and the notion that squalid and charming went hand in hand.

The Last Resort had at least the redeeming qualities of cuspidors on the floor and a bartender who occasionally wiped down the bar with a cloth that had not seen service in the privy. Edward had visited, in his uncle's company, many a saloon that lacked these refinements.

Not too many men sat around the wooden tables, mostly anonymous cowpunchers and traveling drummers. None of them seemed to notice Zan. Edward wondered if Cord had improved the whiskey to the point where beautiful women were accepted as merely a part of an alcoholic fantasy.

He glanced at Zan. "Do you see Mr. Taylor?"

"Nope, maybe he's in Mr. Spencer's office. I'll ask Mr. Thompson. What do you want to drink?"

"I'll get it. You sit down."

"Thanks. I'll take a slug of the usual."

The black man behind the bar greeted him with a smile. "Nice to see you back again. It's been a while. What can I get for you today, Mr. Winchester?"

"Two glasses of whatever Miss Lind usually orders, Mr. Thompson, thank you."

"Okay," Charlie said, looking past Edward to give Zan a nod. He lifted a stoneware jug onto the bar and poured out a gush of brown liquid into a pair of glasses. The color reminded Edward of the dark ales he'd often drunk during festivals at home, brewed by the local tenantry, even to the creamy foam that floated on top.

He shot Zan a doubtful look. Perhaps she was used to liquor. He hoped he wouldn't have to support a drunken Venus home. Moreover, he hoped this "usual" was not too strong. He had enough trouble holding on to his dignity when alone with her without adding alcohol to the mix. The incident by the river never should have taken place.

He paid and bore the two glasses over to the table. "Would you be so good as to exchange chairs with me?"

"What for?"

"A young lady shouldn't be forced to . . . sit opposite such a painting as that." He glanced briefly at the garish canvas above the bar. A woman sprawled on her stomach, supported by a cushioned divan, the scene depicted in the brightest possible combination of flesh-pink and crimson.

"It's not like I haven't seen it before." With bad grace she pushed herself out of the chair and walked around the table. "There, happy?"

She lifted her glass to her lips. Edward could see her throat working as she swallowed. "Ah," she sighed, putting down the glass. "That's good on a day like this."

Edward sipped more cautiously, first inhaling the bouquet, then rolling the flavor on his tongue. The strange, spicy taste surprised him. Even more surprising was the lack of any tang or sting that might indicate the presence of liquor.

"What is it?"

"Sarsaparilla. It's kind of a sissy drink, but I like it. It's even better when it's been in the cellar so it's good and cool, but I'll take what I can get."

"Sarsaparilla is a root of some sort, is it not?" He took another sip, the various flavors blending. Concentrating, he thought he could make out a hint of cinnamon and some taste reminiscent of ginger, though it was difficult to be certain.

"I like it," he pronounced finally.

"Are you allowed to do that?" she asked, a twinkle coming into her eyes. "It's American, you know."

"I don't dislike everything about this country, Zan."

"Just most things," she added. Then she laughed and said, "Are you sure you didn't want to swap places with me so you could look at her?"

Edward realized his gaze had been straying to the painting over the bar. He felt his face color. "I was merely comparing her to the original."

A cowpoke on the way back to the bar for a refill turned at these words. "You know her? What's her name?"

"The young lady and I were having a private conversation, sir."

"Young lady?" The other man pushed back his hat. "By jingo, it is. Say, you wouldn't be the one that sat for that there picture, would you?"

"Doesn't look like anybody 'sat' for it," Zan said, with a nod and a grin toward the shapely pink posterior raised in the center of the painting.

Edward scowled at her free and easy ways. She shouldn't even be speaking to a stranger, let alone discussing such a topic. Hoping to move the cowpoke along, he said glacially, "Permit me to buy you a drink."

"Sure, friend, even if you do talk mighty funny. First, tell me her name, 'cause I'm just plum wild about her."

Zan looked at him no less expectantly. Glancing around, Edward saw that everyone, even the three men playing cards in the corner, had stopped their game to listen. Reluctantly he said, "Her name was Louise O'Murphy."

"O'Murphy?" the cowpoke asked. "Irish? Well, I'll be jiggered."

"Where'd you know her from?" Zan asked, propping her chin on her hand. She looked fascinated at this seeming revelation of his baser nature.

"Munich."

"She lives in Munich, Tennessee?" the cowpoke said. "Boys, I'm moving out."

"No," Edward said. "Munich, Germany. The original of that painting hangs in a museum there, though it was painted in France by François Boucher." And, he thought, if Boucher could have foreseen what some butchering hack would do to it, he would have given up his oil painting for knitting.

"Germany, huh?" the cowpoke said. "It's a far piece, but for a woman like that, no ride is too far."

Zan shook her head. "It don't sound to me like she's among the living any more, eh, Edward?"

"Edward?" the cowpoke said, changing the subject. "What kind of damfool name is that? And why do you talk so funny and know so much about . . . about everything? I think I better punch you right in the nose." He very slowly folded one set of hairy fingers into a fist.

Charlie the barkeep shook a bottle so the amber liquor inside swished and gurgled. "Hey, Slim, let me pour you one on the house!"

Like a lonesome calf hearing it mother's bellow, the cowpoke turned blindly toward the sound. "Don't . . . hic . . . mind if I do," he said, stumbling in his haste.

Zan said softly, "You've got a real knack for making friends right quick, Edward."

"I've no interest in striking up friendships with drunken transients. As we are here to find Mr. Taylor, let us do so, transact our business, and go home."

"All right." She turned around in her seat. The cowpoke stood transfixed at the bar, his glass raised in salute to the lovely late Louise. Zan shook her head in wonder, then said, "Hey, Mr. Thompson. Is Mr. Taylor here?"

"Sure is. He's talking to Cord about buying and selling. Mrs. Taylor's got a down on us these days, you know? And Mr. Taylor's taking plenty of noise about doing business with our kind of people. 'Wine is a mocker, strong drink is raging.' "

The cowpoke said, "Don't start talking Bible-talk. It's too much on top of that feller over there."

Charlie just smiled. "Mr. Taylor should be out soon. You want some more of that gas juice?"

"You bet," Zan said. She drained her glass. "Won't be long before it's all you're going to be able to sell. Might as well get mine while there's still some to get."

"Funny, that's what the men were saying about whiskey. Before we're all much older, this state's going to be drier than an old bone in a windstorm. How about you, Mr. Winchester? Would you care for another shot?"

Half an hour went by with Zan and Charlie discussing the temperance movement, aided by occasional hiccuping commentary from the cowpoke. Edward sipped his peculiar beverage and tried to hold on to his patience. It seemed twice eternity before the door to Cord Spencer's office opened. The gambler and the merchant stepped out, shaking hands.

Mr. Taylor turned around and saw Zan. "Hello, there, Miss Lind. Guess you're hunting me down for my answer. Now, I'll tell you like I told your mother. If you're willing to do the work to clean up those rollers and that evaporator, I'm willing to rent you the mill at a fair price."

"What's fair?" Zan asked.

The merchant beamed, sticking his thumbs into the armholes of his waistcoat. "Knew you was smart as a whip! What do you say we discuss the price when we see how much sorghum molasses is selling for at the end of the season? It may go down, you know, and I'd hate for you to be stuck with some high number."

"And what," Edward asked, turning around in his seat, "if the price continues to climb? Then you adjust your rate upward, leaving us with less of a profit?"

"Oh, uh, didn't see you there, your . . . uh . . . knightliness. It's a reasonable point. But you can't expect me to go to the trouble and expense of handing over my property to you without some kind of guarantee I'll make money out of it."

"You just said that we're supposed to take all the trouble and expense ourselves," Zan put in.

A slightly hunted look came into Mr. Taylor's eyes as they shifted again from Edward to Zan. Patently, he would have preferred speaking only to one party. "There's that, 'course.

But still, sorghum milling is a dirty, sticky job. You might not take care to keep my property in the best condition."

Zan stood up straight, her tanned skin taking on a tinge of rose as the blood came to her face. "I'm Inga Lind's daughter," she said, her voice ringing. "And my mother would skin me alive if I didn't leave your mill cleaner than it is now. So state your price, Mr. Taylor, or we'll ship to Hays City or Salina for the processing." She glanced at Edward. "Right, partner?"

"Absolutely."

"Now, don't be so quick," Mr. Taylor said, waving a hand in surrender. "I'm sure we can come to some arrangement. Something that suits you and me both."

Cord Spencer laughed and patted the merchant on the shoulder. "Remind me to have her do my haggling for me, next time. You won't get away with so much, you rapscallion."

She stopped him short by saying, "I'll need to talk to you, too, Mr. Spencer. I want to take all those empty jugs in your storeroom off your hands. Can I see you later?"

"Take 'em," he said. "If I start trading with you, you'll have my vest buttons and my back teeth before I can say 'knife.' You got yourself a fine partner, Mr. Winchester. Hope you appreciate her."

"More all the time, sir."

"Good to hear it." Cord went into his office.

Though he'd had little contact with him, Edward could see more that was likable in the southerner than in most of the people in Harmony. Prior to the War Between the States, there'd been many Americans from the southern states making what amounted to pilgrimages to Britain. Most of them had been raised on Sir Walter Scott and his tales of chivalry.

Edward didn't know if Cord Spencer or his family had

been among the tourists, but having met many a Southerner in his own country, he knew that they usually had qualities of gentility and culture that most Americans sadly lacked. Furthermore, Spencer had recently married the former Samantha Evans, possibly the most truly cultured woman in the town, Lillie Taylor's pretensions put aside.

After coming to a satisfactory agreement with Mr. Taylor, Zan and Edward left the saloon. She said, "That was a lucky break; Cord handing us the jugs without charge. The distilleries pay him two cents each to send 'em back, but they don't pay for shipping 'em on the railway. It doesn't make sense for him to send 'em unless he's got a ton of 'em."

"So they sit in his storehouse until he has enough to send back profitably?"

"Yep. Now my brother-in-law happened to hear Cord say once that the bugs were getting real bad in the summertime in his storeroom, unless Charlie rinses each jug out awful particular. Even then, one missed jug and you've got drunken ants all over the place!"

"But now this is our sticky problem?"

Zan glanced at him doubtfully. Could he have been making a joke? But his face hadn't changed. "It's not a big deal," she said. "A couple of nickel's worth of candy, and I'll bet my little sister Sarah, and Amanda, Faith's stepdaughter, would be willing to wash 'em for us."

"For so little?"

"Little? I would have taken on an easy job like that when I was ten, and done it for two cents' worth of licorice. But the kids today are smarter than I was."

"I don't know about that," he said. "The way you manipulated Mr. Taylor was masterly."

Zan passed her hand over her hair, uneasily pleased by his compliment. "Wasn't much. I've heard he's been losing business to some of the bigger outfits down the line, that's all. I tell you, though, you could have knocked me down with a feather when he said that about Mother. *I* didn't know she'd talked to him about using the mill."

"I thought perhaps you'd suggested it to her."

"Nope. She must have come up the notion on her own. She didn't mention a word to me. I kind of wonder if she might be on my side about Quintus."

Zan stopped opposite the barbershop. "Let's cut over here, so we don't have to run past the boardinghouse again."

"Very well. One Inquisition a day is enough for me."

" 'Sides, long as I'm down here, I might as well stop in to see Faith. We can cut through the alley."

Edward paused. "I think I shall stop in to visit Dr. Tanner. Perhaps he can make some recommendation for a suitable treatment for Buck."

"Buck who? Oh, your ox. I don't reckon the Doc'll mind prescribing for a dumb animal, considering some of the people around here. I guess I'll see you tomorrow, then."

Suddenly Zan felt a little shy. Last night he'd kissed her. Today, he'd shown her a much better way of keeping her face clean than using a napkin. Though he'd seemed sorry for each incident, Zan knew she was far from feeling regretful. She had to wonder what would happen tomorrow. Looking up into his dark eyes, she said more softly, "So long. Till tomorrow."

He nodded gravely, then raised one slanting eyebrow. "Not before eight, however. I want your word, Zan."

"Aw, heck, you're not still worried about what folks are going to say? You heard Miss Minnie and Miss Maisie. A feller wants something soft on his lap after a hard day."

"If that were all a man wanted, he could obtain a cat. For my own peace of mind, Zan, you will not come to the house before eight o'clock in the morning, nor will you stay after dark." His eyes burned intently into hers for a moment.

Zan found herself nodding involuntarily.

CHAPTER
6

Zan found Faith stretching her arms and a piece of knotted string in the parlor of the new Harmony hotel. Without speaking, Zan took one end and held it up against the wall.

Faith blew a strand of blond hair off her hot forehead. "Thanks, Zan. Hold it there while I count it off."

Wrinkling her face in concentration, she walked up the room, counting knots. "Thirteen. The last two times it came out twelve and fourteen, so thirteen is probably right. Close enough, anyway."

"What's all this for?"

"Wallpaper," she said, as one would talk of plague. "It's fast becoming the bane of my life. And, of course, dearly as I love Kincaid, there's no denying men are very little help when you must decide between one pattern and another. I can't tell you what I went through to get him to help me choose these drapes." She looked fondly at the heavy red material that hung to either side of the windows.

In all her visits to the hotel, this was the first time Zan had seen sunlight streaming into the parlor. It showed up the quality of the blue upholstery on the furniture, but also revealed

the bare wooden boards of the floor. The long-expected carpet
from Chicago still had not arrived.

"I probably won't be much more help than a man," she
said, "but why don't you show me what you've got?"

Her sister looked at her in some surprise. Then she said,
doubtfully, "If you'd be interested . . ."

A "wish" book lay open on the round table in the center
of the parlor. "Now, I've pretty much narrowed it down to
these two," Faith said, putting her slender forefinger down
on the open page.

Zan looked over her sister's shoulder at the black and white
sketch. "What's it supposed to be?"

Bending over the book, Faith read aloud, " 'A pleasing
shade of maroon, marked by representations of wrens, oak
leaves, and acorns. Flocked.' "

"I guess so, if there's a bunch of birds."

"Flocked means raised and cut like velvet," Faith explained
in the tone of the schoolmistress she used to be.

"If you say so. What's the other one like?"

" 'A bright russet, smooth, with vines, roses and mourning
doves.' "

"Sounds to me like they're pretty much the same," Zan
said, sticking her hands in her pockets.

"That's just what Kincaid says." Faith looked at her younger sister with a mixture of exasperation and amusement.
"You're always going to be a tomboy, aren't you, Zan?"

"Least I don't think I'll ever tear my hair out over wallpaper. I like paint. It washes, or if not, you just paint again.
As for choosing between these two . . ." She shrugged and
said, "Why don't you ask Mrs. Taylor to help you? She's
always trying to make the town better looking."

"Yes, and take a good look at what she's done to it! Pink
and purple buildings! Bright yellow and brighter blue side by
side! And Kincaid can't understand why I want to change the

outside of the hotel. Tell me, don't you think a nice medium brown picked out with yellow would look much better than this awful pink?"

"Like you say, Faith, I'm a tomboy. At least pink's a cheerful color."

"Cheerful!" Faith scoffed. "I'd prefer dignified to looking like a . . . house of ill repute. Anyway, I think I can manage to decorate the inside without Mrs. Taylor's opinion."

"Well, then, what about Edward?"

"And who is Edward?"

"Oh, come on. Edward Winchester, my boss, or I guess I should say partner."

"His Eminence? He'd never concern himself with . . . and since when do you call him Edward?"

"I can't run around calling him Your Earldom every time I want to talk to him, can I?"

Faith peered closely at her sister in the strong sunshine. "Zan, you're blushing!"

"No, I'm not." Her hand crept to her cheek. She did feel warm. "It's just hot in here, and stuffy. Why don't you open those windows, for goodness' sake?"

"They're painted shut. Kincaid hasn't gotten around to fixing them, what with all the other things that need doing. I don't see how we're ever going to get every room completely ready before the Fourth."

"Why the Fourth, in particular?"

"With all the folks coming in to celebrate, Kincaid figures there'll be more than a few who will want to stay overnight. If we make a good impression on them, who knows? We may be actually showing some kind of a profit before the end of the year." Faith looked around and sighed. "But never mind that! What's all this about . . . *him?*"

"There's nothing to say. Golly, make a mountain out of a molehill, why don't you? I only mentioned him at all 'cause he knows all about stuff like art."

"He does?"

"Yeah, plus, he's got better eyesight than anybody I've ever met up with, and maybe he can make out which one of these bird papers is better. There doesn't seem to be anything about birds that he doesn't know." Zan told Faith about Edward's excitement at spotting the hawk.

"It seems he's impressed you. Soon you'll be telling me that he's not really rude or arrogant, and that he's much nicer than the poison ivy he so resembles."

"I figure we can get along all right until the crop's brought in. He can be as nasty as he pleases, so long as I get my money and my cut." She couldn't help thinking about how nice he could be, and how passionate.

"Has it gotten even warmer in here, Zan? You're blushing again. Is something going on between you two that Mother or Father should know about?"

"No," Zan denied, shaking her head so vehemently that her long braid slapped against her shoulders. "Not a thing. We're just working his farm together. I got more to worry about from Uncle Fred than from Edward."

"You surprise me! I wouldn't of thought any harm of that sweet old—"

"Boy, your fancy's working at full steam these days, Faith. Tell that husband of yours you need to get out more. I just meant that Uncle Fred's cooking is so good, I may bust the freight scale next time I stop in to the depot."

Faith relaxed as she waved away her joke. "I don't think you'll ever grow up. You know, Mother's worried that you won't ever settle down. Don't you ever wish for a home and a husband of your own?"

"If I did, it wouldn't be Uncle Fred."

"I'm serious," Faith said. "You're eighteen now; it's time to be thinking of these things. Don't you want children?"

"I figure I'll pick 'em up ready made, like you did. Where are Amanda and Kincaid, anyhow?"

"They went to the depot to collect some packages. Joseph Taylor didn't let us know they were there until today. Honestly, that boy gets dreamier and dreamier. Sits there all day with his nose in a yellow-back novel and hardly looks up, even when the train goes through."

"Can't blame him. I've never wanted to go much beyond my backyard, but there's plenty of folks who do. Look at Edward. He's just eaten up with a longing to go home to England. Maybe I can help him do it."

Zan realized she probably shouldn't have mentioned him again. The bright, interested look was back in her sister's eyes, after she'd been to so much trouble to dim it. But somehow Edward's name just slipped out, as though her every thought were connected to him.

"Speaking of home, I'll be getting along now."

"No, wait. I want you to try a piece of my rhubarb pie. I've been experimenting with larger batches of pastry and other things, to prepare for the bigger groups I'll be feeding."

"It's kind of close to dinner, but I'm willing to try anything once. If it doesn't kill me, I'm even willing to try it again."

Leading the way through a swinging door to the kitchen, far more completely finished than the parlor, Faith said, "Oh, I don't imagine it will kill you. I was extra careful to strip off all the leaves and small stalks."

She cut and served Zan a modestly proportioned slice. "Now be honest. You may not know much about wallpaper, but you do know eating. Almost everything about it. Tell me how my pie compares to Uncle Fred's."

"All I've had of his was blackberry. No, come to think of it, that was made by either Miss Minnie or Miss Maisie." She took an ample bite.

"I've heard the way they run after him is simply shameful

71

for women of their age. Why, Zan, what's the matter?"

Zan put her fingers over her mouth and shook her head. With an effort, she swallowed. "Kind of sweet," she said in a strained whisper.

"Too sweet?"

"Water?"

Faith poured her a glass from the pitcher on the table. "I know I doubled Mother's receipt exactly. You'd think if anything it would be too tart."

After drinking thirstily, Zan said, "You don't believe me; you try it."

"All right." Almost as soon as she chewed, her eyes bulged and she put her hand to her throat. Zan handed her the glass of water.

When her sister had finished choking, Zan said, "Faith, it's not fit for people to eat, unless maybe you could squeeze a lemon over it. This under crust is good though. Darn good. Not soggy a mite."

There were tears in Faith's eyes that couldn't be accounted for by the throat-closing sweetness. "I did so want to have some for Kincaid. He says rhubarb is his favorite."

Zan stood up from the table. "If I ever do marry, maybe it should be to Uncle Fred. At least he could do the cooking."

Smiling through her disappointment, Faith said, "I confess I can't see you in a 'kaliker' apron, making biscuits for a large family."

"Neither can I. But I tell you what . . . why don't you scoop the filling out from the crust and stew it up? Add lemon, like I said. At worst, you'll be out a couple of lemons. Maybe, though, it'll work as a side dish."

"Oh, Zan, what a ridiculous idea! It's ruined and that's that. I'll feed it to the pig. He won't mind."

"Is that anyway to talk about your new husband?" She

72

gave the confounded Faith a lively grin. "You deserved it! Well, I'll say hello to the folks for you."

But Faith didn't hear. She'd turned toward the back door as a heliotrope turns toward the sun. In a moment, Zan heard what her sister, ears sharpened by love, had already heard; the laughter of her husband and stepdaughter.

She'd liked the man who was to become her brother-in-law, even when he'd been brooding over the death of his first wife and Amanda's resentments. Since marrying Faith, Kincaid Hutton had become the jovial man nature meant him to be. All the same, Zan knew that even if things had been different, she still could never have felt a particle of attraction toward him.

Faith, of course, had seemed to fall for him like a ton of bricks. They'd married in haste, but showed no signs of repentance. Heedless of her presence or of Amanda's, Kincaid swept Faith into his arms, all but bending her backward as he kissed her enthusiastically.

Zan and the little girl rolled their eyes at each other. "Father! Yuk!" Amanda protested.

When he set Faith upright, Zan saw stars sparkling in her sister's eyes. Obviously he could make her forget entirely about spoiled pies and doubtful wallpaper. There were a few stars, too, in Kincaid's green eyes as he turned to greet Zan. "Staying for supper?"

"No, thanks. Better run on home."

"Suit yourself. What's this I hear about you and a certain gent boozing it up at the Last Resort?"

"Zan!" Faith exclaimed. "You were drinking? Let me smell your breath!"

Zan backed away from her sister. "Get off! We didn't have anything but sarsaparilla. And it's not like I haven't been in there before now, you know."

"What? Does Father know?"

"He ought to; he's the one that took me in the first time. Sometimes when you've been putting in a hard day in the field, you want something with a little more body than just water. So Father'd order a beer and me my sarsaparilla. I must have been five or six the first time."

"And Mother condones this? I can't believe it."

"I don't know if she likes it, but I can't think she doesn't know. She knows everything. And then some. 'Sides, it's none of your business anyway, Faith."

"It most certainly is! How does it look, my little sister going into a low, degraded place like that. This kind of thing reflects on the entire family. Next thing you know, you'll be hobnobbing with those girls at the First Resort."

Zan considered mentioning her business arrangement with Luscious Lottie, but closed her mouth over the words. A tinge of red in Kincaid's otherwise dark face told her that gossip on that point as well must have reached him at the depot. He didn't seem eager to add to the hornet's nest his jesting question had stirred up.

"Well," Zan said lamely, "I might be your little sister, but I'm not Sarah. The Last Resort's never done me a smidge of harm in all the time I've been going there. And if I took it into my head to go to the First Resort, it most likely wouldn't do me any harm, either."

"Not in front of the child," Faith said sternly.

"What's *degraded* mean, Faith?" Amanda wanted to know.

"Never mind. You need to get washed up before supper. Now, scoot." With much foot-dragging, the little girl went out. Kincaid stayed behind, apparently sorry he'd raised the matter.

Faith gave her sister a severe glance. "How can you do such horrible things? Why, even to be seen in front of a saloon is ruinous to a girl's reputation! Even a married woman wouldn't dare . . . unless she were utterly dead to all feelings

74

of morality and decency. The things that must go on in those places . . . I hardly like to think!"

A clever retort came into Zan's mind. " 'Evil to him who evil thinks,' " she said.

As her usually articulate sister gargled a response, Kincaid jumped into the conversation. "You'll never guess what else I found at the depot, Faith."

"Did you hear what . . . What did you say, dear?"

"Down at the depot. Not only did the lamps come in, but stuck up behind some boxes is one genuine turkey carpet, as used in fashionable parlors all across America."

"What? How long had it been there?"

"Joseph didn't know. A while. But it's all right. It was propped up in a dry spot."

"I swan, that boy hasn't got the sense God gave a goose. Well, where is it? Let me see!"

"Out in the wagon." As Faith went out the back door, as eager as a mother to see her far-traveled child, Kincaid winked at Zan. "Maybe you'd better clear out while the getting's good."

"Thanks; I'll do you a favor sometime."

"Would you?"

"Sure. What do you need?"

"Faith's got her heart set on some fancy flowers to line the walk. I'd put 'em in, but no plant I've touched has ever lived a week. I used to try gardening, to please my first wife. I never had much luck. Whatever color my thumbs are, it isn't green."

Zan mentally toted up the time she'd have to put in on the Double B, and the work at the First Resort. "I'll do it, but I don't see how I can before the Fourth of July. But I tell you what . . . you find out what she wants, and if I can manage it before then, I'll come down and take care of it."

"I've got the list right here," he said, tapping his temple. "Roses, daffodils, lilacs, and strawberries."

"Strawberries? I don't know. It's kind of late for those and too early to put out daffodils—they should be planted in the autumn. Maybe I could take a lilac cutting from Mother's plant—it's a good one—but it'll be a while before it takes root. But roses won't be a problem; I know where to get 'em. And you've got shade in the front yard—do you think she'd mind a dozen bleeding hearts?"

"Whatever will work. Do the best you can."

Zan could only say, "I'll try." Then Faith called for her and Kincaid to come out and see the new carpet.

In the end Zan stayed until near dark, helping Faith sweep up the floor and lay down a solid pad of newspaper. Then she and Kincaid stretched and tacked down the carpet while Faith scurried around with alternating squeaks of alarm and delight. Zan left the newly married couple standing in their parlor, arms tight around each other's waist, admiring the latest addition to their home and hotel.

As she left through the main entrance, the foyer lit by a single lamp, she heard a giggle. With a whir and a thump, Amanda slid down the curving wooden banister from the second floor. She stopped dead, halfway through a turn to go back up, when she saw Zan.

"Uh, it's one of my chores to shine the banister," she said defiantly.

"And you're doing a fine job, by the look of things." Zan looked at the gleaming wood disappearing up out of the light. "You know, that's something I've never tried. We didn't even have a rail on our stairs until two or three years ago."

"It's bully fun," Amanda said, warming up. She trotted up two steps and glanced back at Zan. "You want to try?"

"You don't have to ask me twice," Zan said, taking two steps toward the staircase. Then she bolted forward. As soon as she began to run, so did Amanda. They dashed up to the top, neck and neck, both laughing.

She let Amanda show her how it was done, mounting the shining banister as though it were a horse and giving a firm push off from the newel at the top. As the little girl shot out of sight, she whooped with happiness. After a moment Zan heard the patter of Amanda's small shoes coming back up the stairs for another go.

Zan didn't care to be thought of as a 'fraidy cat. She threw her denim-covered leg over the wood. Perhaps she pushed too strongly, or maybe it was the difference between doing and watching. At any rate, she felt as though she zipped through space twice as fast as Amanda. Part of it was from riding backward with no notion of how close to the end she was. There wasn't even time for fear when she bumped over the end post and flew off into space.

"My God," a clipped voice said. "Are you all right?"

She shook away the dancing lights behind her eyes. Blinking, she looked up and saw Edward bending over her. He put out a hand to help her up. Zan grinned and grasped it to scramble upward. Suddenly, however, her knees didn't seem to be working very well.

"Here, now," Edward said, supporting her against his chest. "You took a nasty bump there."

"I'm . . . I'm all right," she muttered into his shirt collar. He smelled of pipe smoke, like Dr. Tanner's office, with his own special tang underneath it. Even if she'd been feeling entirely herself, she could have stood here like this for an hour.

"I don't think you did more than bump it. You must have a rather thick skull." His sensitive fingers firmly yet gently explored beneath her smooth blond hair. Zan relaxed down to her toes, leaning her heavy head into his hand.

Tilting her head back, she gazed up at him through half-

77

closed eyes. The single lamp played up the planes and hollows of his face, and brought out the coppery glints in his hair. "That feels good . . . ow!"

She jerked away, putting her own hand gingerly to a throbbing knot on the back of her head. "Yipes! I really did fetch myself a blow on the noggin. You're right about my hard head, but that hurts!"

From behind her she heard her sister and brother-in-law coming into the registration area, with calls of "What was that?" and "Are you all right?" She couldn't but be glad that they hadn't found her in Edward Winchester's arms.

"What happened?" Faith asked.

Zan couldn't give Amanda away. "I slid down the banister and flew off," she said.

"What?" Faith put her hands on her hips. "I'm ashamed of you! Getting up to tricks like that, and at your age."

"Golly, I'm not ready for a rocking chair yet. What do you want to go and have a banister like that if you don't want anybody sliding on it?"

"No harm done, after all, Faith," Kincaid said. "I've kind of wanted to take a trip down that one myself, but I'm afraid of setting a bad example for Amanda."

"My sister wouldn't think of that!"

Edward said reflexively, "When I was eighteen, I seem to recall my brothers and I riding big silver trays down the carpeted front stairs of the Hall. It had a very bad effect on the butler, as well as on the trays. Poor old Montgomery. What we made him suffer!"

"You sound like a pack of young rowdies to me," Faith said.

"Oh, quite unredeemable characters, Mrs. Hutton. Quite unredeemable." He looked at Zan. "Are you feeling well enough to walk home?"

"You bet. See you later, Faith. Kincaid." She was about to

go slouching out with her hands in her pockets, when Edward crooked his elbow toward her. Hesitatingly, she passed her arm through his. As he led her toward the front door, she glanced over her shoulder at her flabbergasted sister. She winked broadly back at Faith and cherished her amazement.

Outside, she squinted at the strong afternoon sunlight. "I don't know why that sister of mine doesn't open the drapes. She's got all that fancy furniture loaded in there, and nobody can see a thing."

"Perhaps she is concerned her upholstery might fade."

"Then why'd she bother to get the good stuff? She could have gotten cheap cotton coverings and nobody would know the difference, not so long as it's black as pitch inside." She snapped her fingers. "That's right . . . Faith wanted you to look at some wallpaper. She can't make up her mind."

"Why should she think that I could be of any assistance?"

"Well, you know about fancy things like art, don't you? Faith doesn't know much about that kind of thing, though she's had more schooling than me."

"I'm afraid my education doesn't extend to wallcoverings."

Zan took her arm from his. "Now don't be that way! Golly, every time I get to where I might start to like you, you go all high-falutin' on me."

She strode along, outpacing him. But a funny buzzing sounded in her head and she stopped dead, rubbing her fingers over her eyebrows. Edward caught her as she swayed.

"I'm all right," she declared, pushing his hands away. But there was no doubt the world had suddenly begun acting very strangely. "Stand still," she commanded, her eyes rolling, trying to keep up with the seesaw he'd apparently begun to ride.

"I haven't moved. Why don't you sit down, here in the grass? I'll go back to borrow a buggy from Hutton."

"No, don't," she said, grabbing at his arm and missing. "I'll be all right in a minute or two. If I come back in a buggy after setting out on foot, Mother will think I'm either dead or married."

"Nevertheless . . ."

"No, it's okay now. 'Cept I feel like I've got a swarm of bees in my head." Looking past him, she let out a groan and covered her eyes with the palms of her hands.

"Don't look now," she said, "but the devil's dog has come to get me."

"Actually, that's my dog."

Zan opened her hands, keeping her thumbs on her cheeks. "Your dog? I must of banged my head harder than I thought." Like shutters, she covered her eyes again with her hands. "Tell me honestly. Have I forgotten anything else? Like my name, or where I live?"

"You haven't forgotten a thing," he answered, amused.

"You didn't have a dog before, though, did you?"

"No, I . . . er . . . found him. In town."

"Found him?"

She took a quick look at the dog, sitting on its haunches some distance behind them on the dusty road. It was so thin each rib could be counted, as well as the knobs on its spine. The black-and-tan coat seemed a mass of matted tangles, and deep lines of matter were dredged in its fur from eyes to jaw. Faintly toward her came a whiff of unwashed—possibly never washed—mongrel.

Yet, for all that, there seemed to be something almost proud in the way it sat and waited for the humans. Perhaps it was just exhaustion, for the front paws trembled in supporting him, but Zan didn't think so. The dog looked self-respecting, despite appearances.

"I don't recall ever seeing that animal before, and I'm pretty well acquainted with every dog, or cat for that matter, in Harmony. Where exactly did you find it?"

"We'd better think more about getting you home in one piece than about him. With some food and a bath, he'll be fine. You, on the other hand . . ."

"First oxen and now dogs. Edward Winchester, I'm beginning to think you're a soft touch."

"Soft in the head, perhaps," he mumbled. "Do you want me to carry you?"

She laughed shortly, only to press one hand to the top of her head. For a moment, she could have sworn it was about to come off. "You couldn't even lift me."

As easily as though he'd paused to pluck a flower, Edward swept Zan off her feet and into his arms. Her knees dangled without dignity over his forearm and her bottom sagged toward the ground.

"Stay still," he said, started forward.

"Put me down," she demanded, wriggling. "I can walk!"

"Stay still, or I'll drop you on your head again."

Something in his tone told her he meant what he said. "If anybody sees me like this," she said, subsiding, "I'll never live it down."

"There's no one to see."

This close she could see the brown in his eyes and the small freckle under his eyelashes on the left. Even with his skin still faintly reddened by his sunburn, he was, she realized, a particularly good-looking man. She liked his hair close-cropped at the temples and the long, straight nose that made his face so much more intense than the others she'd seen. She never could abide a man with a little nose. Not even the lazy droop of his eyelids when he was being sarcastic could really spoil him.

Zan experimented with putting her head down on his shoulder. She remembered the sight of his body, strong and lean. A warmth started under her breastbone and spread to the rest of her body. It suddenly seemed too much effort to struggle.

Then her head jerked up. "You promise to put me down before we get to the house?"

"At the far end of your lane."

"My brothers might catch sight of us. You put me down by the big cottonwood."

She put her cheek on his shoulder again, comfortably. Looking back, she saw the dog coming along behind, limping a little on its right foreleg. "A soft touch," she said again in a low voice.

She raised her head once more. "I remember what else I forgot. The picnic basket. It's still shoved under the bridge."

"I'll get it tomorrow. Stop squirming."

CHAPTER
7

"Did I not tell you to stay at home today?" Edward gave Zan a look as swift and piercing as an arrow.

"You said if I felt unwell. I'm healthy as a horse. Ate fifteen flapjacks for breakfast and still have room for a stuffed buffalo with all the trimmings." Zan tapped herself on the chest and took in a lungful of Kansas morning air.

"What a constitution," Edward said, but not as though he admired her for it.

"That's me. Why, I dug twenty feet of irrigation trench when everybody thought I'd die of whooping cough. Course I was only three at the time, or I would have managed a sight more."

"How precocious." His tone was dry. But a glimmer in his eyes told her that he was amused by her tall tale. "I shan't ask so much of you as that today. If you would care to continue what you were doing yesterday . . ."

"Is Buck well enough to plow?"

"The ointment the doctor gave me seemed to do much good. I thought perhaps I shall try him out this morning. If all is not well, I shall come and help you, instead. I should very much like to learn your technique with manure . . . I mean fertilizer."

"Sounds fine and dandy. Meet you later, then." She gave him back the coffee cup he'd handed her when she'd stepped up onto the porch. Walking away, she could feel his eyes on her back. To prove herself in excellent health, she squared up her shoulders and put a little swagger in her walk.

If she were standing before God and had to tell the truth, Zan would have admitted feeling more than a little queasy this morning. Though she didn't think she'd faint, she had a headache that seemed to reach from her feet to about three inches above and around her head.

However, she'd looked at her eyes in the mirror when she went to bed and when she got up. The pupils seemed right and had shrunk when she'd moved the candle closer. When one of the thrashers last year had hit his head on the edge of the machine, his pupils had been different sizes and only one of them changed with the light. She'd heard later that he'd died, though she didn't know if it was true.

"Looks like we'll have a good day for it," she said, checking Hank's throat latch.

The sky appeared faded, as though washed by too hot a rain. A few thin clouds were the only cover between the earth and the sun. When she followed one cloud with her eyes, the sun dazzled her, the light stabbing right back to her brain. Without knowing how, Zan found herself sitting on the ground.

"That's the final straw," Edward said. She knew he'd run from the porch to her side, though she'd not seen him do it.

"I'm all right," she said. Her voice sounded tinny and as though it came from a long way off. She tried again, but she seemed to have forgotten whatever it was she'd meant to say. The buzzing of the cicadas kept her from hearing his answer.

The front door slammed. "What's the matter?" Uncle Fred called, coming down the steps.

Once again Zan found herself cradled against Edward's chest. "This little idiot nearly fainted, that's all," he said, sounding savagely impatient. "I told her to stay at home."

"I couldn't," she tried to explain as he carried her toward the house. To her horror, her eyes filled with tears that she could not control. When she blinked they spilled over, wetting the shoulder of his coat.

The interior of the house was cool and dark. The buzzing of the cicadas faded, though she had a frightening feeling they'd start again at any second, this time from within her own head. Edward carried her back to his room and put her gently down on the dobby white bedspread. She'd never felt anything smoother or more soothing that the clean pillowcase under her cheek. If only these foolish tears would dry!

"There now," he said, in a rough voice that was oddly comforting. "There's no need to cry."

"I know that! And I'm not crying, exactly. I just can't stop them from coming down."

"Here." He offered her one of his handkerchiefs, his monogram satin-stitched in one corner.

Zan mopped at her eyes and cheeks. "I'll be fine in a minute; never mind about me."

"Your head hurts, I take it?"

"I wish you could take it." She sighed.

Leaning forward, he laid his palm over her forehead. Zan closed her eyes. "So cool . . ."

"Perhaps you should undo your hair," he suggested softly. "You do wear a tight braid."

"Keeps it back." She turned her head so his hand rested on her right temple. "That feels so good. . . ."

A little rap at the door made her start. "What's that!" Edward took his hand away. Zan opened her eyes, blinking.

"I brought some cool water," Uncle Fred said, poking his gray-fringed head around the half-open door. "And some eau de cologne for your temples."

Despite her headache, Zan grinned at the older man. "I knew you were a lady-killer."

"Oh, no, it's mine. But a very pleasant scent." He handed the glass of water to her. Then he, too, pulled out a hand-kerchief from his pocket, unstoppered a glass bottle etched with flowers, and shook some of the herb-infused liquid onto the cloth. A scent of lemon grass wafted toward her, calming her spirit.

With the two handkerchiefs and the water, Zan had her hands full. She laughed. "If I'm ever really sick, remind me to come stay with you."

Edward said, "I'm sure you would be all too easily killed by kindness."

She glanced up at him, where he leaned on the brass headboard, surprising on his face a look of indulgence. As soon as their eyes met, he ceased slouching and said, "The very moment you feel able to get up, you'll go home."

"I can't. I didn't tell my parents about my fall yesterday."

"Why not?"

" 'Cause of how it happened. I feel awful foolish anyway, and telling them would only make me feel worse."

"All the same, they've got to know."

Uncle Fred looked anxiously between the two younger people, like a family pet disturbed by raised voices. "Perhaps if dear Zan stayed quietly here for a few hours, there'd be no need to worry the Linds."

"And what if she's seriously ill? She must go home. I'm sure her parents will understand and not blame her for her foolish behavior."

"I'll keep a careful watch over her. If there's any change for the worse, I'll go for Dr. Tanner myself."

"Excuse me," Zan said loudly. "Stop talking about me like I'm not here, would you? I'm not in any danger of kicking the bucket. . . . least not now." She caught Edward's eye, reminding him of the bucket she'd kicked before in this room. "All I got is a headache. Nothing hard work won't cure."

Both men said, "No!"

In the end she had to agree to lie quietly and be good at least until noon. Zan made a show of reluctance, yet she was not really unwilling. Partly it was the unsettling feeling that at any moment the bed she lay on and everything else in the room was going to slide down a big black hole.

The other reason for her cooperation, and she admitted this only to herself when she was alone, had to do with the odd feeling of satisfaction she had whenever Edward glared at her. She even kept up the argument a little longer than she ordinarily would have just to see how dark a look he could muster. Far from being intimidated, she struggled to keep back a laugh of delight every time he glowered.

She only wished that he could have stayed longer. The cool touch of his hand had done more to relieve the throbbing in her head than all the water and cologne in the world. Taking his advice about her hair helped as well. Undoing the braid and letting the pale waves spread out on her pillow took about all the strength she had left. She lay down and dozed off at once.

A jingle of harness awoke her some hours later. Thinking it was Edward bringing in the team, she sat up. "Noon already?" she said aloud.

Her head felt much better, except for a tender spot on the back. The dizziness had gone, taking with it the notion that her head had swelled to two or three times its usual size. A sound like distant thunder reminded her that she'd not eaten much breakfast, despite her boast to Edward. As she rubbed her noisy stomach, she wondered what the chances were that

Uncle Fred had whipped up another delicious meal.

As she stood up, she realized that someone had taken her boots off. They weren't anywhere in the room. Zan walked out into the hall. Hearing voices, she went on into the main room of the small farmhouse.

Miss Maisie and Miss Minnie turned as one.

"Oh, my!"

"Oh, dear." Their shocked expressions were condemning enough, but Miss Minnie added a *tsk-tsk* that seemed to put Zan beyond the company of decent women forever.

Fred, in the act of accepting their shawls, said hurriedly, "Miss Lind felt a trifle under the weather this morning."

Both pairs of crystal blue eyes dropped instantly to Zan's waistline. She snatched her hand away from her stomach, knowing a blush had flared in her cheeks. The only thing to do was to pretend she hadn't figured out what they were thinking. "Hey, Uncle Fred, I'm starving. . . ."

"I'm not surprised," Miss Maisie said, sniffing.

Too late, Zan understood her simple statement would add color to their notions. "Uh, I think I'll go outside a second. You seen my boots?"

"I believe Edward put them in the . . . they're in the kitchen," Fred said, the top of his head turning pink. "I cleaned them for you."

"Say, thanks. I guess they were mucking up the coverlet. That is . . . I'll just go and get them."

Giving the censorious ladies a meaningless smile, Zan headed for safety. "Oh, mercy," she said, jamming on her boots, "and to think I didn't want to tell Mother when I'd only hit my head. Just wait till she hears about this!" If she and Edward weren't real lucky, she thought, they'd find themselves being hitched by the Reverend Shotgun before the week was out.

The best thing to do would be to go back into the house and brazen it out. She was powerfully hungry. If she could do justice to her legendary appetite, then maybe the two busybodies would realize nothing had changed. Especially if Edward came back for lunch. Anybody should be able to tell that nothing lover-like existed between the two of them, that their arrangement was business and only business.

On the other hand, it didn't seem hardly fair that Edward should walk in cold to a setup like the one in his own house. If she knew Maisie and Minnie, they were waggling their eyebrows as hard as they'd go, and whispering frantically every time Fred left the room. It would be a kindness on her part to go out to meet Edward. She'd warn him that they must be ice-cold polite to each other as long as the sisters were in the house.

Just then, Miss Maisie appeared in the doorway. "Are you feeling sick to your stomach?"

"No, ma'am," Zan said, standing up. "Never felt better."

"Then come on in. We're waiting for you. And do up your hair, Zan; you look like an unmade bed."

Hurriedly, Zan caught up the loose strands and knotted them. Her hair was fine enough to be wrapped around and stuck up without pins but thick enough to stay up. It still hung precariously, but was no longer streaming over her shoulders.

Miss Maisie cast her eyes over the backyard. "What's that?" she said, pointing a bony finger.

Zan squinted. "It looks like a dog, Miss Maisie."

"Don't be fresh! I can see it's a dog! Whose is it?"

"Edward's, I reckon."

The animal lay, head on crossed paws, in a patch of shade that Edward had rigged by stretching a piece of canvas over two bushes. A deep bowl of water sat beside him. Zan barely recognized the dog as the one that had followed Edward home yesterday and then only by the shape of his narrow head and the still noticeable air of self-possession.

Other than that, he'd completely changed. The black and tan coat now shone black and white. Long banners of fur waved from each leg and lay fanned out next to the lengthy tail, like feathers on an Indian's coup stick. Though every bone he owned was still visible, the dog had the makings of a handsome creature. As if aware they were speaking of him, he raised his head and thumped the ground two or three times with his tail. Then he went back to resting with a concentration that reminded Zan of old tired men basking in the sun.

"So it's true," Miss Maisie said, pursing her thin lips.

"What's true?"

Miss Maisie didn't answer. She turned and went into the house, her high-button shoes sounding resolutely on the floor-boards. Her curiosity piqued, Zan followed her.

She saw her take the lid off a pot to inhale the steam arising from the bubbling contents. "Not bad, but he's got this damper set all wrong. It'll never get done." She fiddled with the sliding plate. "That'll fix it." Miss Maisie went into the other room. Taking just an instant to slide the damper back, for she'd bet Uncle Fred knew exactly what he was doing, Zan went to find him.

In the entrance to the main room, Zan stopped, her mind boggling at what she saw and heard. Could that high, piping voice really be Miss Minnie's? Could she really be leaning, almost coquettishly, toward Uncle Fred? And most unbeliev-able of all, she could not really be saying, "Oh, no. Maisie's pastry always comes out so much lighter than mine."

Staring at Maisie for her reaction, Zan saw her take a seat equally close to Uncle Fred. "Don't be so modest," she said sweetly. "Why, my own husband would never take a bite of my pie, if Minnie had one on the table. How mortified I used to be at the sociables when all the men would flock to her blackberry tarts and leave mine sitting!"

Zan knew now that the bang on the head had scrambled her wits. What other explanation could there be? Miss Maisie and Miss Minnie were decidedly billing and cooing! Now Miss Minnie praised Miss Maisie's gardening; now Miss Maisie couldn't say enough about her sister's skill on the pianoforte.

"Oh, I haven't played in years, Minnie. Whereas nobody in church sings half so sweet as you. When you hit the high notes on 'A Mighty Fortress,' I feel closer to God."

Minnie did not appear thankful for this extravagant compliment. The glance she directed at her sister had more venom in it than appreciation. Moving closer still to the sole man in the room, she said, "But you can tell me, Mr. Winchester. Don't *you* think Maisie bakes a tastier pie?"

Uncle Fred ran a finger around under his collar. "Ur . . ." he gargled. Then he caught sight of Zan, goggling in the entry. With the air of a man reaching for a life preserver in the midst of a relentlessly sucking swamp, he said, "Ah, there you are! Excellent! Most excellent!"

He came out of his overstuffed chair as though a spring had sprouted through the cushion. "If you wouldn't mind keeping our guests entertained while I see to luncheon? And if Edward comes back, give him a glass of the sherry, won't you?"

"Sure thing," Zan said, never one to refuse a helping hand especially to someone suffering as much as Uncle Fred. Crossing to the sideboard, she pulled the stopper out of the cut-glass decanter, the glass ringing slightly. Then she poured out a dollop of the straw-colored liquid, to have it ready when Edward showed up.

Turning around with some light comment about the weather on her lips, she saw the two other women staring at her in disapproval. "Should you be drinking that?" Miss Maisie asked.

"Oh, heck. It was just a little bang . . ."

Two matching sets of blue eyes nearly jumped from their sockets.

"On the head," Zan finished, wearing a grin. "I slid off the hotel banister and whacked my head on Faith's fancy hall table. Those ball-and-claw feet sure hurt if you hit 'em wrong." She figured she'd be better off sacrificing her own stupidity to the gossip mill than handing them Edward on a skewer.

Where was Edward? She could imagine him overlooking his own hunger pangs, but he wouldn't be likely to work Buck or Bright too hard. Looking out the single window for him, she missed what Miss Minnie said next except as a background noise. "Sorry, what?"

"I said, you seem awful at home here."

"Yes," Miss Maisie echoed. "Calling Mr. Winchester Uncle Fred, for instance. Do you think that's respectful?"

"Oh, you know me, Miss Minnie, Miss Maisie. I can get along with pretty near everybody, even folks that are downright determined to be disagreeable."

"You mean 'His Lordship,' I take it?" Miss Minnie asked.

"No, ma'am. I didn't mean him particularly."

The front door opened and closed, and he was there. Zan smiled to see him. Though she'd been giving about as good as she got, it never hurt to have an ally walk in. She did not examine too closely her reasons for thinking of the two of them as being on the same side.

"How'd it go?"

"Very well, thank you," he said, his precise tones so different from Miss Minnie and Miss Maisie's nasal twang. "I hope I see you much recovered?"

"I told you . . . I've got a head that could take a kick from a Missouri mule." She lifted the glass from the sideboard. "Uncle Fred thought you might like this."

He half reached for the delicate glass and then glanced at his hands. "Perhaps after I wash," he said. "Good afternoon, Mrs. Hastings. How pleasant to see you again, Mrs. Parker."

Zan had all but forgotten they had an audience for this meeting. Judging by the ladies' narrow-eyed expressions, they were not yet ready to condemn Edward and herself as illicit lovers. Neither, however, did either lady seem completely convinced of the innocence of their relationship. Zan knew that last was too much to ask. If she'd been one hundred and two and Edward the last survivor of the War of Independence—even if from the wrong side—Miss Minnie and Miss Maisie would still wonder and whisper.

Throughout the meal, Miss Maisie and Miss Minnie continued to extend their strange charity to each other. However, any other person mentioned did not receive so much consideration.

"I hear Samantha and Cord Spencer had a big old fight last night."

"Hmmm, serves her right for marrying him, if you ask me! He's much too handsome ever to be trustworthy. I never have liked a man to be *too* good-looking."

"Well, goodness knows you never had a trouble like . . . I mean," Miss Maisie said, coughing discreetly into her napkin. "I mean to say that you never were one to be swayed by a pretty face. Solid worth . . . that was Mr. Parker."

"Not as solid as your Hastings," Minnie said quickly.

But Maisie leaned confidentially closer to Fred. "She's always had much better taste than me. I'm weak as water when a really good-looking feller comes by. Minnie can't be fooled like I can by a pretty face."

Zan exchanged a look with Edward. He seemed as startled by the change in the two sisters as she was. Without being too obvious, Zan tapped her temple significantly. It seemed a day for the unbelievable. For one instant, she saw something very like a smile flash across Edward's dour face.

Miss Maisie noticed, too. "You're in a mighty good humor today. Is there a reason for it?"

"Only the charm of the company present here this afternoon," Edward said gravely.

Miss Minnie favored him with a sour smile. "I guess you must mean Zan. She is a pretty thing, or would be, if she ever made out which sex she was going to be."

"Is she?" Edward asked, giving his whole attention to his plate. "I can't say that I have paid any regard to that."

"Sure I know what I am," Zan said cheerfully. "I'm a farmer."

"Girls should be wives and mothers. Only men can be farmers. You might as well want to be president!"

Unnoticed, Uncle Fred said, "Anyone care for more baked beans?"

"I don't know about that," Zan said. She knew Edward was in sympathy with Miss Maisie's opinion. It was as much to him as to the older lady that she spoke.

"I figure if Samantha can run the newspaper, and if my sister can run a hotel, and if my mother can manage a mess of kids and a house and never know how many folks to expect for dinner . . ." She drew a breath. "Not to mention the two of you taking care of a boardinghouse and all the guests. Any way, compared to what you all do, farming should be a Sunday walk in the park."

"But all on your own?" Miss Minnie asked. "You're bound to find yourself needing a man around the place. Who's going to . . . well . . . kill your pigs?"

Zan couldn't keep a bubble of laughter from breaking. "Is that all a man is good for? You could have fooled me."

Both ladies drew back, pressing their thin hands to their bony chests. "Suzanna Lind!" Miss Maisie cried. "You should be ashamed of yourself."

"Yes, ma'am." She pushed back her chair and stood up. "You sit tight, Uncle Fred. I'll bring in the sweet stuff."

"I'll help you," Edward said, leaving his napkin neatly beside his plate.

Safe in the kitchen, he asked, "What's going on?"

"Well, they think I'm expecting, you're the father, and Uncle Fred's aiding you in your vile seduction. Or, they're trying to match up you and me, and toss for Uncle Fred. Though why in that case they keep building each other up is beyond me. Oh, and Miss Maisie seems mighty interested in your new dog."

"She saw the dog?" Edward opened the back door. "No, don't get up," he said in a conversational tone. "I'll bring you some more food in a few moments."

Zan shook her head. "You mean out of all that, the only part you heard was about some stray dog you picked up? Edward Winchester, you take the cake. Here," she added, pushing a platter at him, the plain pound cake on it as fat and golden as a princess's pillow.

"Well, you see," he said, shuffling his feet. "The dog isn't exactly mine."

"Not yours? Don't worry. The owner's bound to come looking for it sometime."

"He may very well. You see, Zan, I stole that dog."

CHAPTER
8

She nearly dropped the china boat of thick raspberry sauce. "You what? How could you steal . . . ?"

"I had an excellent reason for my actions. I couldn't stand idly by, allowing—"

"Oh, gosh," Zan said. "Tell me later. If we don't get back in there, they're bound to think the worst. Even in a kitchen. And I'm not having my reputation ruined till I've had the fun that goes with it."

"I'm not surprised you shock Harmony, Zan. Often you shock *me*, and I have seen much of the world."

"You can tell me all about it the same time you tell me about stealing the dog. Now, come on with that cake."

"Here we are," she all but yodeled as she went back to the others. Only Uncle Fred did not cast a chiding glance her way. He sat, white-faced and sweating, between the women, like a mouse between two cats.

The appearance of the cake set off another meeting of the Hastings-Parker Mutual Admiration Society. "Did you make this, Mr. Winchester?" Miss Maisie marveled, savoring a bite. "You and Minnie ought to spend a day alone together comparing recipes. She knows the pound cake that Andrew Jackson's own cook made for him. Don't you, Minnie?"

"Yes," her sister said, preening. "Mr. Parker's mother wrote it down from General Jackson's own cook herself and taught it to me, having no daughters of her own."

A shade of vexation passed over her dry face as she realized she'd been forced to acknowledge that she knew something Maisie didn't. Almost instantly she recovered, flashing a sweet smile around the table. Zan was still at a loss to understand why the two sisters had suddenly changed their tune from carping criticism to love and light. She had to admit, however, that the change might be good for them.

As Minnie pressed her fork down into the moist cake, she glared at her smirking sister. She couldn't keep the acidity from her tone. "Though I must say, nobody makes a better white icing than Maisie. I've often begged her to tell me her secret . . . I'm sure you could persuade her, Mr. Winchester, if you had her all to yourself for even a minute."

Uncle Fred looked more hunted than before. "I shouldn't like to persuade anyone to betray a secret. It wouldn't be cricket. Would anyone care for coffee?" He fled the room.

In a little while the ladies from the boardinghouse took their departure, saying goodbye many times at the door and always finding one more flirtatious word to say to Uncle Fred. At last, out in the yard, Miss Minnie actually took up the reins. However, in the very act of stepping up into the buggy, Miss Maisie said to Edward, "Oh, by the way . . . Sheriff Miller would like to have a talk with you. Just if you can spare the time."

Zan felt Edward's eyes on her, of all people. Looking up into their depths, the color of a stormy sea, the dizziness she'd experienced before returned. Only instead of centering in her head, it seemed to come from her heart. She strove to keep her face from betraying any untoward emotion, very aware

97

of the two sisters watching her every move, whiskers and tails a-twitch.

Maybe she was learning to read him. Though his face did not change any more than hers, she seemed certain he asked silently if she felt up to taking over his work. She gave him a bright, confident smile.

Edward said, "Certainly. If I may accompany you into Harmony?"

"I reckon we can make room," Miss Minnie said grudgingly.

As the dust from their departure swirled in the hot, sticky air, Uncle Fred asked, "What do they do to people who steal dogs in Kansas?"

"You know about it?"

"Edward has always brought home strays, and if anyone mistreated an animal . . . it is one of the few things that makes him truly angry. From his boyhood, he has been willing to stand up to even the biggest and the strongest to see right done to the helpless and weak. It's an admirable quality, but rather trying for anyone who must patch his wounds."

He turned to go inside. "Uncle Fred," Zan said, putting out a hand to stop him.

"Yes, my dear?"

She wanted to ask whether Edward had ever talked about her. The strength of this longing to find out what he thought, even what he felt about her, scared Zan half to death. She had to grip hard and wrestle with it before it let go.

Changing her mind at the last possible second, she asked, "Do you mind me calling you that? Uncle, I mean."

The top of his head turned pink with pleasure. "Not at all. I only wish my other nieces would call me that."

"What do they call you?"

"Uncle Frederick," he said, screwing his gentle face up like he'd bitten into an underripe lemon. "Usually long and drawn out, disgust ladled into every syllable, and often followed by 'How could you?' "

"They don't sound like much fun. At least you've got nephews to take the sting off."

"My nephews, believe it or not, are often worse. Hale and hearty fellows most of them with only two subjects acknowledged to be of any importance—politics and cricket. As though politics matter."

"Even Edward?"

"Ah, no, he almost makes up for the rest of the family. Edward's 'a Corinthian, a lad of mettle, a good boy.' *Henry the Fourth, Part One.*"

"A boy? How old is he?"

"Twenty-eight, I believe. But to an old man like me—"

"You seem younger sometimes than he does. But you like him, and that's why you came to Kansas with him." She leaned against the porch post, willing to stay all day if necessary if the conversation was going to be about Edward.

"I've always been interested in America," Fred said. "And I couldn't very well let him travel all this way alone, not after that fiasco with that girl."

"What girl?" She realized she sounded too eager. "I don't want you to gossip, Uncle Fred, but I've got to work with this man and I don't hardly know a thing about him."

"He knows even less about you. He said he's never met anyone quite like you before. I believe he is beginning to admire you for your good qualities."

She supposed there might be a compliment in those words, if she were willing to dig for it. "There's not much to know about me. I don't have any mysteries in *my* past. But what girl?"

"Her name was Nerissa Sinclair. Edward wanted to marry her, only there was some sort of hitch. My information is somewhat vague, I'm afraid. It did not come from Edward, as you may imagine. One moment the engagement was on the point of being announced, and the next thing anyone knew she was engaged to a rather desiccated peer."

"Is that bad?"

Uncle Fred looked fiercely off into the distance. "It all too frequently happens in England that some elderly but titled bachelor will totter down the aisle with some fresh flower, usually a girl with money. Nerissa Sinclair's husband must be older than I am by a good few years, for he had already a evil name in society when I left school."

"Seems kind of funny a girl marrying somebody like that when Edward—I mean—with a nice young feller wanting her."

"Oh, I don't know if it was Nerissa's own choice or if her parents suggested it. Dreadful people . . . *parvenus* of the worst type. Only interested in advancement. Saw the chance of a richer match than the third son of an earl and snatched at it. Bellworthy's a viscount in his own right, you know."

"Is he really? What's a viscount?"

Uncle Fred blinked and seemed to remember he was not in a drawing room conversing with his equals. He smiled at Zan. "English titles are a trifle complicated, my dear. Suffice it to say that even so lowly a rank as viscount makes a man a greater matrimonial prize than the Honorable Mr. Edward Winchester. If you see only in terms of material wealth, that is, as Mr. and Mrs. Sinclair so obviously did."

Zan scratched her head, wincing as her fingers encountered the lump on the back. "Is that what he means when he says he's honorable? That's what folks ought to call him? We all just thought he was bragging."

"It's not used in conversation. Mr. Winchester is all Edward and I are entitled to. The lordships and graces are our oldest brothers and our fathers, and sometimes even our cousins. An honorable is utterly outranked by nearly everyone. And any children Edward might have wouldn't own even so much distinction as that."

"I prefer plain ordinary Mister," Zan said decidedly. "I wouldn't know what to call my kids if they were all running around as little lords and ladies. And when you start having to figure out what to call the rest of them . . . well, it passes me."

"I should be honored," the older gentleman said, bowing, "to remain Uncle Fred."

By the time she finished enriching the first field, Edward still hadn't come back. Jumping down from the wagon, Zan wiped the running sweat from her forehead with her sleeve. She tried to convince herself that her desire for a cool glass of sarsaparilla at the Last Resort was nothing out of the ordinary. In her heart, however, she knew she wanted to go to town only to find out what had happened to her partner.

Taking the mules back to the barn, Zan saw Uncle Fred quickly crossing the yard as though he'd been waiting for her. "He hasn't returned as yet," the older man said worriedly.

"I don't reckon the sheriff threw him in the hoosegow, or anything like that. But if you want—I can't do much else until Edward's got the next field plowed under—I could mosey on into town and see what's up. Most likely, he just got to talking with someone and lost track of the time."

"Indubitably, that is the answer," Fred said, though they both knew Edward had no soul mates in Harmony.

Pushed by an anxiety she did not try to explain to herself, Zan unhitched Hank. Straddling his broad, bony back, she made better time than she would have on foot, though she couldn't help wishing for the quickest-trotting Arab ever foaled. Maybe her urgency conveyed itself to Hank. He moved along at a decent clip instead of dawdling along trying to eat the wildflowers, his usual tactic when anyone tried to ride him.

So intent was Zan on urging him onward that she passed her barefoot brothers without noticing them. They waved and Ben called, "Hey, Zan, wait up a minute!"

She waved back but didn't stop. Then she realized they were walking *away* from the town. With any luck, they could tell her what she wanted to know and save her from making a fool of herself by inquiring around after Edward. She tugged on the mule's mane. "Hold up, Hank."

As the boys were only a year apart in age, many folks found it hard to distinguish Ben from Gary or Gary from Ben. They were both towheaded and blue-eyed, with snub noses liberally bedewed with freckles. Mrs. Lind did her level best to keep them clean and neatly dressed when school was in session, but in summer they wore tattered overalls with nothing beneath but their evenly tanned skin. Any attempt to put them into fancy clothes in the months between May and September would be repelled tooth and claw.

Today, Zan noticed, their faces and hands were smeared with blue-black juice. Ben, the older, carried a galvanized pail full to the top with juicy blackberries, gleaming like black sapphires in the strong sunlight. Gary held an empty pail, though streaks on the interior showed it had once been as full as the other.

"We made Faith pay a whole dime for those," Ben said, throwing out his skinny chest.

"Who are the rest for?"

"Mother."

"Are you going to make her pay you, too?" Mr. Lind might have hopes that Ben would be a farmer, but Zan saw her little brother more as a natural-born businessman, if not a downright flimflam artist.

"I don't guess we will. Though she's usually good for a couple lumps of sugar." Behind Ben, Gary's eyes lit up, even as he rubbed at a long bramble scratch on one bare arm.

Obviously, appeasing his sweet tooth was worth any pain.

Zan asked impatiently, "Did you see Mr. Winchester while you were in town?"

"Nope. But we heard tell about him." Ben didn't say another word, just stood there digging his bare toes into the dusty road. His shyly upturned eyes were utterly innocent, though they never moved from her face.

"Well?" Zan demanded.

"Guess it all depends on what's it worth to you."

Fighting the urge to get down from Hank and shake her brother, Zan said, "One willow switch."

"I don't want no willow switch."

"Well, you'll get one where it'll do most good if you don't start talking!"

Cord Spencer waved her over to the table where he sat with two other men. His ordinarily neat clothing seemed creased and dirty, most unusual in a man so fastidious in his habits. "Charlie," he called, "get Miss Lind her usual."

"No thanks, Mr. Thompson," she said quietly as she passed the long bar. The bartender stopped rubbing a beer mug with his bar towel to stare after her.

She stood above the round table, looking each man in the face. Zeke Gallagher, deceptively jolly, with something so mysterious in his past that he never spoke of it; lanky Travis Miller, swigging beer despite the bright star hanging off his buckskin vest; and Cord himself, wearing the look of the cat who owned the dairy ever since he married Samantha Evans, arguments or no arguments. Right now, all three of them seemed extra-pleased with themselves, chuckling and grinning up at her.

"Hear you took real good care of Ed Winchester," she said slowly.

"Yes, indeed," Zeke said. "And if he stays out there another half hour, I get all the beer I kin guzzle."

"On the other hand, I'm bettin' he won't find his way back till long 'bout dark." Travis leaned way back in his chair, the front legs coming up off the floor.

Cord shook his head. "To tell the truth, I was surprised he fell for it. That any man in this day and age would agree to go on a snipe hunt!" The three men laughed, enjoying the joke.

"How'd you ever think of that one?" Zan asked, her hands resting on her hips. It took hard work to keep her false smile stretched in place.

"Never would have thought of it," Zeke said, "iffn your brother-in-law didn't of come into the shop for a shave and a haircut. Hutton was going on 'bout how Sir Fancy-pants had a real sharp interest in birds. So when he started gettin' hisself high and mighty over that dog he stole, a snipe hunt just seemed right natural somehow."

"So you got him all dressed up in heavy winter clothes . . ."

"Got to," Travis said with his slow smile. "Disguise the man-scent. Them snipes can smell a human being from a hundred yards away."

"And took him out into the fields . . ."

"You shoulda heard him," Zeke said, starting to grin even more widely, all the way back to his missing molar on the right. "Jabberin' all the time 'bout how he never done heard tell of a snipe what didn't live by the water."

"I can't think I've ever had a harder time keeping a straight face. . . ." Cord added.

"And then you left him holding the bag while the three of you took off 'to drive the snipe toward him.' "

Just then, Charlie came up, taking a mug of her special drink off a tray. "Here you go, Miss Zan," he said, putting it down on the table in front of her.

"Sit down and join us," Cord urged her. "You'll want to see his face when he comes in. I'm expecting to see him mount his high horse."

"Nothin' funnier than a greenhorn who loses his temper over a little ol' trick like that." Zeke scratched himself through his shirt.

With the back of her hand Zan knocked her drink over. The three men leaped up, brushing the foaming beverage off their trousers. One splash stained Zeke's crotch as though he'd been caught short on the way out back.

"Hey, what do you think you're doing?"

"Are you loco?"

"God, I'm soaked!"

Zan stood back, ignoring their cries. "So he got 'high and mighty' over that dog. A poor skin and bones critter, limping along . . ."

"It weren't his," Zeke complained.

"Now, just a minute," Travis said. "I could of run him in, you know, for stealing ol' man Grasse's dog. Grasse wanted to press charges, claiming Winchester knocked him down."

"Ol' man Grasse owned that animal? Well, I can't say I'm surprised." Zan glared even more fiercely at the men. "But I'm downright flabbergasted that the three of you would take his side against Edward. Knowing that Grasse is the meanest, lowest . . . kicked his own son out-of-doors in the middle of a January night 'cause he came home from Wichita a Baptist. Ol' man Grasse who hasn't paid a bill in this town for twenty years without a struggle. Didn't he run up a bill of fifteen dollars for haircuts, always promising to pay and never doing it till you went after him with an ax handle?"

"Yes'm," Zeke said, turning pink behind his white beard.

"And doesn't he haul you out to his place every time he thinks some boy might have stolen a pebble off his drive? Once he even tried to get you to throw his daughter in jail for spilling milk when she was eight, didn't he? Said that was the way to teach a child not to waste food. And it was skimmed milk, at that."

"Well, maybe he's been a pain once or twice. . . ." Travis admitted. "But that doesn't give Winchester the right to steal his dog!"

"Wait a minute," Cord said, holding up his hand. "How bad a shape is this dog in?"

"What difference does that make?" She shook away some of her aggression and answered honestly, "Not too bad, now that Edward's taking care of it. 'Cept it doesn't look like it's ever had a square meal, or a bath, or any kind attention."

"You can't fault a man because he don't wash his dog. Hell, ol' man Grasse hardly washes hisself," Zeke said.

"What I want to know," Zan went on, "is why you didn't ask Edward his reasons for stealing the dog. Why'd you decide to just go ahead and punish him?"

The men sat down again, Charlie having gotten a rag to mop off the chairs. "I don't know," Travis answered. "It's just his way of talking that gets a feller's back up. And there was ol' man Grasse hollering at me, claiming he'd sue the town and the state and who knows who if he didn't get some satisfaction. I wasn't about to throw Winchester into jail on Grasse's say-so, but in comes His Lordship with his nose in the air, talking like I'm nothing but dirt . . . tossing Grasse a couple of dollars like . . ."

"What did he say?"

"Nothing, I guess, now that I think on it. But I always feel small when he talks to me . . . maybe 'cause of his accent."

" 'Sides," Zeke added, "we never meant no harm. We was just havin' a little fun with the boy."

"Fun!" Zan scoffed.

Cord Spencer looked up at her with a teasing twinkle in his dark eyes. "You know, if I were of a wondering turn of mind, I might be wondering why you're so worried about Winchester. He's a grown man . . . or is that the reason?"

"Whoo-doggie," Zeke said, cackling. "Say, is them wedding bells I'm a-hearing?"

"You want me to lock Winchester up till you can throw a rope around him, Zan?"

"He's my partner," she said levelly, "and the way I see it, partners are meant to look after each other, at least until the harvest's in. Now, which way did you take him?"

"Out near Grasse's, 'course," Travis said. "That seemed like justice."

Walking out from the relative cool of the Last Resort, the heat hit Zan in the face like a hot washrag. Hank stood in a patch of shade against the side of the building and with true mule stubbornness and good sense refused to budge. Zan couldn't be brutal toward the mule, so she left him where he was. She turned and headed out of town.

Down the road the heat drew all the strength from her body. As though she moved in a nightmare, she strove to hurry, yet seemed to make no time. Sweat trickled down between her breasts, and she tore open the top button on her shirt. Meanwhile, on a thin, laughing note, she heard herself saying, "So you got him all dressed up in heavy winter clothes . . . dressed in heavy winter clothes. . . ."

Had it been Edward or Fred who told her that if the weather turns too hot, the English start to drop dead?

CHAPTER
9

Up ahead, she saw him, stumbling out from among the dense cornstalks that lined the road. Zan called his name as she began to run toward him.

Edward seemed not to hear. He staggered around in a circle, tearing at the woolen muffler wound about his neck. Travis's heavy sheepskin coat trailed from his hand. Tossing it to the ground, he clutched his brow like a madman, tottering blindly.

Just before she reached him, Edward fell over backward. He lay spread-eagled in the dust, his face upturned to the merciless sky. His body jerked once or twice, his arms pounding the ground. Then he lay frighteningly still.

"Edward!" Fear clutching at her throat, Zan dropped to her knees beside his body. She leaned forward, her hands on his shoulders. Only the rising and falling of his chest, exposed by a wrenched-open shirt, reassured her that he still lived. Shaking him, she said again, "Edward, please . . ."

Frantically she gazed around at the blank landscape for aid, knowing it was hopeless. There wasn't even a patch of shade to drag him into, or any water. The only thing to do was to try to get him on his feet. She'd never felt so helpless before.

His lips moved and on a tiny sighing breath came her name. "Yes, I'm here," she said, bending low to hear what he wanted to say. Her hair, loosened by running, fell to sweep his cheek.

Powerful hands locked around her wrists. Already off-balance, Zan found herself pulled around. The next thing she knew, she was flat on her back, looking up into a laughing pair of gray eyes. Smiling like a champion, Edward asked, "Come to view the corpse?"

Zan couldn't answer. Her mind, absorbing the full wonder of Edward's smile, could form no words. He had dimples! Two deep dents, just about the size of her fingertip, revealed themselves either side of his mouth. To add to their charm, the left one was somewhat lower down than the right.

"I suppose humiliating me wasn't enough," he said. "You had to come and witness it. I've spent the last half hour planning how to get even with them; now I shall have to make a plan for you, too."

Though she lay passive beneath him, her heart thumped crazily. As he held her wrists, he, too, must have been aware of the erratic beat. Softly she asked, "What've you got in mind?"

"I hadn't thought," he answered, his smile slowly fading. His eyes searched her every feature before fixating on her mouth. With excruciating, teasing deliberation, he bent down to seize her in a kiss.

Zan made no move to free herself, even though the numbing grip on her wrists was gone. She realized she'd only been living for him to take her into his arms again, though lying on her back in the road wasn't exactly how she'd pictured it. But she wasn't about to quarrel with his method.

When he nuzzled her mouth open, she gave in willingly, imitating whatever he did, even to the playful flicks of his tongue against hers. Yet somehow, even that didn't relieve the strange pressures that built inside her. She felt like a steamboat ready to blow the main boiler.

Zan moved her hands restlessly on his back, making no distinction between his shirt and his skin. The sweat on his back gave slickly under her fingers as she pressed upward over the hollows and ridges of his muscles. Edward groaned and rested his forehead against hers.

"So much for punishment," he said with a laugh that sounded like despair. Lifting up, he looked into her eyes. "How easily you can make a victor sue for peace."

He tried to sit up, but Zan held him. One of her legs was all tangled up with his. A hardness rested between them, below the buckle of his belt. After eighteen years of putting two animals, whether cattle or horse, together in mating season, she knew what that length meant. She'd never before imagined, though, the pictures her mind presented now. Tail-tilted Louise O'Murphy at the saloon was nothing compared with them.

"What do you want, Zan? Do you want me to apologize?"

She shook her head irritably, ignoring the small rocks crunching and grinding their way into her hair. "No, I want . . . Kiss me again."

"You shouldn't ask things like that," he said, even as his arms tightened.

Everywhere his lips touched, Zan felt as though that part of her had just been called to life. He swept kisses over her eyelids, and she could see for the first time. The sky above had never been so brilliant, the corn never so green. When he teased her ear with his teeth, the earth began to sing for her. A peck on her nose and she could smell their bodies, the dust and the free-growing flowers not a yard away. And when he came to her eager lips, she could taste only him, as sweet and juicy as peaches in summer.

More than that, Zan felt she could sing with the blossoming earth. Hymns of pleasure broke from her lips as she lay back in his arms. She wanted more than anything else to awaken his senses as he'd aroused her. Almost carelessly she worked free the buttons on her shirt.

"What are you doing?" he asked.

The sun pouring down upon her skin did not feel half as hot as his gaze. She offered herself proudly to his raking vision, glancing down at her firm nipples pushing against the soft whiteness of her cotton undershirt. "Don't you like it?"

"Oh, God," he said, closing his eyes, his weight heavy against her. Somehow Zan knew, however, that he could still see her, imprinted on his inner eye. "Zan . . ."

"I think . . . I think I'd like it if you'd touch me. You know . . . here?" She pressed her own hand to what she'd exposed.

Opening his eyes and sitting back on his heels, he glanced around, at the sky, the field, the empty road stretching on to eternity in both directions, anywhere but at her.

"This is madness!" he cried, as if in defiance.

Up on one elbow, Zan took his hand, clenched in a fist against his thigh and gently spread open his fingers. New calluses, rough on the smooth surface, rasped against her palm. Deliberately she placed his hand over the roundness of her breast. She felt no shame, only a shuddering that racked her as he moved his fingers inside the cotton.

His gaze fixed on her face as he circled the sensitive tip. Aware of his scrutiny, Zan tried to give him an encouraging smile, but the tingling sensation that he created began to grow stronger, and she could only concentrate on that. She frowned and shifted restlessly as the reaction spread throughout her body. It wasn't enough—even his touch where no one had ever touched before wasn't nearly enough.

"Oh, sweet mercy! I want . . ."

"Yes," he said in a deeper voice. "So do I."

With sudden decision he pushed the shirt back from her shoulder. With his other hand, he dragged Travis's sheepskin coat to lie behind her. When he pressed his lips to her shoulder, Zan couldn't seem to support herself anymore.

She lay back. He followed her down, biting her throat tenderly. Zan wrapped her arms around him, moving her legs restlessly under his. The sound of his urgent breaths excited her as much as the eager touch of his hands impatiently disposing of her shirt.

At the very moment when Edward slipped his finger under the wide strap of her undershirt, Zan said, "Wait . . . wait! Somebody's coming!"

He had to shake his head to clear it from the muzzy effect of passion. "What?"

"The ground's shaking! Move . . . hurry! Hurry!"

Jumping up, Edward could see a plume of dust rising in the air. Zan didn't wait to look around for that. She snatched up Travis's coat and scrambled onto the waste ground beside the road. "Don't stand there," she said. "Come on."

In a moment a loaded wagon rattled past. The withered old man on the seat poked his head out the merest bit, like a malevolent tortoise. He spat in their direction, a long brown streak of tobacco juice zipping through the dust. Then he cracked his rawhide whip over the backs of his straining horses.

"Ol' man Grasse," Zan said. "But I guess you know that."

Even on one of his good days, Grasse could make a wedding seem like a funeral, or change the burgeoning Kansas grassland into the Great American Desert. His one glare around in passing had taken the passion from her. No one could possibly want to kiss and hug with *his* image in mind. She had to wonder how Mrs. Grasse ever managed to have two children by him.

"I don't blame you one bit for taking a swing at him," Zan said, staring after the wagon in disgust.

"Who told you that I did? I may have restrained him from beating his dog, but I should never hit a man more than twice my age. Such a thing is unthinkable."

"You stopped him beating that dog . . . and then you took it with you so ol' man Grasse couldn't hurt it anymore. I figured it must be something like that."

"Thank you for your concern." Edward began to straighten his clothing with automatic gestures.

"I even tried to explain it to 'em at the Last Resort. But they were too busy being awful pleased with themselves over the trick they played on you to listen."

"I suspected their 'hunt' was some sort of japery," he said, smoothing down his ruffled hair with the palm of his hand. To look at him, no one could guess he'd been rolling on a dirt road with his hired hand. "Zan . . . I wish to say . . . to express . . ."

She did not want to hear a gentlemanly apology. She'd liked what they were doing, and the strong yearning to have gone on with it hadn't faded when they'd stopped. Somehow, however, the right moment for dragging him bodily into the cornfield had slipped by.

"So if you knew they were tricking you, why'd you go along with it?"

"It might have been a chance to discover some new variety of bird." He tapped his foot and gazed off into the middle distance. "Miller, Spencer, and Gallagher," he mused in an undertone. "I shall have to give thought to the manner in which I even the score."

"No, you don't want to be doing that." She tossed her hair back from her shoulders. "You've got to act like a good sport about this snipe-hunting business. Laugh it off or they'll go on making your life a misery." From the direction of his gaze, Zan saw that he wasn't listening.

"Kindly button your shirt," he said, dragging his eyes away from her body. He studied the grass under his feet, his smile nowhere to be seen.

With her long hair off her shoulders, Zan realized the extent of her undress. Not only was her shirt hanging from her, but the undershirt she wore in lieu of more formal undergarments had been pulled all to one side. The whiteness of her skin where the sun never touched made the demarcation between allowed and forbidden territory very clear.

As she buttoned and tucked, Zan learned that hiding her body did not undo what had happened. His hand really had roamed under her clothes, had awakened and roused parts of her that had slumbered until now. What was stranger still was that even parts of her he hadn't touched were tingling as though he had.

"You're buttoned all wrong," he said.

Edward stepped close to her and with a face as cold as a doctor's undid the skewed buttons. The drag of the fabric over her sensitized flesh reminded her of his touch. Zan wet her lips, longing for one more taste of him. But his face stayed stern, though his hands trembled.

He still hadn't controlled them when he lifted one hand to pick away a piece of straw that clung to her hair. "Zan, I wish I knew what to say to you, to reassure you that what happened . . ."

"Just forget it." Damn! Why did he always feel the need to apologize? Couldn't he have guessed from her response that she loved his touch?

"I wish I could."

"You're not the only one," she grumbled. "But right now the big question is . . . what are you going to do about Gallagher and Company?"

"You know these people better than I. What would appeal to their primitive sense of humor?"

"I don't know. When you come right down to brass tacks, they're all men. And I never have understood what makes men laugh, 'specially when they get together and swallow a couple of beers. Seems to me about half the time even a decent man will laugh at three things . . . a drunk, a green-horn, and a woman."

He ran his fingers back through his hair. "It all sounds rather sophomoric to me. Let me see . . . what did I find amusing during my undergraduate days?"

Remembering other snipe hunts, Zan said, "I'll tell you one thing . . . you've got to do something against yourself. Show you don't take yourself so all-fired serious after all."

"Perhaps I should set myself on fire in the middle of the street. Would that be self-deprecating enough?"

"Now, see, that's just the sort of thing that gets these folks' backs up. It's the big fancy words and the highfa-lutin' air, like you think you're better than everyone else." She touched her teeth to her bottom lip in thought. Feeling his eyes upon her mouth, she hastily released the captive curve.

Zan said, blushing, "Maybe the best thing to do is to make you more of what you are."

"More of . . . I fail to comprehend."

"Well, they all think of you as a stuck-up prig, with your brain jammed stupid with book learning and a real chip on your shoulder."

"Thank you for the portrait; it's very lifelike," he said dryly, bowing from the waist.

"And they don't like how you always seem to be making fun of us. We may be ignorant, but we're good-hearted, mostly."

"I've never doubted it."

"They know you don't like being called Ed and that you dress mighty fussy for a feller that says he wants to be a farmer."

"You might add that they seem to know of my interest in birds and also, regrettably, of my gullibility where practical jokes are concerned."

Thinking hard, Zan walked out into the road to pick up the muffler Edward had dropped in his mock seizure. The scarf was roughly twice the length any one would need. She knew the story behind it. "See this here?" she said.

"It reminds me of my aunt Letitia's attempts at knitting, when she decided to give up the comforts of money and regular baths. Needless to say, the experiment did not last long. I think chiefly it was having to live on unbuttered parsnips that changed her mind." He took the muffler from Zan. "As I recall, Aunt would always run out of wool halfway across and have to complete the item in whatever came to hand. Rather like this sorry object."

"I'll tell you why it's two colored. See, Miss Maisie and Miss Minnie have always tried to get Zeke interested in 'em. They're always taking him cakes and bread and cookies. Well, last winter Miss Minnie takes it into her head to knit Zeke a muffler. Course, right after, Miss Maisie starts into knitting one, too."

"Have they always been like that?"

"Ever since Hector was a pup. Though, I never saw them behave like they do around your uncle. They were like two different people. Anyway, you can allow how it was a quandary for old Zeke. If he wore this orange scarf, Miss Minnie might get encouraged, and if he wore this purple and green one, Miss Maisie would get ideas about walking down that aisle again. And if he didn't wear either of 'em, bang goes the gravy train."

"So he sewed them together and wears them both always. A cunning solution and explains away my puzzlement. I couldn't imagine where in Harmony someone was keeping a giraffe with a putrid sore throat." He measured the knitting between his hands. "Six feet if it's an inch. Interesting, but hardly solves my problem."

"Maybe it does at that. . . ."

It had gotten quiet in the Last Resort since Zan left. Cord had broken out a pack of cards, and the three conspirators played listlessly, their beers at their elbows. In another hour some of the girls from across the street would come in looking for well-breeched cowboys to lean on. John Klinger hung over the bar, already bleary with drink. Charlie still polished glasses beneath the pink-and-crimson painting in the heavy gold frame.

The door swung open and Edward appeared in the opening. Zeke slewed around in his chair to stare pop-eyed at him, and Travis and Cord half rose from their chairs. Edward tossed Travis's coat over a vacant table. In his most precise and clipped tones, he said, "I want to thank you chaps for a most interesting afternoon. But you left much too soon. Shortly after you departed, I captured a live snipe."

"What's that 'round your hand?" Travis asked. "It looks like Zeke's scarf."

"An amazing coincidence. Someone knitted the precisely right manner of rope, a very special type of rope, designed to catch elusive creatures." He tugged on the multicolored rope, and Zan stumbled into the saloon, her hands tied before her with the other end of the muffler.

All three men rose from the seats in surprise.

"That ain't no snipe," Zeke said. "That's Zan."

"No, no, quite wrong, I assure you. It's a snipe—*Apex gutterlorum*. Rare in this part of the world, of course." He peered at her, behaving exactly as the fussy, persnickety citified gent should. Zan struggled to keep a laugh from breaking out.

The three townsmen exchanged glances. "Reckon he's gone funny?" Zeke asked in what he probably believed was a whisper.

From behind the bar Charlie said, "I certainly wouldn't mind finding a wild animal like that, Mr. Winchester. If I weren't a happily married man, that is. Maybe you can show Mr. Gallagher and Mr. Miller where you found her. There may be a couple more for them."

Finally getting the joke, the sheriff said, "Hey, any out there with fancier feathers?"

"And I like mine with more meat on her bones," Zeke riposted. He dug his elbow into Cord's ribs. The saloon owner grimaced and stepped away from the barber. Cord frowned at the spectacle before him as though it confused him.

"No, no, gentlemen," Edward said. "She's a very rare bird, indeed. The only one, as a matter of fact. I really couldn't share her."

"Ain't enough there for more'n one feller anyhow," Zeke walked up close to Zan and squeezed his fingers over her upper arm. "Tough and stringy, too."

Edward gave Zeke an up-and-down glance. "Judging by the birds that follow you, my friend, tough and stringy is the only kind you can attract."

"Whoo-whoo," Travis mocked, grinning. "He's got them twin crows of yours pegged there, Zeke."

"Aw, shucks," the barber said, his face turning crimson. "You know I ain't never done nothing to lead 'em on. I'd shoo 'em off, iffen they'd go."

Standing there, with her hands tied, listening to their banter, Zan suddenly knew that her idea to help Edward gain the friendship of these men hadn't been a good one. She'd always been part of the circle before, her femaleness ignored, no one treating her any different than if a teenage boy'd walked in. In truth, a boy would have had to take more guff than she ever did, for she'd always been accepted here.

Now they looked at her and talked about her, but in a different way, discussing her as if she really were some kind of strange animal. Was it that her hands were tied, and the tie held by a man? Was it that because she'd allowed herself to be "captured" that they were looking at her as a woman and not as Zan Lind?

She met Edward's eyes and knew her face burned. The wool around her wrists dragged as heavily as an iron chain. Half lifting her hands, she knew a hint of pleading had entered her expression.

Suddenly Edward began to twist the muffler around his arm. Zan had no choice but to walk forward. A strange jumping heat began to boil just under her breast. At first she thought it was fear. Then she realized it was the same excitement she'd felt in his arms. Even while hoping he'd kiss her again—even here in front of everyone—she trusted him enough to know he wouldn't.

When she stood quite close to him, he dropped the muffler. Abruptly he spread open the loop that enclosed her wrists. "Fly away, little bird."

"Yes," Cord repeated. "Fly away. Right now. And you, Ed, come on over. Your drinks are on the house."

As Zan stood there, the four men sat down at the table. Charlie was already carrying four fresh beers over to them on a tray. Not even Edward took any more notice of Zan. Slowly, with several backward glances, she walked out of the saloon.

CHAPTER
10

Zan stood outside the Last Resort, looking up and down the street. Though the buildings were in their accustomed places, and the signboards swung and creaked to their usual rhythm, everything seemed different to her eyes. Not a soul was in sight, for one thing, not even a dog or a cat.

A hollowness dug its way into Zan's chest. She tightened her lips and crunched her brows, angry that in another minute she'd start to bawl. Stupid, she thought. I'll go back tomorrow and they won't think a thing of it.

She went to the end of the boardwalk to collect her mule and go home. Then a voice called to her from the Last Resort. Though she knew at once it was Charlie, she couldn't help wishing Edward had come out to see if she was all right. That aborted wish made her angrier still. Of course, there was no point in taking it out on Charlie.

He stood there in his bright red vest, cradling a jug in his arms. "Mr. Spencer said I'm to give you this with his compliments. I'm sorry, Miss Zan."

"It's none of your fault, Mr. Thompson. It's my own." She took the heavy jug of sarsaparilla from him. "Tell Mr.

Spencer thanks." The bartender nodded, his deep brown eyes contrite.

"And," she added, "you can tell him I don't need to be hit over the head, either. I understand what he's trying to say with this. He won't be seeing me in there again."

Charlie looked at her as if he were proud of her. "I'll be keeping the jugs for you, Miss Zan. You let me know when you want to pick them up."

Trying hard to remember she was a businesswoman, Zan thanked Charlie and walked away. All the same, what she really wanted to do was to throw herself to the ground and beat her hands against the unyielding dirt. Leaving the jug beside Hank, she walked across the street. Throwing a tantrum wouldn't be very smart, but she could do the next best thing.

An hour later the gravel path that lead down the tiny rose garden behind the First Resort had been raked. Around each bush a circle of darker earth had been turned up to the light and the weeds plucked away. Now as Zan bent over each plant, picking off the tiny white aphids and dropping them into a pan of kerosene, a waft of fragrant smoke told her she was no longer alone.

"Hiya, Miss Lottie," she said, without looking up.

"I've been watching you, girl. You been working like you've got a serious mad on."

Zan shrugged. "I hate these little bugs."

"Now, if it was me, I'd guess there was a man behind it, but if you want to say it's bugs, it's bugs."

Miss Lottie leaned against the back doorframe, her cigarillo held between thumb and forefinger. She wasn't dressed to receive company as yet, wearing a loose wrapper of filmy material draped with somewhat dingy lace. Raising the little brown cigar to her lips, she inhaled and then blue plumes trickled from her nostrils slowly. "Yeah, I'd have to guess a man."

Zan moved on to the next rosebush. The large white flowers were as untidy as Miss Lottie. Yet within the hour the older woman would be powdered, painted, and tightly corseted in anticipation of a working night. Roses could not recapture their beauty, but Miss Lottie could, if the inspection were not too close.

Realizing this was someone who could tell her things even her own mother couldn't, Zan said explosively, "It's not a man . . . it's men!"

"Ah, the little dears. What gets your goat specially? There's an awful lot on that menu to choose from!"

Zan told her what had happened from the time she first entered the Last Resort looking for Edward. She omitted what happened after she found him lying in the road. It wasn't that Miss Lottie wouldn't understand—who would understand better?—but that Zan couldn't find the words. She skipped to when he had lead her into the saloon.

Miss Lottie's dark brows, strongly contrasted to her red hair, lifted as she whistled softly. "You let him tie your hands? I'd heard that about the English. Interesting." Her slow smile made Zan feel very young.

"Anyway, now I've been kicked out of the Last Resort, and Mr. Spencer has made it pretty clear I'm not welcome to come back any time soon."

"You might have Mrs. Spencer to blame for that. It don't look right a nice young thing like you sitting in a dirty bar room, though maybe I'm not the best one to be talking to you about such things. Or maybe I am. I've spent more of my life than I like to remember in those kind of places."

"Yes, ma'am," seemed the most polite answer.

" 'Sides, I'm surprised your mama didn't put a stop to it before this."

"My father never objected to my going in there."

"That was when you were an itty-bitty girl. You're all grown-up now, Zan Lind. Anybody with even one eye could see that. I'm kinda having second thoughts about you even working here in my rose garden."

"I don't see why," Zan said, inspecting the undersides of the leaves.

"No, of course you don't." Some sad note crept into Miss Lottie's husky voice. "I wouldn't want you to. You go on tending these flowers. You do have a way with 'em."

"I like gardening. Not as much as farming, of course. A garden is a good thing, but a farm is like a whole world, if you know what I mean."

"Nope, I don't." Miss Lottie took a last, long draw on her cigarillo and then dropped it on the step. Crushing it out with her feather-trimmed mule, she said, "How do you like working with His Lordship? Except for today, has he been treating you right?"

"Edward? He's all right, once you get to know him." She bowed low over the final bush in the row, hoping the brilliant red of the blossoms would be blamed for the color in her face.

"You've got to know him pretty well, I'd say. Better than anybody knows." The laughter was back in the madam's voice. Zan's head jerked up to stare at her. How much did she guess?

"Oh, yes, child. I haven't been in my line of work so long that I don't remember the first one. A tall lanky feller name of Joe Cartwell. I was younger than you, but I would of walked barefoot over broken glass if he'd so much as wiggled his finger at me. Didn't work out—he was no good and I was one dumb baby-child." She chuckled. "Lordy, but I was dumb!"

"I can't imagine you being stupid."

Miss Lottie's plump shoulders moved under the wrapper. She tugged the lacy edges together. "We're all dumb when it comes to a man's sweet-talk, darlin'. Did he kiss you?"

There didn't seem to be a reason to lie, though she glanced over her shoulder before she said, "Yes."

"Did you like it?" Zan nodded with a smile that was only half-shameful. "Can't say I blame you. Those clean-cut, fancy-talking ones always did something extra to my insides. But you watch yourself, Zan. You want him, you get him, right and proper. Shiny gold on your finger and a proper roof over your head. Don't make the mistakes most of my girls made."

"But I don't want to marry him, Miss Lottie."

"Why not? You're in love with him."

"No, I . . ." Zan meant to protest vigorously, yet the words died on her lips. Could it be true? She never thought of herself being in love with anyone; it seemed so sloppy, like falling into a mud-hole and not troubling to clamber out.

Testing her feelings, she pictured in her mind the men she knew. Some she liked well enough—like Joseph Taylor and Otto Krensler, boys her own age. Some she even found good-looking—Travis Miller and that traveling salesman who spent one night a week at the hotel.

But when she thought of Edward, all the others dimmed in her mind like the flame of a kerosene lamp turned too low. He, however, burned bright and steady. She didn't think it was just his kisses, either. A woman, she knew instinctively, could spend all her days and nights with Edward Winchester and never stop finding new things about him to love. Why, just look at what he could do to her with a smile!

"Close your mouth, darlin'," Lottie said, chuckling again. "You're catching flies."

Wildly Zan said, "Miss Lottie, I can't really be in love with him! Can I?"

"It sticks out all over you like a rash. Let's hope you only catch it once."

"But . . . but what do I do? What if he finds out? Oh, mercy, this is terrible!"

Miss Lottie came down into the garden. "You want him to find out, don't you? How's he going to do anything about it if he doesn't?"

"No, he mustn't. I told him . . . well, I said a lot of things to him 'bout how I don't care if I ever get married and he knows all about Quintus . . . 'Sides, he'd never be interested in me. I'm not what he wants. He wants a lady."

"Hold your horses. Who's Quintus?"

Catching a shaky breath, Zan said, "He's the son of one of my father's friends in Sweden. He wants to come over, to set up a homestead of his own. Father has hinted that he'd be welcome to marry me."

"Fathers are the kind of men we avoid in my business, and for good reason. They always try to do right. If I was you, I wouldn't worry about this other feller till he gets here. But what do you mean—'bout his royalty wanting a lady?"

"Well, you know he doesn't much care for America, and he thinks American girls—ones like me anyway—are awful. He wants somebody who can flirt and play pianos. And he likes girls who listen to their folks and don't run wild."

Miss Lottie showed her slow smile again and patted the hair at the side of her head. "I don't know about that other stuff, and I never much needed to play a piano, but any time you want to learn to flirt, you don't go to anybody but me. And, you know, no man ever turned down a girl 'cause she knew how to run a little bit wild."

By the time Zan stopped at the Double B to collect Herman and to reassure Uncle Fred that Edward was well, though he would be home late, dusk had begun to close in. As she drove into her yard, the sun sent orange streamers through low clouds to the west. Walking to the house after caring for the animals, Zan squinted up at the clouds, ignoring their beauty.

"Doesn't look like it will rain," she said to her father.

He sat on the porch steps, his big brown hands dangling between his knees. "Rain? No, not for a week. Maybe more."

"That's good. Seems like Edward and me haven't done half as much work as we should have this week. We've got catching up to do. Well, I better get washed up for supper." She stepped around him.

Mr. Lind swiveled and said, "The boys brought me a letter from town. It's from Quintus."

Zan froze, her hand on the door. "Quintus?"

"Yes. He sent it last month—very good time from Sweden. The ships are so fast now."

"That's what I hear. So, what does he say?"

"I have not opened it yet. I wanted to wait until you came home. But now it is too late. I will read it to you after supper."

She didn't think he did it to be mean. He probably didn't even realize that she'd be nearly too nervous to eat. What if Quintus's letter said that he was ready to leave Sweden? What if the letter, sent to warn them of his arrival, came only a few days before he himself?

Zan pushed her plate away after only one helping of *lövbiff*. Not that her mother had lost her skill, but somehow even her favorite fried beef and onions didn't appeal to Zan this evening. Not even the potatoes, hot and running with butter, could tempt her to eat more than one.

Fortunately, she could rely on her brothers to eat quickly. Living all day in the open air gave them an appetite that could only be satisfied by large amounts of food eaten with all the dispatch of which they were capable. Mrs. Lind did not reprove their table manners. She'd often told them about her five brothers, all big men raised on the solid food of their native land, and how they could clear a table faster than locusts in a melon patch.

Tonight, only Sarah dawdled and pushed at her food. Mrs. Lind asked, "Is something wrong with yours? Or is that you are sick?"

"It's very good, Mother. It's just . . . Faith gave Amanda and me a big slice of cake with sauce. I'm still not hungry."

Zan asked, "Was it rhubarb sauce?"

Her younger sister nodded. "It was good, but kind of sweet. And she put it on real thick. I'm sorry, Mother."

"Oh, never mind. I will keep it hot for you until you are ready to finish."

Zan sighed with relief at this decision. If she'd had to sit there while Sarah—never a swift eater anyway—cut tiny pieces and chewed them well, she'd go mad.

But Mr. Lind said, "No, Inga. She should have known not to eat cake before supper. We will wait for you, Sarah."

"But, Father . . ." the little girl whined, looking at the good-size serving still on her plate.

"We will wait. But I will keep you company." He drew his daughter's plate closer to him. "Come . . . bite for bite as when you were a baby."

He scooped up a heaping forkful of the beef and guided it to his own mouth. Then, chewing hard, he dipped the fork into the plate again to take up a dainty morsel. With a smile, Sarah took the fork from his hand and nibbled the little bit.

Mrs. Lind leaned across Gary and whispered to Zan, "Why rhubarb sauce?"

"I'll explain later," Zan answered. Her smile was mechanical, for she counted each forkful and tried to estimate how many more remained on Sarah's plate.

Even the boys were wiggling with impatience, but the rule had always been that everyone stayed at the table until all were satisfied. Mrs. Lind, however, calmed their eagerness to be gone with the magic words, "Who wants cake?"

Sarah shook her head mutely, looking a little sick, but every other eye lit up. Zan decided that she could wait to discover her fate until she could devour a piece of layer cake, sticky with caramel glaze. And if she could hold out for one piece, she might as well keep her patience for two!

Replete at last, Mr. Lind sat back in his chair and patted his overhanging stomach. "*Det var en utsökt måltid. Tack, Inga.* Nobody, not even my mother—rest her—could make *lövbiff* better than you."

His wife dimpled at the compliments. "Your mother taught me how to make it her way. I only changed the potatoes."

"That must be the difference. A very good meal, though, as I said."

"Father," Zan said, unable to wait any longer. "What about the letter? From Quintus?"

A glance passed between her parents. She could read the surprise in her mother's eyes and the hope in her father's. How to tell them it was not anticipation that compelled the question but fear? How much time did she have? Would there be enough time to bring in the sorghum crop?

Slowly Mr. Lind reached into the pocket of his old brown coat. He put the folded paper on the table. Then he began to pat his other pockets, saying, "What have I done with my pipe? Inga . . . ?"

"It's with your tobacco pouch."

"Ah, where is that?"

"I don't know . . . wherever you left it." This was the oldest joke they shared together, even older than their marriage. Long before his blond hair had begun to lighten further with gray, he had never known where his pipe or pouch were to be found.

Zan held on to her patience with both hands as her father

continued to search himself. At last he found the pipe in the same pocket from which he'd withdrawn the envelope. Filling the bowl with thorough pokes of his forefinger, he peered at the address on the letter.

"This is a wonderful thing—mail. Not six weeks ago this piece of paper is lying maybe on a table in Sweden—maybe even the table I used to put my hat on when I go to see my good friend Widstrand. And now look. It is on my table, this table I make myself, waiting for me to read. Wonderful thing."

"Yes, Father," Zan said. She scooted the hurricane lamp closer to her father's end of the table. "Is that better?"

"Very good."

Finally he reached for the letter. Sliding one finger under the fold, he opened it. Fine lines of closely written ink covered the page, first horizontally and then vertically. Mr. Lind tilted the page toward the steady light of the lamp. He read silently for a moment. Then he *tsk-tsked* under his breath. "Oh, too bad."

Zan reminded herself that he didn't know he was being difficult. Her mother, however, couldn't control herself. "What is it? Don't sit and make *tsk* noises like an old lady. What is too bad?"

"He is a nice, polite boy. You two, Ben, Gary, you could learn from this boy. He says . . ." Mr. Lind lifted the letter again, his lips moving as he read the Swedish. "He says, 'My heart fills with longing to see your beautiful country. All my friends who have gone write to say that nothing can equal the richness of America. My joy will be great when I reach your silver shores.' "

Zan's brothers rolled their eyes.

"He sounds like a poet," Mrs. Lind said.

"He is like his father. Widstrand could charm the birds out of the trees, and the girls . . . he always had his pick."

"Hmmm, between you, how many hearts did you break?"

For a moment Mr. Lind's smile was that of a man who looks at burning memories. Hastily, however, he cleared his throat and said, "None, Inga. I promise you."

"Read the rest of the letter. Promises later. You still haven't said what is bad."

"He says, 'Regrettably, my mother has taken ill. For a time I must work for her keep. I pray she will soon recover her health. With my sister gone to work in France, there is no one else. My sister will be back in six months, so I cannot go before then. It is difficult to have no wife. . . .' " Mr. Lind turned the page to read the lines that crossed the first set. " 'It is my wish that soon after arriving in your fair nation, I will find a good Swedish girl—Lutheran as we all are—to take to wife.' "

Zan hardly heard anything after "six months." She wanted to whoop and holler. Six months! If in that time she didn't own the Beakman place and have half an orchard planted . . . She thought of Edward. In six months would he be gone? Funny how heavy a heart could suddenly become, sinking down into a meal she wished now she had not eaten.

Ben and Gary begged to be excused, and Sarah went upstairs to nurse a full stomach. Mr. Lind refolded his letter and tucked it carefully away in an inside pocket. "It will be good to see Widstrand's boy, whenever he comes. Maybe we can find a good Swedish girl for him, yes, Zan?"

"Ol' man . . . that is, Mr. Grasse's daughter is twenty, Father. I'm sure she must be thinking of marriage. And, you know, he has always refused to attend the Methodist church."

"One day we will have enough families to start our own church," Mr. Lind said, reiterating a long-held dream of the Swedish families around Harmony. "But no one can say we are not good Lutherans when we worship God every week, even if it is in a Methodist church. Quintus will not think the less of us . . . not any of us."

Mrs. Lind stood up and began to stack the plates together. "Here, Mother," Zan said, "I'll do this. Why don't you sit down in the parlor and let Father read the newspapers to you."

"No, I want to bake my mother's *kaffe-kaka* that you like so much. Maybe you have time to learn how to make it yourself?"

Zan's interest in food extended only to eating it. Ordinarily she would have waved away her mother's suggestion as she often had before. But after feeling the sting of rejection at the Last Resort, she hadn't the heart to inflict the same pain on her mother. She even tried to put a little enthusiasm in her tone as she said, "Sure, okay. After all, it can't hurt me much to know one recipe."

Mr. Lind said, "Every girl should know one good cake. A man likes his wife to make sweet things. Even more, he likes her to say them."

Mrs. Lind rested her hand on her husband's broad shoulder. "I want to talk to you later about those girls you knew in Sweden. Maybe I, too, can learn how to talk sweet."

"You do, Inga, you do." He patted her hand and stood up. "I will go read the newspapers to myself." Zan knew her father only pretended to read the papers he held up before his face after supper. He would sleep in his comfortable chair until his wife reminded him to go to bed.

"Go and wash your hands again." Mrs. Lind peered at her daughter. "And what is in your hair? Grass? I did not see that before. You'd better get it out. Grass does not belong in baking."

Though she'd braided up her hair before letting Edward tie her hands, Zan hadn't had the chance to brush out the accumulated debris from the road. She'd returned so late that there hadn't been time to look in the glass before supper. At least there hadn't been any ants or beetles where'd she'd been lying. Or so she hoped. Just thinking about it made her scalp tingle as though little feet walked all over it.

She went up the stairs. Mrs. Lind, listening to the heavy feet of her usually heedlessly swift child, shook her head as she lit the black stove. Always Faith had brought her girlish troubles to her while Zan sought the advice of her father. But the estrangement between them over Quintus Widstrand prevented them from talking about anything else.

Mrs. Lind vowed that she'd corner her husband again tonight and try to convince him that, while Quintus would be welcomed on the farm, there should be no more promise of a marriageable daughter. "Unless he's willing to wait for our little Sarah," she'd say after the candle was out. That would make him laugh, and once he laughed, he would listen to her.

Zan watched over her mother's shoulder as she cracked eggs, mixed, and beat. "When my father tasted this cake," Mrs. Lind said, "he knew he'd found the wife for him. He did not take very long to ask her to marry, though she made him wait two years before she agreed."

"Why'd she do that? To test whether he loved her?"

"Yes, and to finish her sewing. In those days, a girl would never marry without a chest full of embroidered pieces. There is some of her work in the chest the Bible sits on."

Zan had seen the precious objects before, at Christmas and other special days. What impressed her the most hadn't been the bright flowers painstakingly set on a long black vest or the white linen blouse overworked in white thread with which the vest would have been worn. Rather, she'd marveled at the size of the woman revealed by the dimensions of the clothing her daughter cherished. The owner of this eighteen-inch waist and narrow shoulders had become the mother of eight, only to see them all emigrate to a new nation.

"What do you miss most about Sweden?" Zan suddenly asked.

"Miss?" With firm strokes of the rolling pin, her mother flattened out the dough into a rectangle. "I miss nothing. I have everything I have ever wanted right here. Now watch."

Deftly she spread cold butter over the surface of the dough, leaving a narrow unbuttered edge. She folded the dough like an accordion, making three layers. Then she turned it a quarter of the way around, rolled it flat, and repeated the buttering and the folding. "This makes it light as air."

"I see. I know what I'd miss if I had to leave Kansas."

"You want to leave?"

"No, I was just thinking how hard it would be to leave. But if I had to, I guess I'd miss the—"

"Cloudberries," her mother said, holding the rolling pin in midair for a moment. "I miss the cloudberries the most."

"I've never heard of those. What are they?"

"Little fruit. They look like plump raspberries, only they are a little yellow and sweeter. I have never seen them in America. I don't think they grow here." Firmly she rolled out the dough. "Do this four times," she said.

Mrs. Lind explained that it was best to let the dough rest after the buttering and rolling, but sometimes, if it were cool enough, the cook could continue without stopping. She showed Zan how to mix the cardamom filling and how to roll up the filling in the ring.

Zan concentrated, yet some of the instructions must have slipped in one ear and out the other. For when her mother put the glazed ring to one side and said, "Now you make one, too," Zan had no idea how to begin. Mrs. Lind laughed. "Now we do it together, I think."

Zan found she could do it, if she kept her mind strictly

on what she was doing. No time to daydream as she did driving the mules or pulling weeds. The worst mistakes she made happened when a thought of Edward would drift across her mind. That is when she grabbed the wrong spice for the filling, or forgot to roll the dough out again before adding more butter.

In the morning, however, the family ate her coffee ring with as much enthusiasm as they ate her mother's. Zan set off for the Double B filled with confidence, feeling that the world had grown larger overnight. This sensation lasted until she reached the farm and saw Edward, standing motionless in the barn as though he'd been waiting for her.

The world contracted around him. Nothing else seemed to have shape or weight. She knew that last night she'd played with the thought of being in love with him. Today, seeing him, she knew this was no game. This was a battle she could lose, and the forfeit would be all her dreams.

"Are you ready to start work?" he asked. "We've been slacking off, taking too much time away from the fields. I foresee many long days before us if we are to put this crop in the ground in time."

"That's what I've been saying."

"I realize that, and, if I may say so, Thierry and several other authors agree with you."

"That's a mercy, anyhow." Trying hard to sound as though nothing had changed, Zan realized she spoke more harshly than she'd intended.

"I only hope that you can keep up with me," Edward said, striding off.

Zan said quickly, "You just let me know when you're beaten."

CHAPTER
11

"That sounds like a challenge," he said, facing her across fifteen feet of barn floor. His hands rested over his narrow hips, and he tossed his head back pridefully.

"If you want to take it as one, fine."

"What's your wager?"

"My what? Oh, a bet. I don't need to bet a thing. I'm bound to win."

"No woman can work harder than a man."

"Are we back to that?" She'd thought he had come to accept her as an equal. Apparently her behavior yesterday had put her under the necessity of proving herself to him all over again.

"You are, after all, a woman, Zan."

"I know it. You've done your best to make me know it."

Zan took a few steps toward him, her eyes narrowing with suspicion. "All that kissing and hugging . . . all that pretty talk . . . was that just to get rid of me?"

"No, not in the least." But he couldn't bring himself to meet her eyes.

"You figured I'd get scared and hightail it home the first time, in your room. It must have been a real disappointment when I showed up here the next morning. And by the river and yesterday . . . Well, I'm awful sorry, Mr. Winchester, I just don't scare that easy."

What did frighten her was that even standing here, seeing all the interest he'd shown in her for a counterfeit, she could still look at him and want him. Even while she planted her feet and took pride in the strength flowing through her, a daydream ran through her mind.

She wanted to lie down with him in the prickly hay and do wonderfully forbidden things with him. Her breast tingled where he had touched. He'd surely do that again as well as other things she couldn't begin to imagine. Pushing the thoughts out of her mind was like closing a barn door in a tornado.

"Zan, it isn't what you think at all. I admit that at first, I thought you would run away. A well-brought-up English girl indubitably would have. And by the river, yes, it's true that the reasons I had for kissing you had nothing in truth to do with you. But—"

"Please," she said, holding up her hand. "Don't flatter me anymore. You think I can't do what I need to do 'cause I'm just a girl."

"I thought that once, but I don't anymore."

She didn't hear his handsome admission. "But I'm not going to run away, Mr. Winchester. I'm going to work like the devil, whether you like it or not. We've got an agreement and I'm going to hold you to it."

She walked past him as though he were one of the animals. Only at the doorway did she turn back, giving him a long look. "Come hell or high water, Mr. Winchester."

From then on, it seemed more like war than farming. Utterly disregarding Edward's rules on her working hours,

Zan showed up at the fields long before dawn and kept working until long past owl-time. Her hands developed new calluses, and muscles she did not know she had protested forcefully every night.

"My dear Zan, you can't go on like this." Uncle Fred made a habit of bringing her cool drinks and food at noon. Today he'd found her leaning against the back wheel of the grain drill. He had to touch her to get her attention. Coming upright with a start, she stared around with sleep-bleared eyes.

"Huh? Oh, thanks." She knocked back the drink and dragged her hand across her lips. "I'm okay, Uncle Fred. Just haven't been getting much sleep, I guess. Glad tomorrow's Sunday."

"You can sleep in on Sundays?"

"Nope, but church is kind of relaxing. Nothing to do but sit there and listen to the sermon. Course, there's no getting out of dressing up. Long white dress, shined shoes, and hair ribbons. I purely hate hair ribbons. They pull your hair, and you can feel the tug even after you take 'em off."

"I wouldn't know about that," he said, passing his hand over his pate, all bald save for the gray fringe that encircled it. "But you cannot very well attend services in dungarees."

"I've never understood why the Lord would care whether I came in denims or a skirt starched so stiff I can't sit down."

"Perhaps he wouldn't, but people would. Mrs. Hastings and Mrs. Parker, for instance." He said their names in the same way that a man tests a sore tooth with his tongue.

"Hey, what is going on with them? Have you been slipping 'em a love potion or something?"

Uncle Fred dug the shiny toe of his boot into the loose topsoil. "I don't know what you mean," he said feebly.

"Oh, come on. When they're in town, they're as ornery as ever. But when I saw 'em out here, they were handing around the sweetness and light like cake at a wedding."

"I cannot say that I've noticed anything strange. . . . Yes, I admit it. Their behavior has been odd, most odd."

Zan took a sandwich from the basket he carried and waved it. She could take five minutes for lunch and his problem. "Go on. Are they hunting you?"

He did look like the rabbit who hears the hound. "That is as concise a description as there may be. But the hunt seems . . . altruistic. Excuse me, unselfish. Neither Mrs. Parker nor Mrs. Hastings seems to be interested in me for herself, but rather for her sister."

Her mouth full, Zan mumbled, "I don't get that." She swallowed. "Wait. Do you mean like the way they can't seem to say enough nice things about each other when they're here? I couldn't believe my ears. Miss Minnie saying how wonderful Miss Maisie is, and Miss Maisie being sweet as sugar pie right back. I thought they'd been out in the sun too long."

"It is certainly unusual for them. And, you know, I don't believe either of them actually are wishful to marry me, even were I remotely concerned with finding another wife."

Uncle Fred turned his light eyes toward the horizon. "My wife did not live very long after our marriage. 'Momentary as a sound, swift as a shadow, short as any dream, brief as the lightning in the collied night. . . . ' She can never be succeeded by another."

Zan patted his arm, her eyes suddenly moist. He hadn't even remembered to mention which play he was quoting. "She must have been great."

Mutely he nodded.

After a brief silence she said, "I wonder if their paying court to you has anything to do with Zeke Gallagher. You know, the pair of them have been after him for the longest time with neither of 'em having any luck. It's almost like another one of their contests—who can bake the best biscuits, who had the most worthless husband, who can land the barber?"

Uncle Fred came back from a long way off and gave a boyish grin. "Ah-hah! You feel that if one of them gives in to marriage with me—though as I say . . ."

"Then the other one could get her hands on Zeke."

"The poor beggar."

"Oh, he hasn't done so bad. He hasn't had to buy a loaf of bread or a cookie in years."

"But what action to take so as to prevent this disaster from overtaking me?"

"You could tell them straight out that you're not going to marry either one. That'll stop 'em in their tracks."

"I could never do that," Uncle Fred said, distressed. " 'I am the very pink of courtesy.' *Romeo and Juliet,* Act Two."

Glad to see him his usual self again, Zan said, "Maybe I can help you think of some way out. At any rate, they can't *make* you ask either one of them, not if you don't want to."

"I suppose not. Yet they possess great strength of mind. Many a man's foot has been caught in such a trap before he knew what he was about."

"What play is that from?"

Uncle Fred fairly sparkled. "Oh, it's not Shakespeare's. It's a little thing of my own. Did you truly think it one of the Immortal Bard's lines?"

"Sure sounded like it to me. But then, all you English fellers talk funny. Like you think out what you're going to say ahead of time and get it off by heart." She finished her lemonade, wondering if the man in the other field would ever say anything from his heart to her.

She stretched, one hand planted in the small of her back. "Got to keep working. Thanks for lunch, Uncle Fred."

A few hours later she saw Edward head his cattle in. With a laugh that jarred her sore stomach muscles, Zan kept on working. Though she never lashed Hank or Hermann—she'd much sooner lash her brothers—the mules would work longer for her even than for her father. But even a mule has limits, and they seemed to know it was Saturday. When the sun began to redden and sink, the mules stopped dead. Nothing could persuade them to take another step.

Giving up, she turned their heads toward the house. Now they stepped with enthusiasm, high, wide, and handsome. Zan had begun leaving them in the pasture behind the barn, instead of running them home each night. Soon her father would need to use the team. In the meantime, as Edward was getting the use of them, he could feed them.

Zan figured Edward had gone into the house already. She toyed with the idea of going in and flaunting her hard work as she put the mules up. But as she crossed the yard, she heard hammer blows ringing in the air.

She looked all around and then up. Flat against the sloping barn roof, his toes barely touching the thin edge of a nailed-on board, Edward hammered shingles into place along a row. Zan had never seen a man more precariously placed. Compared to his position, a boy taking a dare to a walk the ridge-pole of a church stood on safer ground. As if she weren't worried enough, he chose that moment to edge along on tiptoe so he could reach another course of shingles.

Not daring to call out a warning—for a startle would be sure to send him crashing down—Zan sank to her knees in the grass. Her eyes fixed on Edward, she hoped God would forgive her for not closing her eyes in the prayer she set up for his safety.

"If I take my eyes off him, Lord, he's sure to fall. I'll keep my eyes on him; you tuck a hand beneath him."

Behind her, she heard the house door slam. From the front porch, Fred clapped a pair of pot lids together, making a noise like the Last Trump. As the deafening echoes fled, he shouted, "Are you almost finished? Dinner will be ready momentarily!"

Zan clamped her fingers over her mouth to keep back her scream. Surely with such a sudden noise, Edward would let go and fall. There'd be nothing left for her but to weep over his shattered bones.

By some miracle, however, he didn't even slip. "Very well," he called down. "I shan't be long."

"Where's Zan?" Uncle Fred asked. "I wished to invite her as well. I feel as though she has somehow grown to be a part of our family group."

"She's right there," Edward said, pointing over his shoulder with his hammer. "Watching to see if I'm doing this correctly, no doubt."

Zan scrambled up, though she didn't take her eyes off Edward. "Thanks for the offer, Uncle Fred, but it's Saturday night. If I don't get home in time to take a bath, my brothers will use up all the hot water in the stove's reservoir. Nothing worse than a . . ."

Her mouth went dry. Not from fear, but from pure desire. Using only the strength in his arms, his firmly muscled legs held out in a stiff line from his hips, Edward climbed hand over hand down a dangling rope. Every motion he made was under his complete control.

Zan had never seen a more assured display of pure strength. She couldn't have done it. Jake Sutherland, the blacksmith and popularly accepted as the strongest man in Harmony, couldn't have done it. Even if he had, Jake had never created the feeling of excitement that leaped and boiled behind her breastbone as she watched Edward.

"At one point, at age thirteen or fourteen," Fred said quietly, noting the direction of her gaze, "he left school for a time to run away to sea. Three months passed before his father discovered where he had gone. I believe Edward learned much during those months."

"What are you telling her, Uncle?" Edward said, coming closer.

"I merely mentioned your seagoing adventure."

"Oh, that! A schoolboy's folly. I hardly think of it."

"What made you give it up?" Zan asked breathlessly. She could see him, like the hero of one of Joseph Taylor's yellow-back novels, fending off Barbary pirates and bending beautiful princesses over his knee to tame their wild spirits.

"Hardtack and cold boiled beef made the dull food at school seem like a gourmet feast. I had never been so pleased to see my father as the day we docked and there he stood beside the wharf. I didn't even mind the caning I received. Seagoing discipline can contrive far worse than a mere cane."

"I loathed being caned," Uncle Fred put in. "It was the unfair caning of a classmate that prompted me to lead a revolt at Eton . . . oh, years before your time there, my boy."

"We still honored your generation for its bravery, sir. Though we often wondered how you came by the gunpowder."

"A revolt?" Zan asked, more confused than ever. They were so proper always . . . or nearly always . . . that she couldn't tell whether they really were as delighted by their memories as they seemed. It all sounded pretty horrible to her.

Uncle Fred smiled modestly. "No, no, my boy. That was not my class's work. I believe there used to be a revolution at Eton every twenty years or so. It was the brave lads of '89 who blew in the headmaster's door with gunpowder.

My class had not their boldness. However, we did throw barricades about two buildings and did not surrender them until our terms were met. We had the headmaster on the run that day, I can tell you!"

Maybe it was after they grew up that English boys became stiff and proper like Edward. In their maturity, if Fred was any example, they mellowed again. Sooner or later Edward might become more Fred-like.

"What were your terms?" Zan asked.

"Let me see if I can recall them. They seemed vital at the time. Chiefly we wanted caning by the headmaster only and never before twenty-four hours had passed between the sin and the execution. No chalk on the cane. . . ."

"Chalk?"

Edward said, "To strike the same place repeatedly, which hurts more than random strikes, the master would sometimes chalk the cane, leaving a line on the boy's jacket to help in aiming more precisely."

"Ow!" Zan exclaimed, screwing up her face.

Uncle Fred said, "Our final demand was for spotted dick twice a week rather than only once."

Now Zan felt certain they were pulling her leg. "Spotted what?"

"That's it!" Edward said, clapping his hands together once. "The perfect name for the dog, Uncle. He's definitely spotted, now that I have cleaned him up."

"Seems like he's got more patches than spots," Zan said.

"Perhaps, but it will be his name, I think." Edward started away. "I must go see if he'll answer to it."

"What is 'spotted dick,' anyway?"

Uncle Fred answered, "A type of pudding served with custard that is very popular with schoolboys. I shall make if for you one day. Speaking of which, I must just see if my biscuits are burning. Are you certain you cannot stay?"

"Thanks, no." Had Edward looked back before turning the corner? Had there been disappointment in the set of his shoulders when she did not follow? Zan knew she should hurry on home. Yet, when she got moving at last, it was to go into the backyard.

The dog danced around Edward with straight front legs, its feathered tail sweeping through the air. Red tongue lolling, the dog showed its teeth in a grin of idiotic delight. Edward patted the black-and-white coat, saying happily, "Good dog. Uncle Frederick gave you scraps, I see. Did you like them? Yes, now, get by, Spotted Dick, get by."

"Does he like that name?" Zan asked.

Edward looked around, his face instantly composed as though he'd never even think of talking to a dog. "I believe he will come to know it in time."

The dog sat down as soon as Edward spoke to Zan, as though waiting his turn for the man's attention. He kept his brown eyes fixed on Edward's face, though the long silky ears twitched when Zan said, "He's not a bad-looking animal."

Coming closer, she held her fingers out, backs forward for the dog to sniff. As regally as though he'd never gamboled like a puppy, he condescended to twitch his black nose. Accepted, she stroked the top of the flat, almost square head.

"Kind of a rough coat you've got there, boy." She glanced up at Edward. "Our dog, Gulbrun, his head's as smooth as ribbon. I guess 'cause we pet him all the time."

"I would say Mr. Grasse never troubled himself to show kindness to anything. There is nothing that angers me more than to see an animal mistreated. I realize, of course, that some creatures work for man, and others are destined for the table, but to beat a fine, loyal dog like this . . ."

He shook his head grimly. There was something magnificent about Edward Winchester when he got riled. His gray eyes seemed to flash like lightning through the clouds, and his firm chin stuck out as if he were daring the world to strike at it.

"Do you know," he said, "I believe Spotted Dick here to be at least partially an English Setter?"

"He looks like he sets just fine."

"It's a type of hunting dog, used primarily in water. When they spot the prey, they point out its position by turning entirely rigid and holding up one foreleg, the foot turned back at the wrist."

"Oh, come on. No dog could do that."

"Like you, Zan, I never feel the need to lie."

"Well, not out loud. Sometimes you act one out."

He didn't give her time to regret her bitterness. His fingers closed around her upper arm, and he held her so that he could look into her face. With the edge of his finger he tilted her chin. Reluctantly, slowly, Zan lifted her eyelids to meet his stormy gaze.

"If I kissed you before for all the wrong reasons, then why do I kiss you now?"

Against the warm persuasion of his lips, she could raise no defenses. The best she could do was to remain passive and doll-like, yet that strategy failed the moment he nipped her lower lip. She gasped and wrapped her arms around him to bring him closer to her.

Whenever he took her in an embrace, he forgot her unwomanly strength the moment she yielded. Now, the soft weight of her breasts against his shirt and her hips curving out from beneath her ridiculous clothes reminded him of her sex. Plunging into her mouth, tasting her sweetness, he craved to perform with his whole body the actions of their dancing tongues.

When he broke off the kiss, her stifled moans of pleasure changed to protest. But he had only given up her lips to bite her throat, tasting the salt of her sweat as though it were a delicacy too rare to give up to any other man. Then he returned, like a gourmet, to the wetness of her mouth. He filled his hands with her breasts, and emptied them for the pleasure of filling them again.

He'd once called what happened between them madness and he'd been right. At this moment he was willing to be mad. Only the dim memory that they were not alone on the farm kept him from taking Zan by the hand into his bedroom. He could see her so clearly, her white and golden body naked on his sheets, that it pained him to realize this dream wasn't ever likely to come true.

Spotted Dick barked. Half-blindly, Edward glanced down at the dog. Exactly as he described, the setter stood rigidly, as if from nose to tail-tip he'd been carved from stone. The raised front paw pointed at the back door, which still bounced from being closed hard.

"What is it?" Zan asked, looking over her shoulder. "Oh, Uncle Fred."

"Why do you call him that?"

She shrugged, her eyes still aglow. "It just seems right. Edward . . . what are we going to do?"

Though it had never been how she saw herself, with all her heart Zan wanted him to ask her to be his wife. She didn't believe there could be this much heat between a man and a woman without both of them feeling the same way about each other. Since she loved him with all her heart, it seemed sensible to think that he loved her, too.

"Do?" he replied, stepping carefully away from her. "The answer's quite simple. We must never be alone together again. These encounters always begin innocently enough, but I cannot trust myself to keep my distance. You . . . It seems very odd. Usually, I have extraordinary self-command."

"I can't say I've noticed." Zan couldn't feel her heart beating through the ice that accumulated instantly when he spoke so coldly. "But I guess you're right. I'll stay as far away from you as I can, considering we're both working here."

She turned away, surprised to find that she could still move. Maybe a heart wasn't a necessary piece of equipment for a farming girl. She hoped that it wasn't, for she'd given it away to someone who'd just trampled her gift into the ground. She hadn't another to spare.

CHAPTER
12

"Ow!" Zan protested as her mother tipped another kettle of steaming water into the tub.

"Hush, and scrub your neck."

"I'm not a potato, Mother, in case you forgot."

"Such a fuss! Even the boys do not complain so much."

"You don't make their water this hot, I bet. They don't come out boiled."

"Everyone should be clean for church. No, scrub harder." Mrs. Lind took the washcloth from Zan's lackadaisical hand. With determined strokes, she rubbed at the girl's long back.

"Yowch!" Zan twisted, trying to escape her fate. But her mother had her free hand on her shoulder and controlled all her determined wriggling.

"There! Now I'll wash your hair."

"I'm going to be wearing a hat," Zan said, just to keep her spirits up. She knew, however, that protests were pointless. To her mother, it was a greater sin to go to church without being clean from the skin out than to rob or to covet thy neighbor's anything. Her hair would be washed, and rinsed with vinegar to make it shiny, though her mother always smoothed on rosewater afterward to take away the smell.

Even then, Mrs. Lind was not finished with her efforts. Glancing around to be certain Mr. Lind was nowhere in sight, she fetched a small box from the depths of the pantry. When the purple glass bottle within was uncorked, a sharp smell of camphor wafted out like a malevolent genie.

"Ah, that will take care of anything," Mrs. Lind said, as she did every Sunday.

Zan screwed up her eyes and scrunched her nose. "I don't think it does much good, Mother. I'm always going to be tanned no matter how much Lily Lotion you use on me."

Mrs. Lind read out the testimonials printed on the side of the box with a tremulous hope in her voice. " 'I never found a beau because of my rough red skin. Then I used Benbrick's Patented Lily Lotion. Now I have five strapping sons. M.J. from Billings, Montana.' "

"I hear any woman can get a husband in Montana, even old maids," Zan said. "I wonder if she lived there before she started using this stuff."

" 'Though neglecting to take my parasol on a church sociable, one application of Benbrick's Patented Lily Lotion turned my brown hands to white silk once more or at least that's what my gentlemen callers say. A.K. from Sedalia, Missouri.' "

"A nice flirt she must be. Going to church sociables and still seeing more than one boy at a time. I wonder what she uses on her other face?"

"Hush, now." Tipping the bottle to let the thick white stuff pour onto her hands, Mrs. Lind smoothed the lotion on her daughter's face. "Don't frown so; you will make wrinkles."

"I'd rather be sprayed by a skunk on an August high noon," Zan said. The lotion stung, and the smell made her eyes water. Soon enough, however, her mother rinsed it off with cool water and patted on more rosewater.

The box and purple bottle were once more tucked out of

sight in the pantry. "When the butter and egg money is a little more, I will buy another bottle. This one is almost empty."

"You shouldn't, Mother. I don't think it makes any difference, and you know Father would think it a foolish expense. I'll try to remember to wear my hat more. I should any way; it gets so hot out there." A memory of Edward, the sweat trickling down his naked chest, flashed over her.

"Your face is no whiter," Mrs. Lind said, "but it has a lovely color now."

"Hadn't you better bathe, Mother?" Zan asked, changing the subject. "It'll be time to go soon."

"Yes, yes. You go and get dressed. I will be up soon to help you with your corset."

Up in her room, more evidence of her mother's love and concern lay spread across her bed. Stockings, petticoats, and dress lying in a patch of sunlight dazzled Zan's eyes with their hard-won whiteness. It seemed almost sacrilegious to put them on, even to go to church.

But as the white linen slid over her skin, she wondered if Edward would notice how smooth her hair lay and the softness of her complexion. Stooping to look in the mirror, Zan knew she looked healthy. There'd be no need to pinch her cheeks to make them pink. Just the thought of Edward's cool hands roaming on her body made her blush like an artificial poppy.

The sky arched overhead, bright and clear as they rode together in the wagon. Ben, Gary, and Sarah, scrubbed so that they fairly shone, sat on clean feed sacks in the back. Usually Zan rode back there, too, but today her mother had scooted over closer to Mr. Lind and patted the wooden seat. Holding up the white batiste to keep it clean, Zan climbed up.

"Why do you sit so close, Inga? My arm will be cramped, and how am I to drive then?"

Mrs. Lind gave him a look from under her golden lashes.

"When you and I were young, you could drive very good with only the one hand. Have you forgotten how?"

With a bashful grin Mr. Lind quickly decided that he could be comfortable by putting his arm around his wife's still-cuddly figure. Zan turned her head to watch the fields go by, to give her parents at least a pretense of privacy. She pretended not to hear her father's Swedish endearments, murmured in a rumbling undertone.

The sight of the fresh green fields, however, were not going to take her mind off the perfect planting weather that she was wasting by going to church. Nearly all the sorghum seeded had been sown over the last two days. One more would see every available inch planted, the rich dark earth nurturing the seeds. Then let it rain, but just enough, and her future would start to come up green. So great was her impatience that it took about all she had to stay on the seat, when what she wanted was to leap down and run all the way back to the Double B.

Arriving at the white church, standing in contemplative solitude at the end of town, Mrs. Lind looked at their four children. "Does everyone still have his penny for the plate? Good. Now, Ben, there will be no sliding into base today. I cannot patch your clothes again. And Gary, you will not pull so much as one braid—or pigtail." The two boys hung their slicked-down heads, not too shame-faced. Zan knew they'd find plenty of mischief not covered by their mother's restrictions.

"Sarah . . ." The youngest of the Lind children turned pink with embarrassment. But Mrs. Lind simply said, "You are a good child," and Sarah's round cheeks turned pinker still with pleasure as she showed her small, even teeth in a shy smile. Zan had long been afraid that Sarah would turn out to be just as beautiful as Faith. Now she knew it would be true.

Zan straightened up like a soldier on parade as her mother's loving eye passed over her. Reaching out, Mrs. Lind twitched the blue satin ribbon that ran through the lace across Zan's square neckline into a more becoming bow.

"Doesn't Zan look nice, Father?" Mrs. Lind asked.

Her husband looked up from tying up the horses. "She looks clean anyway."

The church bell chimed. The people who stood around in twos and threes, or family groups, began to move toward the white building with unhasty steps. Not long into the service, the temperature would begin to rise and the interior would soon be unbearably stuffy. A good Christian wouldn't complain about such a minor aggravation, but it didn't mean they had to be in any hurry to suffer it.

"Mother!" Faith called and waved. She left her husband and daughter to go on in as she walked quickly toward her family. "You're all coming to the hotel for supper after church. The dining room's all done now, and I want you to see the parlor. It looks so fine with the carpet down."

"Some job Kincaid and I had getting it to stay," Zan put in.

Her sister smiled at her. "You look like a real lady today. Such a change from those awful dungarees."

Half the brightness went out of her day. Sure, she knew it was unusual for her to wear such feminine clothes, but she had hoped that no one would mention it. She wanted Edward to see her like this, to know she could be presentable if not as beautiful as Faith. If only Edward could be the only person to notice! Zan knew, however, that she was already being discussed in the pews as the ladies of the town sat down.

"Thanks, Faith," she said, putting on a good face. "You look dainty as a cat's paw yourself." Her sister's tight, heavily flounced dress showed off all her curves and brought the light up in her gray eyes.

"Yes, Jane Carson certainly knows fabric. Mother, you

ought to have her make Zan's clothes from now on."

Zan snugged her arm about her mother's waist. "I like Mother to make my clothes. I don't need fancy duds like you and Samantha Spencer. They're too much trouble."

"But how are you ever to catch a man . . . ?" Faith began.

Mrs. Lind said mildly, "It is no day to talk of clothes and men. Sunday is for pure thoughts of the one who died for us."

Chastened, Faith walked along silently. Zan tried to think as her mother directed, but the sunshine made it difficult to consider anything but the waste of a good planting day. Maybe Edward, with no mother to insist on attendance, had stayed home to finish the job. It rankled that he would be able to work an extra day that she couldn't, yet she acknowledged that the important thing was to get the seed in the ground. Not even their rivalry was more important than that.

Then she saw him. He and Uncle Fred stood by the cemetery gate, removing the dust from their boots. Uncle Fred saw her first and touched Edward on the arm, saying something. Edward glanced up idly. Across the distance between them, Zan saw the shock of her finery hit him when he suddenly jerked backward as if he'd been shot.

"There's Edward," she said to her mother. "You go on. I've got to ask him something."

"It can wait till after church," Mrs. Lind answered, linking her arm through her tall daughter's.

"But I—"

"No man ever thought less of a girl through her making him wait."

"No, it's not like that," Zan protested, though she knew it was. She hadn't anything really to say to him. She wanted to see the surprise in his eyes, and maybe admiration would be there, too. She wanted to walk into church with him, and let everyone in Harmony see them together.

"A girl may feel eagerness," Mrs. Lind said in a tiny voice, too soft to carry even so far as Faith's ears. "But it is wrong to show it."

Zan's fingers and face felt frozen as they stepped into the dark interior of the church. Though a moment ago she would have given the world to step high, wide, and handsome into the church on Edward's arm, she now wished the floor might open and take her in with a giant burp. How many people were staring at her! How many were speculating that these fine clothes were merely to entrap a husband for poor, boyish Zan Lind? And if her mother's ploy was that transparent, wouldn't Edward see through it as clearly as everyone else?

She opened her white leather Bible—given to her on her fifth birthday—and stared intently at the first passage. Though she knew the instant he put his foot over the threshold, and could have repeated the names of the people he passed on his way up the aisle, she did not raise her eyes as he went by. He could have been on the other side of the world for all the interest she showed. If everyone was watching, they'd see there was nothing between them. Only she knew how her pulse raced as his step hesitated the slightest bit as he passed where she sat at the end of the pew.

Edward knew it was against the Code to speak of a lady in public. Yet he couldn't keep himself from turning to his uncle and saying in an undertone, "Did you see Zan?"

"Yes, she's sitting over there." Uncle Fred nodded discreetly in the direction of the Linds.

"I mean, did you *see* her? The change is . . . remarkable. I very nearly did not recognize her. Only her hair made me think it might be she."

Giving him a very pointed look, Uncle Fred said, "I don't know what you mean."

"Ah, of course. Excuse me." Edward caught himself up.

A gentleman did not bandy a lady's name even with his closest relation. To do so might compromise her irretrievably. Even to look at her for an instant too long might ruin her. The matrons of Harmony were no less sensitive to these things than the marriage-minded mamas of the best London society.

After a few minutes, however, the back of Edward's neck began to ache from the necessity of keeping perfectly still. Everything in him yearned to take another glance at Zan. By some magic she had been transformed into a beauty.

From the first, he'd admired the long lines of her body, her high breasts, and straight spine. Her elegance of form would have pleased the most stringent Parisian dressmaker, if he could have seen past the blurring camouflage of dungarees and man's shirt she so often affected. Edward remembered the glimpses he'd stolen around these things. His hands shook suddenly, and he dropped his hymnal into the aisle.

Leaning down and over to pick it up, he glanced for a single instant Zan's way. The Bible she held before her face hid all but the angle of her jaw. Her skin looked as red as if she'd been dipped in boiling water. Edward could glimpse the side of her glossy brown high-button shoe and realized that she had the most delicate ankles he'd ever seen.

Sitting upright, a jolt of desire shook him to his foundations. He was but dimly aware of Reverend Johnson's appearance behind the lectern and the thunder of his opening words. All Edward's thoughts were focused on Zan. He wondered if she were looking at him now, and felt his face turn as scarlet as her own.

As usual, immediately following the service, the women congregated together by the church door, whispering and laughing. The men stood by the horses, presumably to wait for their wives, though the discussion ranged from politics to reminiscences. Adolescent boys showed off to the adolescent girls, keeping a safe distance yet secure in the knowledge that not a handstand or shoving match went unwitnessed by the mysterious opposite sex. Only the youngsters mingled freely, unhampered by custom or self-consciousness.

"An excellent service," Uncle Fred said, shaking hands with Reverend Johnson.

"That's good of you to say."

"Yes, most enlightening," Edward belatedly agreed, though he'd heard little of it. The Linds had already come out. Faith Hutton had taken Zan by the arm and had all but dragged her into the women's group.

Cord and Samantha Spencer stood behind Uncle Fred, waiting for a word with the Reverend. Edward heard her say in a half whisper, "Cord, you've got to do something. They're standing in there—in the church!—arguing about horses! Mrs. Taylor's about ready to hide from shame, and I don't blame her."

"What can I do?" Cord answered.

Edward tore his eyes from Zan. "Perhaps I can help," he said, turning toward the couple.

"Oh, if you could, Mr. Winchester!"

Mr. Evans was only ten years older than Edward himself, though he carried himself with the weariness of a much more elderly man. He wore a black silk sling around his neck, cradling the arm he'd broken a few weeks earlier. At the moment an unwonted enthusiasm lightened his voice and his eyes. "I tell you that high withers are the most important part of a really fast horse."

"Nope," Mr. Taylor said, shaking his head. "It's the length of the bone that matters. You can have powerful withers, but what good will they do you if your horse has got stumpy legs?"

"Ja-a-mes," Lillie Taylor said, mortified. "May we go now?"

"In a minute, in a minute. Let me just straighten this business out."

Edward said, "What a fascinating discussion. Are you referring to specific animals, or horses in general?"

Mr. Taylor frowned at the interruption, but Mr. Evans turned about gladly. "Here you go, Taylor. They say nobody knows more about horses than the English nobles. Here, now, Winchester, what do you say is the most important part of a really fast horse? I'm saying it's the power in the hindquarters, but Taylor claims it's the length of their legs."

"Personally, I shouldn't care to try to race a horse without either part, but if I must make a distinction . . . Perhaps I could see the horses?"

"Dang tootin'," Taylor said, striding toward the door. "Come on, and you'll see what I'm talking about."

His wife turned on Edward a look of gratitude that shone in the dark church. Edward said, "May I offer you my arm, Mrs. Taylor?"

She wanted to apologize to the Reverend. While Edward waited for her, he saw that Samantha was not the only woman who followed Mr. Evans and Mr. Taylor to where their horses were tied. He expected to see Zan already there. But Edward saw that Faith kept her grip on Zan.

The younger girl looked as painfully bored as someone with tone deafness at a two-hour *thes musicale*. She happened to glance around at the same moment he did, and their eyes met across the grass. With his free hand he waved to her, encouraging her to follow the men. When she tried to break away, however, Faith only took a new hold.

Mrs. Taylor said, "I didn't want James to buy that new buggy, you know, Mr. Winchester. I knew if he had a new buggy, nothing would make him happy but a new horse. And could he choose a nice, steady animal that I or Mary could drive? Of course not! The best or nothing—that's his motto. He can't stand to be passed on the road."

"Many men like fast horses," Edward said.

"What difference does it make whether you get somewhere five or ten minutes faster than someone else? We'll all wind up in the same place sooner or later anyway."

"You're quite a philosopher, Mrs. Taylor."

She simpered a little at the compliment. "Do you really think so? You know, I've been thinking about beginning a literary society here in Harmony . . . to read and discuss the great books and thinkers of the past. I hope I can count on your support. We cultured persons must do something to bring the torch of knowledge to this backward country."

"Absolutely," Edward agreed politely. No doubt Mrs. Taylor's plans to educate her friends would come to the same end as her attempt to beautify the town. Many discussions, the consumption of large amounts of cake and lemonade, considerable acrimony, and finally a result that no one particularly cared for but that gave each participant a sense of accomplishment in the face of tremendous odds. He'd always thought the entire process a waste of time and effort. Now he was surprised to find himself thinking that it sounded rather fun.

Zan watched Edward and Mrs. Taylor walk away. Despite Mrs. Taylor's being fifteen years his senior with a son nearly his own age, jealousy stabbed into Zan's heart. She wanted to be the one on Edward's arm, and to have him listen to her with the same deep attention he gave Mrs. Taylor. Instead, she was forced to stand here, in the broiling sun, listening to Netta Jones and her friends slanging everyone who passed before their gaze.

"I don't know what has gotten into Jane Carson," Netta said, narrowing her lips until they nearly disappeared. "She's been mooning around like a crazy woman lately."

"Old maids," her bosom friend of the moment, Mrs.

Winston, said. "They all get a little strange past twenty-five. What is Jane? Twenty-eight?"

"Oh, at least," Mrs. Lansing said. She had a voice as smooth as cream, rather pretty. It was her only beauty, since she'd never lost an ounce of the weight she'd gained with each of her four children. They'd given her wrinkles, too, as well as a permanent glare of fury.

With the air of someone trying to save even a single good from the pit of the world, Faith said, "Jane does sew very beautifully. She made this dress."

Mrs. Winston ran her eyes over the pretty gray dress. "Hmmm, charged you a pretty penny, too, I'll guess. Jane's gotten awful tight-fisted. Desperate to make a future, probably. She'll probably never marry now, which means no security. She'll be hanging on by her fingernails when she gets older."

Zan, who hated to hear anyone attacked without the chance to defend themselves, said, "I don't think she's sour or desperate. Not everybody in the world's got to be married, you know. And not everybody who's married is happy, either."

"Zan . . ." Faith chided, smiling around like a mother whose child is misbehaving in public.

"*I* was taught that an unmarried girl should never be emphatic in her opinions," Netta said. "It's vulgar."

"I reckon the lesson didn't take," Zan said, disliking the woman even more than usual. "You've got mighty strong opinions yourself."

"Zan," Faith said, "apologize."

"Ah, heck! Let's go see what all the excitement's about." Firmly she tugged her arm free of her sister's restraining hold. "Come on, Faith."

For a moment young Mrs. Hutton hesitated between the ladies and her sister. With another apologetic smile, she followed Zan. Catching up to her, she said, with a tear choking

159

her voice, "How could you be so rude! Now they'll never . . . It's so important that Kincaid and I be civil to everyone, or they'll never come to the restaurant!"

"Golly," Zan said, "don't you know that even if you were sweet as sugar to them, they'd still rip you up the second you turned your back? What do you care about them anyhow? The Winstons don't let go of a dollar till the eagle screams, and Mr. and Mrs. Lansing are so busy eating everything in sight that they wouldn't care if you called them names from here to Christmas."

Faith smiled ruefully. "I have to admit you're right. But what about Netta?"

"You'd be lucky if you could keep her out of the hotel. You know she'll come snooping around every nook and cranny just to see what you're doing wrong. Most likely, she'll drop a few of her 'helpful' hints until you're all but ready to drive her out with a pitchfork."

"I'll tell Kincaid we must put a pitchfork in the parlor. She is awful, isn't she?"

"Worse'n a snake. Least snakes catch mice. Netta Jones isn't good for anything but a coatrack—she's skinny enough."

Zan stood up on tiptoe, craning her neck, to see over the crowd. Kincaid Hutton turned around and saw his wife and sister-in-law. He put out his hand, and Faith stepped up to take it. "What's happening?" she asked.

"Mr. Taylor and Mr. Evans called in Ed Winchester to settle which of their horses is faster. He's supposed to be some kind of an expert."

"Why don't they just have a race?" Faith wondered.

Someone standing near took up the question. Soon everyone there suggested, more or less loudly, that the two men should race their horses. Zan, shoved and buffeted by the excited group, found herself pushed forward. She came to rest about four feet from Edward.

PASSING FANCY

"Well, Evans," Mr. Taylor said. "What do you think of a race? Say, down Main Street and back."

Mr. Evans considered for a moment, his frown aging him. "My buggy's heavier than yours."

"No buggy, then. We'll ride 'em. Leastways, my boy will ride for me. I'm too old for such goings-on. Hey, Joseph, you'll do that for the old man, won't you?"

His head filled with dreams of adventure, it took Joseph a moment to adjust to the notion that adventure might be possible in the present day. "Sure thing, Pa," he said, a slow grin showing the gap between his front teeth.

Mr. Evans glanced around. "I guess maybe Cord . . ."

Mr. and Mrs. Spencer stood near to Edward. When her father's eye lit on Cord, Samantha said sharply, "I should say not!"

As a general laugh went up, Cord shrugged. "I don't think so, Alex. Sorry."

A few of the wits in the growing crowd made noises like chickens. Cord didn't seem to mind being called henpecked, for he gazed at Samantha as possessively as if she were his rarest treasure. She said something to him, and he kissed her cheek with a ringing smack!

Alexander Evans said, half-lifting his broken arm, "Well, I can't to do it myself. . . ."

Edward stepped forward. "I'll ride for you, Mr. Evans, if you think I will do."

"Say, there's an idea," the older man said. "I hear you English can ride about as well as any Indian. But can you ride bareback? This beast has never worn a saddle."

"I believe that I can manage."

Zan beamed at him. He might still be stuffy, but no one could doubt his courage. As a matter of fact, a few of the men who'd pooh-poohed his book-learned farming notions were now clapping him on the back, offering rough compliments. Cord shook Edward's hand.

"When do you want to do it?" Mr. Taylor asked.

"There's no time like the present," Mr. Evans said. "But I reckon we ought to ask the Reverend if it's all right, it being Sunday and all."

"That's right, James Taylor!" His wife, obviously waiting for the chance, spoke up, her hands on her ample hips and her voice high. "And you're all sinners for even thinking of such a worldly subject as horse-racing on a sacred day. I'm ashamed of you . . . and you, James, trying to drag my innocent son into such goings-on."

"Come down off it, Lillie. You know full well they had a race at the last camp meeting you dragged me to. And if the good men who put on that revival could allow it, I don't see what call you've got to go objecting. We'll ask Reverend Johnson and whatever he says goes!"

"Perhaps if everyone promises faithfully not to drink," Edward suggested.

"There's an idea, Lillie," her husband said. "That ought to please you; you being so hipped on the subject of a peaceful glass. Come on, let's go find the Reverend."

Unable to walk as fast in her skirt as she could in her dungarees, Zan fell back as the crowd surged forward. She couldn't hear everything, but the Reverend visibly blenched at the size of the group bearing down on him. With all the interruptions, both from Lillie and Samantha, united in opposition, and from the crowd, it took several tries for Mr. Taylor to explain what they wanted.

Then the noise died down, and Zan could hear. "Seems to me that a compromise has already been reached. I see no difficulty in holding a race on the Sabbath, as it will further explain and glorify God's reasons for creating the birds of the air and the beasts of the field. As long as the race is carried out in a decent and *sober* fashion, no betting for instance, then I see no moral objections."

"Knew we could rely on you, Reverend," Mr. Taylor said.

"One more thing," Reverend Johnson said. "I suggest you hold the race after dinner. If I made Mrs. Johnson put back her fried chicken, I should have to sleep in the church."

Amid laughter, it was agreed by all parties to wait until after the noon meal to race the horses. The crowd dispersed quickly, each man knowing the sooner he ate, the sooner the excitement would begin. Many, though, stopped to shake Edward's hand. Even though the majority of them called him Ed, Zan didn't see any grimaces pass over his face. He seemed genuinely pleased and more than a little embarrassed by the favorable attention.

Zan hung back, hoping for a chance to speak to him. But when the crowd cleared, standing between her and him was Faith. With an all-too flirtatious look, her sister said, "I certainly hope you and your uncle will be able to join us for dinner, Mr. Winchester. I won't take no for an answer. It's much too far for you to go home and come back in time for the race."

"I can't answer for my uncle, especially as I'm not quite certain where he is at the moment, but I should be all too pleased, Mrs. Hutton. Thank you."

"T'isn't anything, Mr. Winchester. We'll be walking over in a few minutes, as soon as we can round everyone up. My little brothers are awfully hard to catch!"

"That will give me time to search for Uncle Frederick."

Faith turned and flounced away. As she passed Zan, one bright gray-tinted eye closed in a rapid wink. "Never say I don't do anything for you."

Zan hadn't time to whip back a reply. Edward approached her. "Have you seen my uncle?"

Silly to blush at such a simple question. She didn't, however, seem able to control the hot rush of blood to her cheeks when he looked at her. He always stayed so cool and unaffected, even when she was in his arms. "I . . . I thought I saw him reading over there, under that tree."

Sure enough, the fringed head of Frederick Winchester could just be glimpsed under the dappled light. As they watched, they saw him throw out a hand in a sudden, grand gesture, as though he were arguing or declaiming some brilliant passage. The tumult of the race caucus had apparently passed over him in his absorption.

"Shakespeare, no doubt. He never goes anywhere without at least one volume of his works, though heaven knows he has every word committed to memory."

"I kind of envy anybody who can get that lost in a book."

"You don't read very much?"

"Who's got the time? 'Sides, I can never get the hang of it; I can't ever figure out what they mean when they say something's like something else, when any fool can see that they're completely different. I get disgusted."

"Perhaps, if you are interested, I could lend you one or two of my favorites."

"Those farming books—Porterfield and what's his name?"

"No," he said with a chuckle and a shake of his head. "*A Thousand and One Nights,* or Charles Perrault. Fairy tales, full of magic and wonder."

"I'll give 'em a try, but like I say, I don't have much time for reading. Maybe in the winter." Would he still be around when the winter came?

The Linds had gathered by the church steps, even Ben and Gary. Amanda sat with Sarah, working a string into a cat's cradle across their fingers. Seeing everyone assembled, Edward cupped his hands around his mouth.

"Uncle Frederick!" he called. He had to repeat it twice before the older gentleman looked up. As he scrambled to his feet, he pointed to his chest as though hardly believing it was himself they were summoning. Edward and Zan both nodded, exaggerating the motion widely. Once more Edward bellowed through his hands, "Food!" while Zan waved Uncle Fred in.

As they walked toward the family, hoping Uncle Fred would follow, Edward said, "I wanted to say that you look—"

"There won't be much more to do tomorrow," she interrupted hastily. "Just that last field needs seeding, and then I reckon we pray for rain. But not too hard. A couple of inches is all we need to be sitting pretty."

"Speaking of pretty," he began again, but there wasn't time to finish what he wanted to say in any privacy. He wondered if that was just as well, especially when Joseph Taylor appeared from seemingly nowhere, closely followed by a massive youth with brilliantly gleaming corn-gold hair. He had the awkwardness of an adolescent and the muscles of a man who worked solely with his hands.

"Hiya, Joseph. How ya doing, Otto," Zan said. "Are you invited to dinner, too?"

The one named Otto gave Joseph a nudge that left the boy holding his side. "No, Zan, we just figured on walking along with you as far as the hotel, if that's all right." He glanced at Mr. Lind.

Mrs. Lind, however, answered. "That is very good of you, boys."

So far as Edward could tell, Zan had no clue that her changed appearance might have something to do with the boys' presence. She merely thanked them, saying, "Guess you're darn excited about the race, huh, Joseph?"

"My pa says he'll skin me if I don't win. Mr. Evans bet him a week's groceries for Cord and Samantha, and you know Pa. Credit kind of hurts him somewhere. 'Specially the kind you don't have to repay."

"I understood," Edward said, stepping between Joseph and

Zan, "that the Reverend requested there be no betting."

"Shucks, he meant money, not groceries. And boy, Cord can really pack away the flapjacks. Course, I hear that's all Samantha knows how to make."

"Shouldn't you refer to her as Mrs. Spencer?" Edward asked coldly.

"Till she and Cord married last month, she was just another kid to me. I'm four years older than she is." He tried to look around Edward. "Gee, Zan, I bet you wish you could get in this race. You'd beat us both. She's faster than greased lightning," he confided to Edward.

"Well, I . . ." Zan began.

"No lady could ever contemplate such a thing," Edward said.

Tall Otto suddenly gave an idiotic chuckle, receiving in return the full power of Edward's disapproving glance. The Scandinavian giant said something in a low voice to his friend.

"Otto wants you to know," Joseph said to Zan, "that he only wishes you were riding. He still remembers your wild rides to school and how you'd come whomping into the school yard about half a second ahead of the bell."

"I always beat it, too," Zan said, giving the big blonde a punch in the arm. Otto flushed and his blue eyes took on what Edward privately thought of as a "wounded hart" expression.

Well, he decided, if callow youths are to her taste, I wish her joy of them.

He slowed his pace until his uncle came even with him. Uncle Frederick was reciting to Mrs. Lind. " 'Men have died from time to time, and worms have eaten them, but not for love.' *As You Like It,* Act Four. I have always found that a strangely comforting thought."

Edward was far from comforted.

CHAPTER
13

As Zan stood talking with Otto and Joseph, the rest of the party having gone into the hotel, two cowboys rode by. One lifted his hat and whistled, the notes rising and falling like a train whistle. Zan, without missing a word of her conversation, waved in a friendly fashion.

Edward scowled after the impertinent cowpoke, balling his hands into fists. Once the two men were out of sight, he transferred the scowl to Zan. She seemed to have no sense of shame and was positively encouraging these callow youths to talk freely to her. He said, "Shouldn't you gentlemen be meeting your families?"

Joseph said, "Ah, Ma's making corned beef and cabbage . . . and it's too hot for that. I got some apples down at the depot for dinner."

"Sounds mighty good," Zan said. "I don't know but what I'd like apples better myself. Eating what a newly wedded wife cooks can be a mighty chancy business."

Once again Otto whispered to his friend. "Otto says," Joseph interpreted, "that he's sure you and Faith must both cook pretty good, if you learned from your ma. He can still taste the baked beans she made last harvesttime."

"Thanks, Otto. I'll tell her you said so."

The blond giant's sunburned face flushed, and he tugged on Joseph's arm. "Okay, Otto. We better be getting along. I got a load of stuff to go out on tomorrow's train. Otto's going to help me with the bigger crates—'course, we don't have to do it right this minute."

"Yes, you do," Zan said. "I'm too hungry to stand out here gabbing another second. See you later." Without further ado, she walked into the hotel.

Edward took a moment to pass a critical gaze over each young man. He'd withered dowagers with just such a look, and neither Otto nor Joseph were proof against it. Otto's red face became crimson, and Joseph shifted nervously from foot to foot.

Edward dismissed them, saying, "Until the race, gentlemen."

In the dim coolness of the hotel lobby, Edward caught up to Zan. "I never should have thought of you as a flirt."

She stopped dead to stare at him, her big blue eyes wounded. "A flirt? Me? Have you been standing in the sun too long without a hat?"

"Can you deny that you were encouraging those boys to . . . to . . ."

"To what? I've known Otto and Joseph all my life. They're a heck of a lot more likely to flirt with a fence post than with me." She shook her head ruefully and started toward the back of the hotel again.

"And that cowboy? Is he an old friend, too?"

"What cowboy?" She turned toward him, her hands resting on the firm curve of her waist. Edward forced his eyes up from her breasts, thrusting forward beneath the ruffles of her bodice.

"The one who whistled at you."

"Whistled . . . ? Oh, him. He was just being friendly. Folks *are* friendly out here, you know. All but certain stuck-up fellers who are getting to sound more like my father than my father ever has."

Edward knew perfectly well he was behaving like a jealous swain. With an effort that asked for nearly all of his self-control, he fought down the sudden rush of desire that urged him to take her into his arms. Only her full participation in an extremely passionate kiss would have cooled his jealousy. But he had sworn a silent vow to take no further advantage of her virtue, a virtue which, judging by her responses to his advances, she seemed hardly to know how to protect herself. He struggled a moment with his memories of her responsiveness and only barely managed to strangle his desire.

"Pray excuse me, Miss Lind. It is not my place to order your conduct."

"Darn tootin'!" She let out her breath and her anger in a gusty sigh. "Don't be such a poker," she said, showing her white teeth between curving rose lips. "I guess I don't know how to act even in fine feathers. English girls don't have that problem, I bet. They probably always behave themselves."

"Usually. They are, of course, more closely chaperoned than you Americans." He wished there was some spinster in lorgnette and lace here now, keeping his lust in bounds with her cold-water gaze.

"I'd hate that. 'Sides, I don't see the harm in a whistle or two. It's not like I collect a whole lot of 'em. Come to think of it, I don't think anybody ever whistled at me before." Her smile widened. "Do you really think he meant it as a salute?"

Oh, but it was a struggle not to kiss her! She was such a mixture of woman and girl, of knowledge and innocence. He could almost wish she was a flirt, for then he would know what to do. "I . . . I prefer not to think of such noises in any light."

"You're not cross, Edward. You're just hungry, same as me. Let's eat." Just as she had to Otto, Zan gave him a light, friendly punch on the arm.

Edward couldn't stand it. He'd kissed her, caressed her, and all but taken her, and now she wanted to treat him with affable disregard, almost as if they were merely friends. Vow or no, it was more than merely mortal flesh could bear.

He caught her hand, smoothing it open with gentle pressure. Her breath caught as he raised her hand to his mouth. With infinite tenderness, he nipped and kissed her palm, demanding that every sensitive spot react to him alone. She trembled and sighed as he tugged at the delicate webbing between thumb and forefinger. Her other hand crept to his shoulder for balance as he tasted the ticklish insides of her fingers. Even her calluses could be kindled by firm suction, though the soft cry she gave then almost destroyed his control.

Edward tried not to think how easily he could kiss his way up her arm, arousing each inch, lingering on the volatile inside of her elbow. To put his arms around her and sip her fragrance from the cleavage showing above the line of her bodice would be the work of an instant. More important, he tried to keep his thoughts from dwelling on the hall of empty bedrooms above their heads. He concentrated, as though his life depended on it, on awakening her hand.

Zan could not move. Lines of fire radiated from her fingertips, shooting up her arm. Her knees were barely capable of supporting her. It felt as though a twister were building within her body that would sweep all familiar guideposts away. Frightened and thrilled at the same time, Zan reached to put her arms around him.

Then she heard the rattle of running footsteps over the hard wooden floor. Her brothers were calling her. She had one instant to pull away from him, yet it seemed she moved very slowly.

When Ben and Gary appeared, the two adults stood on either side of the claw-footed table. "Dinner's on the table," Ben said. "Faith says come now or the pig's going to get yours."

Zan tried hard to find enough breath to answer. "Okay; we'll be right along."

As fast as they appeared, the boys tore away. Gary threw over his shoulder, "There's three kinds of cake!"

"Faith must be experimenting again." She met his eyes steadily. "You've got to make up your mind, Edward."

"About the cake?" he asked. His chest rose and fell with his hard breathing.

"No. About me. You can't keep grabbing me and then deciding you don't want to be bothered. And please . . ." She held up her hand, though not the one he'd made love to. That one seemed too sacred for ordinary use.

"Please?"

"Don't apologize anymore. You've got nothing to be sorry for. I'm not going to break when you kiss me, or scream if you put your hands on me. Maybe I'm no lady, but I don't seem to mind one bit. I like what you're doing, so long as it's you that's doing it. Anybody else—I'd cut 'em off at the knees."

She longed to tell him, right then and there, that she loved him. But he was so stunned by her confession of hankering after him that she didn't dare. What if he laughed at her, or reproved her, as he knew so well how to do? She had no fear that he would take advantage of her love-talk to complete the passion that leaped between them like electric sparks. Zan could wish him less honorable.

In the dining room all the family but Faith were seated, the adults at the large center table, and the children at a smaller round table wedged into a corner. Ben and Gary had not wasted any time after calling Zan. They, along with Sarah and Amanda, were well tucked into plates heaped with cornbread, fried chicken, and Mrs. Lind's receipt for *bruna bönor*, that Otto recalled so fondly. The savory odors mingled with the sweet warmth of the pies and cakes lovingly displayed on glass serving dishes on the new sideboard.

When Zan came in to take her chair, Uncle Fred stood up, as though to propose a toast. Mr. Lind, across the way, lifted his glass of amber cider. But Uncle Fred didn't do anything, only watched Zan. Mr. Lind frowned and sipped his drink, as though daring anyone to think anything of his hesitation.

Zan found Edward behind her, pulling back her chair to hold it out for her. She took care to glance back before sitting, just to check that he hadn't jerked it away. Joseph Taylor had done that once to a visiting school inspector's wife. The teacher before Faith's short-lived tenure, Mr. McDugal, had dusted Joseph's britches but good that day. Zan still remembered the look of abject terror on the woman's face as she sat down on the floor in a welter of petticoats. It had been the funniest thing she'd seen in her twelve years of life, but she had no wish to be so funny herself.

As soon as she was seated, Uncle Fred sat down. Edward took the chair next to Faith's vacant one. Kincaid leaned toward him and said, "It shouldn't be too much longer till we eat. But I guess you don't want to stuff yourself too full—what with the race and all?"

"Who are you betting on?" Edward asked, his gray eyes amused.

"Oh, well, just between us . . . I've got a dollar and a half on you. The Taylor boy's good, but he hasn't much experience. Now, I'm thinking that you English lords must know a powerful lot about horses."

"I have ridden, once or twice."

"Don't let him fool you," Uncle Fred said. "He has one of the best bottoms I've ever seen." Zan choked and reached hastily for her water glass. "Are you all right, my dear?"

She nodded, though her eyes were watering. "Just fine. You were saying?"

Looking around the table, Uncle Fred said, "No one can seat a horse like Edward. I've seen him back beasts that a gypsy horse thief couldn't ride."

"Uncle, really . . ."

"Don't be modest, my boy. Unfortunately, I missed the Winchester seat, but you cannot deny that Henry the Eighth himself said, 'The Howards for loyalty, the Percys for building, and the Winchesters for horses.' "

"No, Uncle. I believe it was Elizabeth. And isn't it 'The Sidneys for honor, the Seymours for treachery, and the Winchesters for horses.' Put either way it does seem rather like damning with faint praise."

He smiled at his uncle. Zan suddenly couldn't bear to be so near to him or to see him smile at someone else. She pushed back her chair. "I'll go see if I can help Faith."

Uncle Fred instantly rose to his feet once more, followed by Edward. Zan saw her father glance between the two men, his frown being replaced by puzzlement. He leaned to the side to examine Uncle Fred's chair, then sat back, shaking his head.

Faith scurried between stove and sink, her fair face flushed and sticky curls clinging to her forehead. "Oh, no," she sighed in answer to Zan's offer of help. "There's nothing anybody can do. These biscuits are burnt."

"You've got cornbread."

"I can't serve that to His Lordship! I wanted something special. . . . You say Uncle Fred's a good cook."

"Don't worry about him. It's the rest of us. We're all fainting from hunger. Just serve whatever you've got and get on out there with it in one big hurry." She picked up the small blue willow dish, loaded with fresh peas and carrots gleaming with new-made butter. "Bring that chicken and I'll come back for the potatoes and beans. Nobody in their right mind ever turned down those."

"What about bread?" Faith said in a sharp agony. "I've got to serve some white bread!"

"Why in heaven's name? You've got enough fixings for a feast right here."

"Oh, you don't understand. All the best hotels serve rolls or bread."

"So you'll be a best hotel at supper. I can't help thinking that some food is better than no food. And if Father doesn't get something inside him besides cider, I don't want to stay."

When the two girls carried in the platters, Edward and Uncle Fred once again stood up, this time advancing immediately to take the burdens from them. Mr. Lind demanded abruptly, "What is wrong with your chairs that you cannot be still in them?"

Mrs. Lind reached out with her knife and fork to lift a triangular breast of chicken, the coating tight and crisp, onto his plate. "Eat. Don't ask questions."

Zan thought this excellent advice. Taking a heaping serving spoonful of mashed potatoes, rich with cream, she said, "I can't think when I've been so hungry! I feel like I've been working in the field all day."

Picking up a drumstick in her fingers, she opened her mouth to tear off a bite. Faith cleared her throat noisily and rapped her fork on the table. Zan glanced around. Kincaid and Faith cut their chicken before eating it. Her parents, on the other hand, picked up the pieces and ate them that way. Edward hadn't begun to eat yet. At last she looked at Uncle Fred.

Without ado, he picked up the wing on his plate with his fingers. " 'Old fashions please me best.' *The Taming of the Shrew,* Act Four. A most instructive play."

Reassured, Zan once more lifted the chicken to her lips. But a commotion in the lobby, like an ox let loose in a small room, turned her about before she could more than smell the food. Then Otto Krensler appeared, disheveled and out of breath.

"Otto?"

Zan half-rose from her chair in surprise, the two Englishmen following suit. When the big blond boy waved at her anxiously, for he was too out of breath to speak, she instantly obeyed. He latched on to her arm with one meaty hand. Half-lifting her off her feet, he began to walk away with her.

"Steady on, my boy!" Uncle Fred said.

Mr. Lind, also on his feet, demanded, "What are you doing, Zan? This is not a time for fooling. Dinner is on the table."

"It looks like I'm going someplace with Otto. Keep it all hot for me, if you can." She smiled at Edward, who stood bristling by the table. "Good luck with the race, if I don't see you before it starts. Okay, Otto. Let me walk, will you?"

He all but carried her to the depot. His agitation was such that she didn't have the heart to ask him to slow down, and he never answered a direct question anyway. As his mother said, "Otto can talk . . . he just doesn't speak so anyone can hear him."

Inside, he opened the half-glass door to the back room where Joseph spent most of his time reading yellow-back novels of adventure. The few books Zan had read came from the extensive library Joseph had compiled on the shelves around his desk. Not even the bookstore had half as many titles, though perhaps carrying a wider variety. If it didn't have a cold-eyed villain, a beautiful girl in peril, and a silent but energetic hero, Joseph didn't read it.

Even now, with Dr. Tanner working on the bare foot Joseph had propped up on the desk, his head was bent over a book. Somewhat belatedly Otto knocked on the door. Glancing up, Joseph stuck his finger in the book to mark his place.

"Golly," Zan said, "what happened to you?"

A large gash, still oozing blood, ran diagonally across his foot. Already the flesh around the cut puffed up purple and swollen. Doc Tanner looked up from his examination. "Looks worse than it is. No bones broken, though it feels like it, eh, Joseph?"

"Ah, it's not so bad. I knew that box was too heavy for me to lift, but Otto was busy."

"You dropped a box on your foot and did all that?" Zan said.

"Stupid, wasn't it? But the shipment's okay." He glanced down at his wounded foot. "What's that stuff, Doc?"

The doctor uncorked a bottle half-full of brown liquid. "Whiskey," he said shortly.

"For me?" Joseph asked, struggling to sit up straighter. "Ma said I should never drink, but if it's medicinal . . ."

"Hold your horses. It isn't for drinking. And it's going to sting!"

Zan grasped Joseph's hand. "Hang on tight."

His fingers curved around hers even as he ran his other hand through his dark hair. "Horses . . ." he began to say.

With a jerk of his wrist, Dr. Tanner sloshed a liberal measure of whiskey over the cut. Joseph's eyebrows seemed to tangle in his hair as he sucked in his breath. He squeezed Zan's hand and thrashed around in his chair but didn't utter a sound. When he could talk again, he said, "It'll heal up for sure now. That's powerful stuff, Doc."

"Should be . . . it's the cheapest kind. Now I want you to keep that foot up as much as you can. I'll send some salve

176

over to your mother. She'll change the bandage once a day and smear it with salve. You shouldn't even have much of a scar there."

Joseph looked up at the doctor with hopeful eyes. "Any reason I can't ride?"

"Ride? You mean in that race today? Sorry, son, I don't think that's a good idea."

"Then I guess you'll have to do it, Zan."

"Oh, so that's why Otto came a-running for me. I didn't think it was just to hold your hand." She shook his clinging fingers free.

"Come on, Zan. You know you want to. Pa's horse is the fastest in these parts. Mr. Evans's old mare won't get a sniff of his heels."

"Can't you just put off racing until your foot's better?"

"And give Ma a chance to talk Pa out of it? Even if I can't ride it, I still want to see it. And you're the only one I know of who's even half as good as me."

Zan glanced around. Dr. Tanner had paused in packing his black leather bag, and Otto gave her an encouraging nod. She thought of herself, flashing past the gawking faces of her friends and neighbors. She'd be a nine-day's wonder if she won, and she knew she could win. Maybe they'd even let her into the Last Resort again.

"You've talked me into it."

Otto beamed. The doctor said, "Should be quite a race. I'll be cheering for you, Miss Lind."

Joseph grinned up at her. "Best of all, it'll give you a chance to take that snooty feller you work for down a peg."

She couldn't return his chuckle with one of her own. How could she have forgotten Edward was to ride Mr. Evans's horse? But she couldn't back out now, not after saying she'd do it. They might think she was a coward, or worse. They might conclude that she and Edward were in love.

The silence that fell in the dining room when she went back and announced her intention told her that most people there weren't going to see it her way. Luckily, the small fry were out of the room, so she didn't have to try to tell her family anything so risky over their racket.

Faith said, "Oh, no!" and rolled her eyes heavenward. "Mother! You can't let her do it!"

Kincaid asked doubtfully, "Can you ride all that well?"

"Sure," Zan said with a careless shrug. Her food squatted, cold and unappetizing, on her plate. Nevertheless, she began to eat, anything to avoid looking at Edward.

"I'll withdraw from the race," he said.

"My boy!" Uncle Fred's happy face took on a wounded expression. "You can't simply throw up your hand this way. It's not cricket."

"Girls don't choose to play cricket, Uncle. At least, I've never met any that have. And I cannot race a woman. Think of it. If I win, I've done a thing no gentleman can boast of. And if I lose, the humiliation . . ."

Zan kept her gaze on her plate, pushing a carrot around like a long-boat through the grease. "Nobody'll think the worse of you if you do lose. They know I'm good."

"Mr. Lind, sir, I appeal to you," Edward said. "You cannot permit your daughter to act like a jockey for the vulgar amusement of your neighbors."

Lifting her eyes, Zan held her breath. She had never willfully disobeyed her father, once he spoke his mind. He'd leaned back in his chair and crossed his arms to rest on his abdomen. Slowly he surveyed the faces gathered around his son-in-law's table. His interest lingered longest on Zan's face and, surprisingly, on Edward's.

"I do not approve of what Suzanna wishes to do." Edward gave a triumphant nod. But his satisfaction faded as the farmer went on. "However, she has promised Joseph Taylor

178

that she would race for him. I would not have her break her word."

Mrs. Lind turned to Faith. "She cannot ride horses in those clothes. Go home. Her dungarees are hanging on the line."

As soon as she changed, Zan walked over to the mercantile to look at the horse she'd soon be riding. Mr. Taylor came out to meet her. "Paid three hundred and fifty dollars for him not two weeks ago." Zan whistled in polite amazement. "Yep, and worth every cent. Never owned a piece of bloodstock before. Gentle as a kitten, too."

"He's a fine-looking animal, that's for sure." The horse, standing in a loose box in the shed behind the store, stamped his feet as if in agreement, his long ears twitched forward. His nearly black coat had a glossy light along the short neck and back. "Seems to me, though, he's built more for distance than for speed."

Mr. Taylor blustered, "Not a bit of it—nonsense! I've put a watch on him before I bought him. Those city horse dealers think they can put one over on any feller coming in from the country. But I clocked him myself at four and half minutes, with the buggy, in the mile. You should have heard what Mrs. Taylor had to say about it!"

Zan could only imagine and be grateful she hadn't been around. "I'll do my best for you, sir."

"I know you will. And I want you to know, Zan, that if Joseph can't do it, there's no one else I'd rather have riding for me than you."

"Joseph's going to be terribly disappointed when I win," she said, running her hand along the horse's smooth neck.

"That's what he gets for daydreaming on the job. He couldn't be satisfied working for his old man—knew I'd keep too close an eye on him. Now I'll bet he's wishing I'd been there to tell him what's what. Leave the heavy work to the fellers with muscles, I say, and let them that's got brains use 'em."

"Joseph's got brains, all right."

"Then why don't he use 'em for something 'sides a hat rack? Mrs. Taylor says he's a genius and one of these days he'll stagger all of us. I wish he'd get along and do it, if that's what he's going to make of himself." Grumbling, Mr. Taylor thumped out of the shed.

The horse kept his liquid brown eyes fixed on her. She said softly, "Just you and me, now, boy. I know you're not used to being ridden, but it's only for a couple of minutes. And I'm light as a feather. You won't hardly know that I'm up there, except that I'll help you run quicker. Course, when we win, Mr. Taylor's liable to burst his vest buttons, but that's his risk, not ours."

"The risk," said a cultured voice from behind her, "is negligible. You won't win."

"You're allowed to take that point of view if you want. But I figure I've got as good a chance to win as you do."

She stepped away from the horse and turned toward Edward. The sunlight coming in through the shed door lit the red in his hair and angled along his tight jaw. Though he looked fierce, her heart began to thud in the quickening rhythm of desire.

They were alone and so often he'd been unable to resist taking her in his arms. She rubbed her palms together, as one tingled recalling what he'd done the last time they'd had an instant alone. If only she could entice him to kiss her again, but she had no idea how to go about seducing him.

"So you have every intention of riding today," he said, his eyes flicking coldly over her boyish attire.

"Why not?"

"Because it's wrong! It's not . . . a lady wouldn't do such a thing. Making a spectacle of herself."

"I've done lots of things in my time that weren't ladylike. Some of them with you." When the fire leaped up in his dark gray eyes, Zan realized that she knew at least how to arouse *some* emotions in him. Taken aback by the effectiveness of her words, she retreated. "I mean, spreading manure isn't exactly what an earl's wife would do, is it? What do you call an earl's wife, anyway? An earl-ess?"

She sighed in relief when he smiled, though it was a tight, cold smile entirely unlike the ones that charmed her so. "One refers to her as a countess except to her face, when she would be Lady Whomever. You may as well forget that, now that I've told you. It will hardly have relevance to your life."

"You never know. I might go to England someday. Course, it couldn't be during the summer—there's too much work to do."

He shook his head, still smiling grimly. "I shouldn't recommend that you go. They have standards in England that you could never meet."

"What do you mean? I can do anything I set my mind to."

"I don't doubt it. However, you couldn't survive in London society for five minutes."

As a rule, Zan controlled her temper. If she did get angry, it took her a long time to build up to shouting. But when Edward stood before her, so arrogant and so self-assured, she felt herself go up like a sulphur match dropped into phosphorus.

"Maybe I could, or maybe I couldn't," she said. "Least I can survive in Kansas. Unlike some people."

"If that is to my address . . ."

"If the shoe fits, Your Lordship!"

He couldn't have looked more stunned if she had struck him. "Very well, Miss Lind. If you are so eager to be man's superior, let us begin with this race. But you won't win."

"I don't want to be your superior," she said, anger draining from her like water from a broken pitcher. The hurt in his eyes had only flared there for one second before his pride hid it from her. She knew she'd hit below the belt and was instantly contrite. "All I've ever wanted is for us to be equals—partners. Even friends."

"Friendship?" He laughed shortly. "That is even less possible than equality. Friendship has never been what I want from . . ." Shaking his head, he turned away. "I will see you shortly, Miss Lind. And permit me to wish you the best of good fortune."

CHAPTER

14

"Though Maisie's got awful fond of Fred Winchester," Minnie said, "I never could abide that nephew of his with his nose in the air. So you beat him good, Zan Lind. I've got fifty cents riding on you."

Zan had been cornered by Minnie on her way to the church and the start of the race. Mr. Taylor would bring his horse along himself. "I never would have thought of you as a high roller, Mrs. Parker."

"Betting is the devil's favorite work, most of the time. But I kind of think of betting against Ed as a patriotic duty. Valley Forge! And uh, 1812! After all, the Ever-Glorious Fourth of July is just around the corner."

"I'll do my best to make you and George Washington proud of me, Mrs. Parker."

Zan walked on. Though she'd given Miss Minnie a light answer, her heart felt like a lump of pig iron. She didn't really want to win anymore. She and Edward had been challenging each other from the moment she'd started working for him. Today, she was afraid they might find the finish to their feuding. Zan kicked a rock, and it vanished down between two boards.

All the same, she'd be danged if she were going to give in. Let Edward prove he was better than her, if he believed it. And even were she to be left in the dust, she'd still show up for work tomorrow and every day thereafter. Though owning the Beakman place seemed a hollow dream without Edward to share it, it remained the only dream she held that had any chance of coming true.

Reaching the church, she smiled wanly around at her friends and well-wishers. Then Miss Maisie popped up in front of her, the mound of her gray hair wispily askew. Taking her arm, she lead Zan out of earshot of the others.

"I'm putting my money on Ed," she said without preamble. "But I don't want you to have any hard feelings against me because of it."

"No, Mrs. Hastings, I wouldn't do that."

"It's just that's the way . . . a gentlemen friend of mine told me I ought to bet that way, and I couldn't seem to wriggle out of it. Otherwise, all my money would have been on you."

"I guess Uncle Fred is betting on Edward. Only natural."

"Fred? Most likely. Course that sister of mine has to be ornery and bet against a smart feller's advice. Serves her right for betting so much money."

"What's your stake?"

"Ten cents. Wouldn't be right to waste more'n that, what with times so hard."

Zan rubbed the back of her neck, trying to force down a smile. "I'm afraid you are going to lose that dime, Mrs. Hastings. I mean to win, if I can."

"Wouldn't expect you to say nothing else. You've got spirit, Zan Lind."

Mr. Taylor arrived, leading his blood horse. The slowly gathering crowd clapped as the horse began to strut, showing off, shaking his head as though to dislodge flies. Zan excused herself from Miss Maisie and went up to meet Mr. Taylor. Cord Spencer held the reins of Mr. Evans's white-footed bay mare. The two older men joshed good-naturedly.

Zan glanced around. Samantha Spencer and Jane Carson, the dressmaker, stood under a pair of parasols. Though Zan had never patronized Jane's shop, the You Sew and Sew, she knew her well enough to wave to.

Jane didn't return the greeting, being busy shaking her head simultaneously with Samantha over Mr. Evans's antics. She'd been tending him since he'd broken his arm while operating the newspaper press. Obviously she agreed with his daughter that he was overdoing things now.

Joseph Taylor, leaning on a crutch-handled stick, not only waved, he hollered. "Hey, Zan! Whomp him home!"

Even Otto, standing by his friend, shyly wiggled the fingers on his right hand. Glancing around, embarrassed, he shuffled his big feet. His tiny mother reached up to pat her son's arm comfortingly.

Zan's own family waited by the church. Ben and Gary chased themselves around the grown-ups. Sarah and Amanda were jumping rope with some of the other little girls. They waved to Zan but didn't leave the game.

Mr. Lind looked her over and nodded gruffly. "Hold him in until you make the turn at the end of the street. If Mr. Winchester takes the lead, let him have it until then. You will make it up on the comeback."

"Yes, sir."

"And if you want to race, you must do your best to win. That is the only reason for racing at all." He clapped her on the shoulder. "I want to say . . . you have never done anything that has not made me . . ." He couldn't seem to say anything more. He coughed and turned red.

Zan understood. He had never told her he was proud of her. He'd never needed to. She'd always known it.

Faith stepped forward. "I don't approve of this at all," she said. Then her eyes, so like Zan's in shape, though unlike in color, softened. "But I sure hope you win."

"Thanks."

"Of course, I managed to talk Kincaid out of betting on you. Not that he's betting on His Highness, either. We need every cent for the hotel."

The crowd had been growing from moment to moment. Somehow, the word had spread, and Zan saw people from outlying farms who only came to town on special occasions. A nervous bubble in her stomach suggested that eating a large plate of cold food half an hour ago hadn't been the wisest move.

Something was happening by the horses. The bay mare, not relishing the nearness of Taylor's stallion, had backed and reared. Her high-pitched neigh cut through the noise of the people. The stallion laid his ears back and fought to rear up as well.

The crowd cheered as Edward stepped forward to take the mare's reins from Cord. Zan wasn't near enough to hear what Edward said, but the mare calmed almost instantly, dominated by the man's superior will. For the first time, Zan realized that Uncle Fred had not exaggerated. Edward did know as much about horses as the older man had claimed.

Her mother said, "You'd better get ready."

"Mother, I . . ." She wanted to ask if it was too late to back out. Though she might, through winning, find herself once more plain old Zan Lind, with friends and a place of her own, these things no longer seemed as desirable as they had before Edward. And if she lost, how could she ever be free of the doubt that she hadn't done her best?

"Go on," Mrs. Lind said with a gentle smile. "It will be all right."

Then she was bestride her mount, with no clear idea of

how she'd gotten there, except that she'd needed a boost from Mr. Sutherland, the blacksmith and starter for the race, to throw her leg over the tall creature. Edward had no need of help. The mare stood patiently for him to mount up, as steady as a horse carved for a war memorial.

Her own horse backed and danced. When Edward looked at her and offered his hand, saying, "Best of luck," it took her two tries to reach it. His hand, like his eyes, was as cold as a stranger's. She half expected to see him wipe her touch off on his coat.

Then the men around them dispersed, Uncle Fred giving her a discreet thumb's-up as he stepped back. The burly blacksmith stood before them, a large white handkerchief fluttering in the breeze as he held it up. The crowd noise died away, except for one crying baby.

The instant the handkerchief dropped, Zan clapped her heels to the stallion's belly. Galloping like mad down the dirt street, she began to enjoy herself. All her doubts were blown away by the speed of the wind through her hair. Of course she'd do her darnedest to win, and if Edward didn't like it, well, she was woman enough to turn him around.

Out of the corner of her eye, she saw him surge ahead. Mindful of her father's advice she let him go. The colorful buildings of Harmony blurred like the brilliant shades of sundown.

She came to Zeke Gallagher, holding up a second handkerchief to mark the turn, just past the Last Resort. She caught a single glimpse of Zeke's bearded face as the stallion slewed around. The wild hooves slid and shuffled. Somehow she pulled the horse together, keeping him upright though the reins scorched her fingers.

Edward was no more than a horse-length ahead when she started once more down the straight street. Nothing matters, she told herself, but I gotta catch him. Then, to her amazement, she saw him lean back, dragging on the reins with all his might to stop the furious momentum beneath him.

Zan saw this as her chance. But even as she raised her knees to bring her heels down on the horse's ribs, she glimpsed a small dark animal in her path. She, too, hauled on the reins, willing a halt with heart, mind, and hands.

The tiny kitten, eyes still blue, raised a feeble paw in defiance against charging death. Zan couldn't stop in time, and closed her eyes, not wanting to see the huge hoof smash down. She was nearly thrown over the horse's neck as he put all four hooves down in a scrambling stop.

Gingerly she opened one eye and looked down. The kitten arched its back, the yet unmanageable fur spiking along the curve. Zan's stallion lowered his velvet nose to sniff at the strange creature in his path.

A young girl darted out from among the people watching the race in front of Sutherland's stable. With apologetic grace, she scooped up the kitten. "He's not very old yet," she said quickly. "He doesn't know any better."

"Never mind," Edward answered. "It doesn't matter."

A woman from the crowd called, "Laurian Sawyer, you get back here!"

As she ran off, Zan glanced over at Edward. "What do we do now? Call it a draw?"

"This isn't over, only interrupted."

Something in his voice told her he was not talking about the race. Unable to sustain his gaze, she toyed with a loose strand of hair. "Oh, look," she said, relieved. "Here comes Zeke. He'll start us off again."

A handkerchief was dropped anew. Once more the two horses leaped forward. Try as she could, however, Zan couldn't seem to draw away from Edward, or he from her. Perhaps her stallion and his mare had pleased each other by their refusal to crush the small creature in their way.

Passing the mercantile, they were as perfectly in stride as a matched carriage pair. The judges on either side of the street as they flashed past could only scratch their heads in wonder before they began to argue. Not even Reverend Johnson could call the race.

Cord and Jake were there to walk the steaming horses, while Zan and Edward went to hear the verdict. Half the town stood within earshot. Sheriff Miller gave his opinion that Zan's horse had stuck his nose in front at the last second and there was some excitement. The noise doubled, however, when Kincaid, who had been a judge on the opposite side of the street, said he thought Edward had taken a slight lead. The more argument there was the more firmly each man stated his opinion.

Finally Uncle Fred said, "It must be the difference in perspective. Edward rode on Kincaid's side, and Zan on the Sheriff's. Each man saw the same thing, but from a slightly different angle. I'm afraid the only thing to do is declare this race a tie."

"It wasn't a fair test," Mr. Taylor protested. "They stopped. . . . What'd you stop for, Zan?"

"A kitten." She could tell how foolish that sounded when the merchant's jaw dropped. "I couldn't very well run it over."

"Is that why you stopped, too, Winchester?" Mr. Evans wanted to know.

"Yes, sir. It was right in front of me."

The buzz from the citizens grew louder as each person decided to discuss this development with their neighbor. The word *kitten* passed from lip to ear as fast as a mouth could move. Miss Minnie expressed the emotion of the crowd best when she said loudly, "Never mind a dang-blasted cat! What I want to know is . . . what about my fifty cents?"

Mr. Evans raised his good arm to ask for silence. "We'll run the race again. No, not now. Give the horses a chance to recover, and the riders. But if you will agree, Zan, and you, Mr. Winchester, to ride next week . . ."

"Can't," Zan said, pushing her loosened hair off her face. "I only did it today to help Joseph. But his foot should be healed up fine by next Sunday."

"Sure thing," Joseph said, hopping forward. "Feels better already."

"I shall be pleased to ride for you again, Mr. Evans, against any opponent Mr. Taylor can mount." Edward bowed. "May I suggest that any wagers placed today simply remain in hiatus until next week?"

Though a few disgruntled souls still griped at not having their money in hand, most people seemed willing to accept the judges' decision. Slowly the crowd began to break up, some still arguing about what they'd seen. Zan glanced around for her parents, but couldn't find them at the moment.

Mr. Evans said, "It's good of you, Winchester, to agree to be my rider again. And let me say, I never saw a man with a better talent for riding. You've ridden often, I take it?"

"I believe my father first put me on a horse when I was either six or eight months old."

"That's right," Uncle Fred said. "My brother thinks the only reason a boy can't ride is physical affliction or outright cowardice. And he would be proud of you, too, my dear." He took Zan's hand. "His own daughters are not the most intrepid of horsewomen. Slow ponies are all they'd consider."

"I didn't know you had sisters," Zan said to Edward.

"Two. One older, one younger."

"So you come from a family of five kids, too! Course, we don't have an uncle like yours."

"You do now, my dear." Uncle Fred kissed her hand. "What's this? Blood?"

With a concerned frown marring his forehead, Edward grasped Zan's wrist, taking her hand from his uncle. A tingle of power leaped up her arm at the contact. She knew that he felt it, too, for his hand was far from steady. "How did this happen?" he demanded gruffly.

"Must have been when I pulled on the reins. They must have cut me. There's no reason to make a fuss; it doesn't hurt." She wiped off the slow-seeping blood on her dungarees, wincing as the torn flesh caught on the tough material.

Her mother pushed through the dispersing crowd. "You have hurt yourself?"

"It's nothing. I'll be ready to work come tomorrow. Edward . . ."

"Yes, I know," he said. His ill-humor seemed to have gone, leaving in its place the heart-stealing splendor of his smile. "The last field needs to be sown while we wait for rain."

"Not wait," she said, her heart flying because he was no longer angry with her. "Pray. Any credit you have with God, go ahead and pledge."

" 'The quality of mercy is not strained,' " Uncle Fred said. " 'It droppeth as the gentle rain from heaven upon the place beneath. It is twice blest; it blesseth—' "

Mrs. Lind interrupted, "Never mind that now. Zan, you come along and have the good doctor look at your hands. Why didn't you wear gloves?"

Later, lying in bed, Zan lived what amounted to a waking dream. She thought of Edward, remembering how he'd touched her the day of the snipe hunt. She could recall everything, what he'd done, how it felt, where each kiss had fallen on her mouth and throat.

Pressing her hand to the placket of her simple white nightgown, she relived his fingers slipping inside her undershirt. Even thinking about that moment made her heart beat wildly and her breath come faster. The times he'd touched her since had thrilled her to her heart's core, but the intimacy of his hand on her body had the power to send her reeling, even in memory. Zan resolved that she wouldn't let tomorrow go by without experiencing his touch once again. All she had to, she figured, was to show willing and he'd do the rest.

At her mother's insistence she wore a pair of tough leather gloves the next day, to protect her palms from further damage. However, it wasn't long before she'd stripped them off, finding it too difficult to work in them, especially when brushing down the mules.

Edward picked them up from the tack shelf in his barn. Slapping them against his leg, he said, "Let me see your hands."

"What?" she asked, combing Hank's tail. "Some folks think I'm odd, the way I take as good a care of these two as most folks do a horse. But I figure, they deserve a little fussing over—all the work they do."

"I said, let me see your hands."

After putting down the comb, Zan faced him, her hands hanging limply off the ends of her upturned wrists. They were dirty, black soil accentuating every crease and marking the half-moons of her fingernails. The cuts between her thumb and forefinger were hardly distinguishable from the dirt marks, save that they were dark red.

Edward didn't touch them, only inspecting them with disapproval drawing down his eyebrows. "How will you work if they become infected?" he asked.

"Heck, they won't. It's not like I was working with manure today. Good clean dirt never hurt anybody. My little brother used to *eat* it, and he's never been sick a day in his life."

"You should have worn these to protect them."

"Heck, I can't work in gloves. Mother always tells me I

should—so my hands don't get ruined—but I start to sweat in 'em and the itch drives me so crazy I always pull 'em off. Or I try to pick something up, can't with the gloves on, so they come off anyway."

He hadn't seemed to mind her hands' calluses and rough spots when he'd done those wild things to her fingers in the hotel. A reckless smile came to her lips as she wondered if he was thinking of that, too. "I guess my hands are kind of ugly, though, huh?"

Her hook came up without a compliment on the end. "Very. But one cannot expect white purity from a hard worker such as yourself." Edward held out his own hands. "Once upon a time, my only calluses came from riding horses and writing with pens."

Zan slid her fingers over his. "I like the ones from plowing, roofing, and pumping a whole lot better."

He flinched away from her touch. "Allow me to finish your grooming task. As the fields are finished now, I suppose you will want to take your mules home today?"

"I think so. We won't need 'em again until we cultivate between the rows. Weeds grow awful quick in the summertime." She wasn't hurt by his jerking away. Let her go scrub off this dirt and she'd try again.

After she'd gone to the pump, Edward continued currying the mules. He had never had much experience with mules, but Hank and Herman had, in their week of residence, endeared themselves to him. They were such solid citizens, doing a day's work for little reward and content to go to their rest each evening without getting up to tricks. Edward also suspected that the two of them were smarter than he was.

He knew he kept the surface of his thoughts busy with philosophical musing about mules as a defense against Zan. A thousand arguments against any further physical passion between them could be overset in an instant by her touch.

Striving to fix his thoughts on something beside images of himself and Zan rolling on sheets in naked desire, Edward ticked over in his mind the differences between horses and mules.

The horse race yesterday should have stiffened his resolve not to become more involved with her. But her radiance had enchanted him all over again, her cheeks flushed with excitement and her long hair, like that of a princess in a fairy tale, whipped into a banner by the wind. He'd actually been seething with greed, wanting to drag her away to hide her treasures from the vulgar crowd.

Not even a cold bath, as prescribed by the masters at Eton, served to chill his blood to the required temperature. Nor did sleep banish lustful thought. He'd awakened this morning with Zan in his thoughts, and he suffered a state of almost unbearable excitement, necessitating a second deluge of cold water. It hadn't been nearly cold enough.

Edward faced the truth that his intentions were entirely dishonorable. Whenever he touched her, any ideas he had about the future fled. He wanted to take Zan wherever they met, in the barn, in the church, on the road! Perhaps Kansas had finally succeeded in driving him mad.

When she wasn't near, when he was sane, he recalled what was important. He remembered that his goals were to earn enough money to go back to England, to live in comfort, and to find a suitable wife. He couldn't be such a cad as to seduce Zan and then, without further thought for her, achieve his goals. And although she'd become necessary to his first goal, she had no place in the achievement of the other two.

"That's better," she said, coming back, her skin glowing from the cold pump water.

He did not dare look at her. He concentrated on removing the last flecks of dust from Herman's coat. All the same, he knew precisely where she stood, within arm's reach. And his arms were hungry.

"You've done a good job on this barn," she said, looking up at the roof. "I remember what kind of shape it was in when you came here."

"I don't recall seeing you on the Double B before my uncle hired you."

"Oh, I came here before that. I was thinking about buying this place, before Mr. Beakman decided to sell. That reminds me . . . was it okay when I brought Mr. Beakman out here a couple of days ago?"

"You know you may do what you like." He strove to keep his voice neutral, but his curiosity got the better of him. "Why did you?"

"Well, he's getting ready to clear out of his place for Wichita. I think he's a little nervous about keeping his word to me. Somebody's made him a better offer, and he's not a hundred percent sure I can come up with the price we settled on. He'd like to give me first crack at it, but he won't hold off if there's no hope for me."

"And he wanted a look at our farm to be certain you're good for the money?"

"That's right." A rush of pleasure shot through Zan. Did he really think of her as sharing the Double B?

She moved closer to him, wishing he'd look up. "You've done everything to those mules except give 'em a shoe shine."

"As you said, they deserve some extra care." He leaned down to flick a bug off Herman's knobby knee.

Zan laid her palm on his back. The muscles under his shirt twitched and fluttered. "Edward," she said and stopped, taken aback by the sound of her own voice. She had never cooed before.

Casually he stood up, shaking off her hand. "Of course you should bring Mr. Beakman by again. Perhaps after the sorghum plants have broken the surface of the rows. He couldn't possibly have been impressed with the way the fields look now."

"Edward," she said again. This was more difficult than she would have believed.

"You know, I believe I'd better go up into the loft. I'm not entirely happy about the ventilation up there, and I don't want the hay to rot. Please excuse me. No doubt I shall see you again when the weeding you mentioned is required."

Without further ado, he began climbing the ladder that lead to the loft. Zan picked up the currycomb and brush, cleaned them, and put them on the tack shelf. Then, taking her time, she led the mules out to their temporary pasture.

Entering the barn, she took a deep breath. Climbing the ladder was no challenge to her strength, yet it was one of the hardest things she'd ever done. When her head cleared the piled hay, she saw Edward.

He lay on his back on some loose hay, his hands beneath his head. His eyes were closed and his breathing came deep and slow. It seemed an awful funny place for a nap, as the summer sun had heated the air to the point where it was almost unbearably stuffy. Golden dust motes swirled in the barred light that came in through the vent.

The crackling hay shifted under her feet as Zan made her way toward him. Somehow she knew that he was not as unaware of her presence as he seemed. He hadn't moved, but the pace of his breathing increased. She sank to her knees beside him and touched the center of his chest with timid fingertips.

"Edward?"

Still with his eyes closed, he asked, "What do you want?"

"You."

He lay so still she thought he hadn't heard. The single syllable had slipped out without her conscious will, but she had no wish to draw it back. "Did you hear what I said?"

His breath shuddered. Quick as striking snakes, his hands came up to grab hers. His eyes open, he jerked her off balance and rolled over with her. When his hard, tense body lay on hers, he said fiercely, "I don't want you to want me! You shouldn't even be here!"

He brought his mouth down on hers with a savagery that appalled the gentlemanly side of his nature. Finesse, gentility became sounds without meaning. He insisted that she open to him. When she did, he plundered her mouth mercilessly, demanding her total surrender.

She gave it to him. He held her hands over her head so she could not touch him. Yet Zan couldn't keep still beneath him. The weight of his body pressing her into the hay didn't make her feel trapped but eager. Though not quite sure how she'd gotten into this so quickly, she had no complaints to make.

Mindlessly she stretched out her legs, moving restlessly to bring his hips into closer contact with her own. Her entire body felt alive, from her tight nipples to the heaviness between her thighs. This was even better than her dreams!

Edward dragged his mouth from hers, and she protested with a moan. Abruptly he released her hands. He had every intention of moving away from her and ordering her to go. But his hands fumbled with the buttons on her shirt, seemingly of their own free will. Impatiently he dragged the heavy cotton from the waistband of her dungarees, carrying her undershirt up with it.

"Oh, God, you're perfect," he said almost in pain. Only big enough to fill his hands, her breasts were firm as apples and as white as the flesh of that fruit. The deep rose tips were already hard. He couldn't resist tasting the beauty that she offered to him so proudly.

Zan gasped when he slid his fingers over her, moving his thumb back and forth over her nipple, bringing it to an even keener point. But when he replaced his hand with his firm lips, she cried "Yes!"

Though her hands were now free to roam over him, or to push him away, she only grasped at the hay on either side of her body. Sharp pleasure drove her toward some abyss. She was not afraid of falling. With Edward holding her, she could fly!

Then his hand was down there, his fingers pressing against the center seam of her dungarees. Her blood going wild, she didn't pull away, but gave him all he wanted. His hand moved, his mouth was hot, and Zan couldn't hold on. She launched herself, arms open, into the abyss.

Edward rolled over onto his back, the madness ebbing out of him. She was even more responsive, more passionate, than he'd dreamed. Watching her achieve a climax, knowing she'd never had one before, had been very nearly more than he could stand.

Only the merest tattered shred of decency kept him from tearing off the rest of their clothing and plunging wildly into her sweet warmth. He could but hope that what had happened already would not traumatize her too severely. Taking his arm from his eyes, he saw she lay on her side seemingly asleep. Her lips curved into the smile of an angel as he watched.

Her shirt was still up. Edward tore his eyes away from the glimpse of the smooth underside of her breast. He dared not reach over and tug her shirt down, any more than he dared to inhale too deeply. The secret scent of her filled the hayloft and might send him insane again.

But her face was not any easier to look at. With her golden lashes cast down on her cheeks, and the faint flush of health shining through her skin, she seemed utterly innocent. Edward cursed himself for despoiling her, knowing that when those lashes lifted she'd revile him and rightly. He groaned and hid his eyes again in the crook of his arm.

"What's the matter?" she asked.

In a fluid movement she sat up facing him, her shirt falling to cover all but her midriff. She ran her hand over his sleeve. His body had a firmness that no one would notice until they touched him or saw him without a shirt. Recalling her visit to his room when he'd been sunburned, Zan shivered in delectable anticipation. Soon she'd see him that way again, and even more of him, too.

She sneezed, turning her head away just in time.

"Bless you," he said grimly.

"Thank you. What's wrong?"

"Don't you know?"

"No." She smoothed his shirt, running her hand over the fancy vest, one like he always wore. Tracing the embroidered vines, she ran across a piece of hay. "You've got it all over you," she said happily. "I guess I do, too."

"Don't do that!" He trapped her wandering hand as she followed the vine to the waistband of his trousers. She mustn't understand what the large bulge that distorted his clothing was. He could protect her that much.

"Zan," he said calmly, holding on to her hand. "Zan, I want you to put all this right out of your mind."

"I don't think I can do that, Edward."

"You don't understand." He looked up into her happy face. "It's not a good thing. It's immoral and wrong. And it's all my fault."

She leaned down and kissed his unresponsive mouth. "It's none of that. It's just love. I love you, Edward."

CHAPTER
15

Zan asked herself what she had expected. A passionate declaration? A proposal of marriage, to take place at once? Even the favor of a dazzling smile? Whatever it had been, it wasn't this. A flashing instant of frozen horror had passed over Edward's face. Then he'd forced a smile like the ones that undertakers shape on corpses.

"You don't mean that. Zan, you've had a startling experience, unlike anything you've known before."

"I'll say!" Her heart still pounded. Though the rush of pleasure had left her with a deep contentment flooding her body, at the same time she felt curiously tense and unsatisfied. It was like when someone talked about mountains. She found it pleasing to know that somewhere there were such things, yet just hearing about snowcapped peaks and wild tumbles of rocks wasn't enough. She wanted to experience the wonders of the world firsthand. Somehow she knew Edward had even more to show her than he already had.

"When a young woman experiences this . . . event for the first time, she often feels very grateful to the man who has helped her. She can become confused and believe herself to be madly in love. But . . ."

Because Zan loved him, she could smile at him tenderly when he spouted such nonsense. "Where'd you pick this up? One of your books?"

"Zan, I'm trying to explain that you don't have to say you love me. I know your emotions are clashing together. You feel gratitude toward me and at the same time deep shame at being so vulnerable. Perhaps you resent me for robbing you of a moment that should more properly be experienced only with your husband. I shouldn't be surprised if tomorrow you hate me. This is perfectly understandable."

Her warm, utterly feminine laugh stopped him. "You may know an awful lot about birds and animals, Edward, but you don't know a thing about women."

"I know more about these things than you."

"I believe it. After all, you're older than me, you've been all sorts of places I haven't. I bet there's more than one girl who has had this 'experience', with you."

"That's not anything you need concerned yourself about." He frowned, shocked by her even mentioning other women at a time like this.

She chuckled again. The sound did things to him. How dare she laugh at him, when a moment ago she lay helplessly spending herself in his arms? Underlying his anger, though, was a rising desire to laugh with her until he could bury himself inside her.

"What is so amusing?"

"You are. Don't you know that I wouldn't have had this 'experience' you keep going on about if I wasn't already in love with you?"

"You have no idea what you are talking about. 'Love' and 'passion' are two different things." He stood up, half turning away from her discerning eyes to hide his arousal from her. His body did not seem to understand that this interlude was over. More cold water was the remedy, yet first he had to make things clear for Zan. Impatiently Edward began brushing the hay from his trousers.

"Are you saying that if any man put his hands on me like you did, I'd feel the same way?"

"Of course not. You're no harlot."

"Then explain this to me, if you're so smart. Why did I feel it with you?"

She continued to kneel in the loose hay. Once again Edward could not look at her. The expression of bright inquiry she wore was too eager. That her smiling lips were now on the level of his belt buckle didn't make things easier.

Firmly restraining his audacious imagination, he said, "I think this conversation is leading us nowhere."

"I don't know," she said, still with a laugh in her voice. "I'm learning a lot." She ticked off items on her long fingers. "I'm no harlot, but passion is different from love. Many girls would resent what you just did with me, so it's okay to resent your husband."

"I never said that."

"Didn't you? Let me see—what else? Oh, I'm supposed to forget you've ever touched me, and keep myself for the man I'm going to marry someday, right? So I'm supposed to lie to this poor man who probably won't ever touch me like you have because it's something to be ashamed of. Besides, he won't have your wide understanding of women."

"You're twisting everything I've said!"

"Am I?" she asked, her blue-gray eyes innocent, her lips far from shy. "Why don't you explain it again? Start over again from when I came into the loft."

Zan had never seen Edward angry before. Once or twice, he'd expressed cold disapproval or sneering contempt. However, the blood hadn't mounted into his face, his voice hadn't grown rough and deep. His lips hadn't tightened, nor had his body stiffened. Now all of that happened.

His anger didn't frighten her. Rather, Zan reveled in being the only bumpkin in Kansas who could make His Lordship lose his temper.

"You don't know what kind of a game you're playing!"

"I'm no fool. I do know. You've managed to talk yourself out of believing what I said."

"I don't—"

"I love you."

Without a word he turned and began to go down the ladder. Just before he disappeared, he said, still furious, "You are a fool, Zan!"

She heard him cross the floor, his steps light and quick, as though he were striving not to run. Zan tossed her braid over her shoulder and began picking the hay out of the thick twist. "No, I don't think I am," she said softly.

She had every intention of going home. But when she came down the ladder from the loft and stepped out into the yard, she saw a familiar horse and buggy before the house. Uncle Fred stood on the front steps. On either side of him were the tall, thin, yet imposing figures of Miss Minnie and Miss Maisie.

Zan saw them and felt a pang of guilt. She'd given no thought to Uncle Fred's plight. At the moment faced by his two "admirers," Zan thought he looked like a hangdog desperado between two jailers. He could barely muster a smile to greet her.

Miss Maisie glanced over Zan, not missing a single strand of hay. "What is that truck all over you?"

"I was shaking down some fresh feed for the animals." She wiped her sleeve across her forehead. "Sure was hot up in the loft. Any lemonade going, Uncle Fred?"

"Certainly. Would you ladies like some?"

"Don't mind if I do, the road was terrible dusty," Minnie

replied. "Maisie, why don't you go along and help him?"

"I'll do it!" Zan quickly offered when Uncle Fred turned slightly pale. "You ought to sit down and enjoy the breeze, Mrs. Hastings, Mrs. Parker. Working as hard as you do, you deserve a little sitting down time."

"Hmph! Not everybody can take that kind of time. I noticed Ed walking like the devil was after him when we drove up." Miss Maisie gave Zan a glance. "He looked like he was a-coming from the barn. Was he helping you, up in the loft?"

Zan thanked heaven for the heat. She knew her face was already flushed and hoped her blush went unnoticed. "That's right. It takes two to stack the stuff properly. Let me just go and see 'bout that lemonade."

Uncle Fred had fled inside before Zan finished making her offer to help. He jumped, as nervous as a colt in fly-time, when Zan stepped into the kitchen. "Oh, it's you. I was afraid . . . 'Now I am cribbed, cabined, confined, bound in to saucy doubts and fears.' *Macbeth,* Act Three."

He stirred up the cloudy liquid in the glass pitcher with the same devil-may-care attitude as a suicide mixing up a poisoned brew. "Actually," he said, "occasionally I think it might not be so bad to be married. Doesn't Shakespeare say, 'What is a wedlock forced but a hell, An age of discord and continual strife? Whereas the contrary bringeth bliss, and is a pattern of celestial peace.' *Henry the Sixth,* Part One."

"But they are trying to force you into it. And continual strife . . . and that other stuff would be the least of it. You can hardly squeeze a word in now. What would it be like if you were married to one of 'em?"

"You have a point. Yet marriage isn't all bad, when the people are properly suited to each other."

Zan didn't like the look in Uncle Fred's eye. It had a matchmaking gleam in it. She was reminded unpleasantly of Miss Maisie's and Miss Minnie's own stares when hot on the marrying trail of some perfectly happy single person. They were always arranging impossible matches for unlikely couples. Why, she had even heard that they'd tried to make out that Jane Carson and Alexander Evans were that way about each other!

As she so often had before, Zan began to protest that she was not interested in matrimony. "I guess marriage is all right for some people. But how do you know if you've got the right feller on the hook? Here's my father trying to put me together with someone I've never even met. . . ."

"Marriages are, or at least were, frequently arranged between two persons as yet unacquainted with the other. Kings and princesses, for instance. Even today, marriages are not always for love."

"Like that girl you were telling me about? The one that Edward was all but ready to marry and she wound up hitched to some nasty old man? Her parents forced her to marry him, didn't you say?"

"Yes, but many such marriages turn out quite well. It was the disparity between their ages that doomed that arrangement from ever blossoming into true affection."

"What do you think is a good difference in age, Uncle Fred?" Zan asked, filling a clean plate with gingersnaps.

"Why, my dear, this is so sudden!" The two of them chuckled companionably together over the joke. "I wouldn't suggest that either party be too much older than the other. Perhaps not more than five or ten years. My own dear wife was eight years younger than myself, though that did not ensure her a long and happy life."

"I'm sure it was happy, Uncle Fred, no matter how short."

"You are too kind," he answered, turning away with an emotional sniff. Laying a clean, embroidered cloth on a black lacquered tray, he arranged the plate of cookies, a small basket of berries, and a plate of soda crackers thinly spread with some *hushållsost*, a tangy cheese Zan's mother had sent over with her that morning.

"How old are you, my dear, if you don't mind my asking such an intimate question?" he asked, giving the lemonade a final stir. He sipped from the spoon and smacked his lips in satisfaction.

"I'm near nineteen. September fifteenth."

"Then, if you want my advice, marry someone twenty-eight or twenty-nine. Approximately the age of . . . Edward." His gray eyes twinkling, Uncle Fred picked up the tray and left the room.

Zan brought along the pitcher and four glasses on a second tray. She hoped Uncle Fred was only teasing, taking a shot in the dark. There could be nothing worse than to be so obviously in love with Edward that the whole town would be gabbling about it. Edward would hate it so.

Of course, she thought, it wouldn't be so bad if he were in love with me, too. Then they could talk all they wanted, and I wouldn't care a snap. She began to daydream about how wonderful life would be if Edward loved her. Their wedding day could be this autumn.

The fields would be bright gold with September corn, and there'd be a nip in the air that would make cuddling up with him at night very welcome. They'd have plenty of money from the syrup, and maybe they'd go all the way to Wichita to bank it. That could be their wedding trip, far away from Harmony's prying eyes and wagging tongues.

"You falling asleep, Zan?" Miss Minnie asked, leaning forward, touching the girl's knee.

"I guess I am," she said, blinking. "I've been working hard lately." Though it wasn't the hard work that put the fatigue in her bones, but those heady ten minutes with Edward's hands on her in the hayloft.

"You must be," Miss Maisie said. "I never thought this

farm would ever amount to a thing again. You must be proud."

"I might be, if we ever get some rain. Anyway, it's mostly Edward's doing. You know, he's all but finished putting a new roof on the barn. Done it all by himself, too."

The two women squinted across the yard. "Too proud to ask for help," Miss Maisie said.

"Speaking of Mr. Winchester," Miss Minnie said. "We've got a letter here for him. Foreign-looking, too." She dug into the large bag that dangled from her wrist.

Maisie said, "Now that Joseph Taylor's laid up with his foot, Mary's taking over the depot till he's better. The railroad ought to take that job away from Joseph and give it to her. Maybe we'd start to get our packages on time, 'stead of mercy knows when. And she seems to have some idea where the tickets are kept if not how to fill 'em out."

"Are you planning on going somewhere, Mrs. Hastings?" Uncle Fred asked with a hopeful look.

"Nope! Nothing outside of Harmony interests me much. Could have gone to Chicago with my old man many a time, but I never would. Them big cities are full of nothing but sin and degradation. Opera houses full of half-nekkid gals, open omnibuses with nothing but a strap to hang on to, and fancy restaurants with rooms upstairs."

Minnie stared at her sister. "What kind of talk is that? You'll be giving Zan here ideas!"

"Don't worry about me, Mrs. Parker. I've never cared to be anywhere but right here . . . in Harmony, I mean." But she knew she'd gladly travel to the ends of the earth, if Edward wanted her to.

"Found it!" Miss Minnie said, pulling from her capacious bag the triple-folded page. She held it out to arm's length and read, " 'The Honorable Edward F. Winchester, Harmony, Kansas, United States of America.' " Swiveling her sharp eyes toward Fred, she asked, "What he want an *F* in the middle of his name for, anyhow? Figure a first and last name would be enough for anybody."

"I admit that I agree with you. I myself, Mrs. Parker, have five, you know."

"Five? Names?"

"Yes, indeed. Neville Frederick Ferguson Cabell Winchester. Like many of my family, I had three sets of god-parents, including a bishop. I imagine my parents thought such a family as ours needs all the help it can find."

"Why don't you use Neville, 'stead of Fred?" Miss Maisie asked.

"Would you use Neville, if you had a choice?"

Zan said, "You could always pick your own, like I did."

"Well, this letter's for Ed F. Winchester. Pretty hand-writing, too. Kind of fancy, all them swoops and curlicues." She held the letter up between her eyes and the sunshine, as though to shade them. She apparently had some trouble with the angle, for she kept tilting the letter this way and that, her thin lips moving as if she were reading.

"Why don't it have a stamp?" Miss Maisie wanted to know. "There's nothing in the corner but a John Hancock."

"May I see that?" Uncle Fred held out his hand. Miss Minnie gave it to him, reluctantly. "Pray help yourself to the refreshments, ladies."

He leaned back in his chair and studied the signature. "Braxton Sinclair . . ." he muttered.

"What's that?" Miss Maisie demanded.

"Oh, I was but musing, dear lady, on the workings of fate. 'Let Hercules himself do what he may, The cat will mew, and dog will have his day.' *Hamlet,* Act Five."

"Dang if I can make you out sometimes," Miss Minnie said. Then hastily she added, "But Maisie just thrives on that kind of fancy talk, don't you?"

"Why, you know I like a plain-spoken feller. It's you that . . ."

Gently Zan asked, "What about fate, Uncle Fred?"

"Nothing, my dear. Merely that I see an old acquaintance of mine has achieved his fondest wish and purchased himself a seat in the British Parliament." He surveyed the yard. "I wonder where Edward has taken himself off to? He should read this letter at once; it may be important."

Putting aside their glaring for the moment, Miss Minnie and Miss Maisie pricked up their ears once more. "If this Sinclair feller's a friend of yours," Miss Maisie said, "why's he writing to Ed?"

"And I would've sworn," her sister added, "that there's a woman's handwriting."

Peering over Uncle Fred's shoulder, Zan took a good look at the writing. The lines were very even, written in deep black ink. From the *T* in *The* to the final *S* in *States*, every letter bore a burden of fancy touches, spirals, loops, and flourishes, as though it were written with a loosely trailed ribbon. The writer had really let herself go on the capital letters in Edward's name until it was all but unreadable.

"Kind of a wonder it even made it this far," she said.

Into her head came a picture, very small, but bright and clear. A dainty hand, white as flour with clean, pointed nails, took up a silver pen from a desk made of some highly polished reddish wood. The foaming ruffles of lace and blue satin were shaken back as the writer dipped the pen into a glass ball full of ink. Sunlight streamed in through gently moving curtains, also of lace, and lit the inkwell like the dangling baubles of Miss Lottie's best lamp. The rainbows dancing from the inkwell hurt Zan's eyes, and she couldn't see anymore.

"Well?" Miss Maisie demanded. "Why is this friend of yours writing to Ed?"

"I haven't any idea." Uncle Fred tucked the letter into his pocket. "More lemonade, ladies?"

Zan picked up the pitcher and swished it invitingly. "And you've hardly eaten a bite."

The two ladies exchanged a glance. "Don't mind if we do," Miss Minnie said, making herself more comfortable in her chair. Miss Maisie followed her sister's lead.

They looked to Zan as if they were planning to stay until Judgment Day, if that was the only way to snoop into the contents of the letter. She was a little surprised they brought it all the way up to the Double B, without satisfying their curiosity with steam. The blob of half-crumbled crimson sealing wax on the back wouldn't have deterred them long.

She could understand their fascination. For one thing, nobody knew very much about Edward except Uncle Fred, though she supposed she herself could now set up as an expert on the man. For another, a body couldn't help but feel a thrill at the sight of a letter from a far-off foreign country, as long as it wasn't from Sweden.

Half the people in the county probably knew by now the contents of Quintus Widstrand's latest letter to her father. She could only be glad they hadn't all commiserated with her for still being single. She couldn't act well enough to appear properly despondent at her suitor's nonarrival. It might be hard to convince folks she was unhappy while grinning all over her face.

"I'd like your advice about something, ladies," Uncle Fred began. Zan wondered if he'd come up with a way to distract Maisie and Minnie from their wait for Edward. "You, too, Zan."

"Shoot."

"As you know, the Fourth of July is rapidly approaching."

"What's it to you?" Miss Maisie asked. "You being a Britisher and all."

"I have tremendous admiration for your citizens, your nation, and your founding fathers. Yet I cannot but feel some regret at the failure of our two nations to fuse into one, indivisible whole. To me, your Declaration Day is a sad time."

"Advice?" Zan muttered, seeing the stalwartly patriotic faces before her crumple into disapproval.

"Ah, yes. Do you think it would be acceptable in the community if I hosted a little celebration on the Third of July? Not in any pushing way, you understand. No, rather to commemorate the last day of the formerly happy state of affairs existing between the British Empire and what was to become the Thirteen Original States of your glorious union."

"You want to do what?" Miss Minnie asked, squinting.

Zan said, "I think it's a fine idea, Uncle Fred. Where do you want to hold it? And who are you going to invite?"

"Everyone, of course. I understand from your sister that there will be many families coming in from the outlying farms for the Fourth. And as for location, what do you say to the mill?"

"The mill?" Miss Maisie asked.

"Why not? It has a solid floor for dancing and is not often in use at this time of the year."

"It's not very clean," Zan said doubtfully. The condition of the mill had been on her mind, what little of it she could spare from the farm and Edward.

"Ah," Fred said with the twinkle coming once more into his eyes. "I believe that a few of the younger bucks would not be adverse to lending a hand there, so long as they were promised as a reward the opportunity to squire beautiful ladies about the floor. I am thinking specifically of your friends Otto and Joseph. No doubt their friends would help them."

"You're right there," Miss Maisie said. "Anything for fun."

"Of course," Uncle Fred added with a bow, "I must rely on you ladies' good sense and organizational abilities to lend a style and elegance to little idea."

"I don't know . . ." Miss Minnie drawled.

Miss Maisie said, "Sounds all right to me. Been quite a little while since we had a chance to kick up our heels. You wouldn't guess it to look at her, but my sister used to be able to kick a hat off a feller's head."

"Maisie!"

"Well, it's true, ain't it? I remember once you kicked your husband in the head, but he knew you didn't mean it. He shouldn't of flinched."

Finally the two women agreed to organize with some of the other ladies in town to provide refreshments, though as Maisie said, "You can't expect 'em to lay out as fancy a spread as there'll be on the Fourth. Course, the young girls will most likely go all out, since there's always going to be a chance of catching a man with something particular good to eat."

"Excellent!" Uncle Fred clapped his hands. "And I shall provide a flowing bowl of the warm south . . . the true, the blushful Hippocrene."

"What's that?" Miss Minnie asked. "Some kind of fruit punch?"

"Something like that," Uncle Fred admitted. "Rich and strange, I'm sure you'll find."

Zan said, "You'll have to talk it over with Mrs. Taylor."

"She'll come 'round," Miss Maisie said. "Catch Lillie Taylor passing up a chance like this."

Though the ladies sat until the fireflies began to wink in the early twilight, and every morsel had gone, Edward didn't come back. "Gone to the saloon, more 'n likely," Miss Minnie whispered to her sister.

"Wouldn't be surprised," Miss Maisie replied with a sour mouth.

Zan's quick ears caught the whispers. She caught back a protest. Why shouldn't a man get drunk once in a while, so long as it wasn't a daily thing? Especially when he was as confused as Edward.

She understood his confusion as clearly as if they'd talked it over. He fought against the lure of this land, trying with all the pride and stubbornness he had inside not to give into the richness of the soil and the vastness of the sky. But all she had to do was watch him working on the fields to know how powerfully Kansas had pulled him in. He didn't dare show this country his infatuation because then it would really have him for good.

Looking out into the velvet dusk, the sticky air glazing her skin, Zan felt a kinship with her home even deeper than any she'd known before. Edward felt the same way about her as he did about this country, trapped maybe, struggling still to be free, but slowly becoming unable to resist anymore.

Soon he'd be glad not to struggle. Love would make him forget that he'd not come to Kansas, to her, cheerfully and with a good heart. All she had to do was wait and try to keep her own love for him locked up. It got away from her today, in the hayloft. She had to see to that it didn't slip out again until he was ready to hear.

CHAPTER
16

Miss Minnie slapped at the back of her left hand, then flicked off the dead mosquito with her right forefinger. "They're sure coming out."

Though the faint whines of the long-legged blood-suckers sang in her ears, Zan sat easily. Her brown skin mightn't be ladylike, but fleas or mosquitoes never troubled her. She wiped away a smile as Miss Maisie swatted the side of her face. Would skeeters win over curiosity?

It turned out to be a tie. The two spinsters were settling into their buggy, the patient horse given the order to start, when Edward walked into the farmyard, the dog he'd purchased gamboling around his feet like a puppy. Zan had only to glance at him to see that if he'd not found some decision in his walking, he had at least found weariness enough to stop him from thinking.

Maisie pulled on the reins. "Oh, we forgot! Minnie, wasn't there a recipe . . . ?"

"Why, yes! Uh . . . cocoa cake, wasn't it? Mr. Fred, do you reckon you could write that up for me . . . ?"

Fred's hesitation was visible. He said, "I shall personally

deliver it tomorrow." Zan thought it brave of him to run into danger of matrimony to save his nephew from the ladies' inquisitiveness.

Edward belatedly took off his hat to salute them. "Evening, ladies."

"There's a letter for you, Mr. Winchester," Miss Minnie said. "We brought it out from town."

His gaze went to his uncle, standing on the porch. Uncle Fred put his hand to his breast pocket and showed Edward a corner of the letter. "From England, my boy."

"I see. That was thoughtful of you, Mrs. Parker, Mrs. Hastings. I am much obliged for your pains. I trust you will have no difficulty driving home? It is dark."

"We've often been out later than this, haven't we, Minnie?"

"Oh, often. And I can't go away without that recipe your uncle promised. I want to try it out tonight, so I'll learn it before the party." Miss Minnie held out her hand for Edward to help her descend.

He did not provide the support. "Strange," he said. "Your boarders gave me to understand that you are ever punctual to meals. They are quite worried at your absence now."

"You *were* in town then?" Miss Minnie took in two or three deep breaths through her large nose.

"Your boarders are considering alerting Sheriff Miller to your plight. There was some talk about abduction."

"Gossip's a dreadful thing," Uncle Fred said. " 'I find the people strangely fantasied, possessed with rumors,' *King John*, I believe, a lesser known play but with its own sweet music."

Even with the idea planted that they might be the target of gossip rather than the source of it, the two ladies were visibly torn. The foreign letter was a mystery all but irresistible, but to be chattered over was impossible. Miss Maisie slapped the reins over the startled horse's back.

Zan could sympathize with this frustration. She wanted desperately to know what the fancy Englishwoman had written to Edward. As her heart began to hurt inside, she recognized her own fear. Edward had not yet glanced in her direction. As best she could, Zan shrank into the shadows by the house wall.

"Who's the letter from, Uncle?" He rested one foot on the porch step and absently ruffled Spotted Dick's feathered ears.

"The frank is signed 'Braxton Sinclair.'"

"Is she still having her father do all the dirty work for her, then?"

Zan swelled with hope. That hadn't been the tone of a man sick with longing for a lost love.

"Who can say? All that's plain is that it is not her husband's name across the corner." Uncle Fred pulled out the folded paper and gave it to him.

Edward weighed it in his hand. Then he slid his thumb under the seal. The red wax crumbled and the bits fell to the floor. With an impatient flick of his wrist, he opened the page. He tilted it back and forth in attempt to get sufficient light.

"God, Nerissa's handwriting! Why can a woman never print?"

"There's better light inside," Fred said.

Edward nodded his thanks and strode up the steps and into the house. The thud of his steps shook the boards, and the vibration jogged right up into Zan. She crept to the open door to peek inside.

"My dear," Uncle Fred said softly, "you really shouldn't . . ."

They heard the short, mirthless laugh. Then Edward came stalking back. Once again, Zan retreated to the shadows. Uncle Fred blew out the single lantern on the untidy table. "It's bringing out the insects," he said by way of explanation.

Edward paid no attention. "Rejoice with me, Uncle. It would seem all my difficulties are solved."

"Indeed, my boy?"

"Far be it for me to bandy a woman's name. . . ."

"It is from Lady Dernwood, then?"

"Yes. She writes to inform me that her husband has died."

"Ah, that was thoughtful of her."

Edward strode back and forth between the door and the steps. "Thoughtful? Yes. She writes how difficult things are for a solitary widow—business, ledgers, legal matters. They make her head spin. And how lonely she is." He held up the letter as though he'd read it again in the near dark.

"I imagine the last is true." Uncle Fred began to collect the used dishes, loading them on a tray. "I cannot imagine she and Lord Dernwood had very many interests in common. His friends, those that survive him, would have little time for a young bride, nor, with his choices in friendship, would one wish them to associate with her now that Dernwood is no longer about to protect her good name."

Abruptly Edward stopped pacing. His voice changed, became less brusque, almost sentimental. "Yes, I can imagine that crowd of lechers circling about her. Nerissa was lovely, wasn't she? All that soft black hair, and milk not whiter than her skin. She had one of the loveliest speaking voices I have ever heard. How tired I grow sometimes of the squeaks and rattles that pass for speech out here at the end of the world."

"I admit that the women of America hardly coo like doves. If I miss anything, it is that." Uncle Fred gave himself a little shake, and Zan knew he'd remembered her presence. "Well, what else does Lady Dernwood write?"

"Does it matter? The very fact that she is bold enough to write at all speaks volumes. All this about how lawyers' questions make her head go 'round and how she wishes for someone strong and decisive to help her is just pretense. I feel confident that her father protects her well. This letter, my dear sir, is no cry for aid. It is tantamount to a proposal!"

"And as her father signed for it . . ."

"I cannot imagine Nerissa going so far as to write such a letter to me without Papa's full cognizance. Damn me, he probably stood at her elbow to dictate each word."

"You believe he wouldn't now stand in the way of your marriage with Nerissa?"

"If she's inherited any part of Dernwood's properties, I imagine he's out of his depth. For all his vaunted shrewdness, I cannot imagine Braxton Sinclair dealing well with bailiffs, stewards, and tenantry. Or, for that matter, the *haut monde*. Have you ever had the privilege of watching him hunt? A boy of ten would take his fences with more fortitude."

"I have heard he can put a person's back up."

"Yes," Edward said dryly. "He can do that."

Sinclair had said things to him once which, from a younger man, would have meant pistol shots in a cold, gray dawn. Or at the least, a split lip and blackened eyes. But one did not challenge one's social inferiors or strike men old enough to be one's father. Being a Winchester, he forced his anger and his wounded love into silence, had bowed and walked out. To have Sinclair now acknowledge that a penniless son of a peer might have worthy qualifications as a son-in-law served as very sweet revenge. Nerissa was as exquisite as a painting on china and every bit as fragile.

"What will you do now?" Uncle Fred asked.

"Answer this letter, certainly. Beyond that, I do not know." He glanced again at the paper in his hand. "There's Zan . . ."

For all she knew, her heart had stopped beating some time ago. Now she could feel it again, slamming into her side so strongly that she almost cried out.

"Yes . . . what about Zan?"

"She needs this crop to make her dreams come true, and to escape matrimony to this . . . rustic her father has in mind for her. I cannot walk away from her. She is my partner, of sorts. She would stay to help me—try to be rid of her!"

"She is a most honorable young lady."

"I, therefore, should stay to help her. On the other hand, I could simply make her my steward. Perhaps give her a higher percentage of the eventual profits. My own father couldn't ask for a more efficient employee, though he'd undoubtedly balk at hiring a woman."

"Balk? He'd have an apoplexy at the very thought!" Edward grinned and Uncle Fred said, "Can you imagine his reaction if a young and beautiful girl walked up to him and said, 'I have come to help you with your crops'? At the least he'd burst his collar button, and probably his stays as well."

Edward's smile faded. "I can imagine all too well Father's reaction to Zan. Though, you know, Mother would probably like her, though never as my . . ."

"Yes, my boy?" Uncle Fred asked, giving his nephew a sharp look. But Edward had turned away from even the feeble light that came through the door.

"I shall have to think well on what my reply shall be to this," he said, flicking his hand against the letter. "Cool, I think. It will not do, to be too eager. And if I should go back, it will not be to grovel to Braxton Sinclair."

"Certainly not!"

"But think of it, Uncle! London! The cool, green squares and Georgian houses! The Embankment! Simpson's in the Strand!"

"You almost make me wish I were there again. And then I remember . . . pea-soup fogs, drafty drawing rooms, and insipid conversations in which to mention a leg in mixed company is to bring about social ostracism."

"Is that all England means to you, Uncle?"

"You know it is not. And yet, all that is part of our nation as well as a 'precious stone set in the silver sea.' "

"True, very true. But it doesn't matter. 'Where'er I wander, boast of this I can: Though banished, yet a true-born Englishman.' "

"*Richard the Second*?"

"Exactly." Edward shook his head. "Besides, what else is there for me? I have made no very great success of farming."

"Zan seems to think. . . ."

"Zan is . . . ."

"Yes?"

"She's infatuated with me, I'm afraid." His voice was hatefully amused.

"And you?"

"I? She's a charming child, of course."

"I am an old man, Edward, yet even I can see she is no 'child.' Quite the contrary. I should say she is a woman, and moreover, one who knows her own mind well. Certainly worthy of a good man's affection and name."

"Yes, you're right. But the right sort of man, Uncle. One who wouldn't cringe at the things she does and says."

"Yet you called her charming."

"Certainly, but she is hardly a sophisticate. Tomboy, I believe they call it here. Hoyden, as we should say. She would never fit in at home."

"There is an alternative. You could stay here. There is no country finer in all the world. Take my word for that!"

"I do, Uncle." Edward walked to the edge of the porch and looked out into the darkness. The fireflies winked as they floated through the still air. "And I confess . . . at times . . . this country does speak to a man, even a failure like myself."

He shook his head as though to clear it. "If I had no other choice but to stay, I should stay and be well content. But now—" Edward rattled the letter in his hand. "Now I have a choice. Everything I've ever wanted."

"And if your wants have changed?" Uncle Fred's voice scarcely carried.

"They have not. They cannot." He folded the letter up and slipped it into his pocket. "I shall meditate tonight on how to phrase my reply to Nerissa and her father."

Uncle Fred lifted the tray again to carry it into the house. "You must be hungry, my boy. I've kept something warm for you on the stove."

"Let me see to the cattle first, Uncle." He walked down the front steps. "Did Zan take her mules home?"

"I don't believe that she did."

When Edward was safely out of earshot, Uncle Fred said, "Oh, my poor child."

"He can't mean it," Zan answered, stepping out.

"I'm afraid he does."

"But he doesn't love her! He couldn't. I bet she's awful sappy."

"From what I recall of Lady Dernwood, I believe you are right. Not one of our great original thinkers, to be sure. Very fond of wondering aloud what her papa would say."

"Kind of pretty, though, like he said." She wondered if dying her hair black would do any good.

"Pretty? Yes. But she will never gain true beauty, as you have done."

"And I'll never be a lady like she is." Zan put her fingers to her throbbing temples. "I don't have a chance in hell of keeping him in Kansas, do I?"

Gently Uncle Fred took her hand and chafed it. "My dear girl, being a lady isn't . . . Goodness, Nerissa Dernwood isn't any different than you are. Her father isn't the scion of a hundred earls or anything near it. And her mother is the daughter of a Yorkshire mill owner."

"I don't understand. You all call her Lady."

"Well, yes, because she married a titled gentleman. But her blood isn't one whit bluer than your own. All those other things . . . the air of quality, the refinement, knowing what is what and who is who . . . all were taught to her."

"Yeah, she probably learned it all in her cradle."

"Nonsense. Her father didn't become the wealthy fellow he is today until Nerissa was . . . eight? She grew up barefoot, my child, with her hair in a tangle. And if she can learn all it takes to be a lady, so can you and faster than a child might. Believe me. Believe the Bard. 'She is not so old but she may learn.' *The Merchant of Venice*, Act Three."

"So," Zan said, finishing her explanation. "I thought I should come to you."

"Well, I can't say you were wrong. What I don't know about turning a sow's ear into a silk purse . . . No offense." Miss Lottie toyed with the gleaming gold bracelets on her left wrist, all the while studying Zan through half-closed eyelids. "You're not a bad-looking gal. You just don't make the most out of what God gave you, that's all."

Zan sat up a little straighter in the soft armchair in Miss Lottie's own private room. Everything in her room was soft, from the lace draped over the dressing table to the slightly rumpled covers of the big bedstead. A big red-glass lamp shed a delicately rosy glow. Getting sight of herself in the large mirror by the headboard, Zan saw that the light flattered her skin and made her eyes seem bigger. Lottie must be the right person to consult.

"Course," she said aloud, "I've got to be more than pretty. He wants a lady."

"Pretty never hurt a girl's chances. And as for ladies . . . more 'n one of the girls I've worked with before now have married fine gentlemen and done themselves proud. Why, if the truth were known, I'd bet half the society women in San Francisco started out working on their backs."

Zan paid no mind to Miss Lottie's musings. "Can I wear a dress like that?"

"Nice, isn't it?" Lottie ran a hand over her tightly uphol-stered figure. Zan thought her black velvet dress the loveliest thing she'd ever seen. Spangles flashed even in the low light, all along the shoulders and following the plunging lines of the bodice. Miss Lottie's shoulders and full bust looked very white in comparison with the luxurious black fabric.

"Wouldn't do for you, though," Miss Lottie said, after consideration. "You don't weigh what I do."

"You're not fat!"

"I never said I was. I'm . . . comfortable. Least, I've never heard many complaints. But you want a dress that'll make you look young and sweet. Kind of innocent like. I don't have anything like that around here . . . 'cept that Little Bo-Peep . . . Never mind. You go see Jane Carson tomorrow and have something made up, special. Lots of ribbons and floating stuff."

"Ribbons?" Zan asked, downcast.

"What'd you think, baby? Denim and rawhide? First thing you got to do is dress right. Men are simple, you know? They believe what their eyes tell 'em. Now a woman, 'specially one in my line of work, we know better. Cash down and don't believe nothing you see before he's got his clothes off."

"I guess so."

Miss Lottie smiled. It took all the hardness from her face. "Don't you pay me no mind. I'm just running off at the mouth." She took another squint at Zan. "Just how long *is* your hair, anyway?"

Zan took out the thong she used to hold it back. Shaking out the braid, she drew the thick switch forward, letting the springy waves tumble over her shoulder. "I keep thinking about cutting it off. It gets in the way something terrible and is awful hard to keep clean."

"Don't you dare!"

"That's what Mother says."

"You listen to her." Lottie ran her hand almost reverently over the long golden mass. "If I had hair like that, and your face, there's no way I would of ended up running a house in Harmony, Kansas. Paris, France, maybe. Or New Orleans. Maybe even a palace. Then I'd be a courtesan, not a . . . well, I can't complain. Much."

She stepped back. "Anyway, a squeeze of lemon in the rinse water, a trim to neaten it all up, and then piled up high in a knot on the back of your head. Leave just a few little bits coming down. Men always fall for that."

"My mother rinses it with vinegar."

"No, that's for brunettes to polish up the red. Blondes should always use lemon, to brighten the gold. And I know a way to take the roughness out of your hands and lighten up that tan. Good thing you don't have freckles. They *never* come out."

"Mother also has me using Lily Lotion."

"That stuff! Nothing but fraud in a bottle. You leave all that to me."

"Maybe you ought to go into the patent medicine business."

Miss Lottie froze and blinked as though in a sudden strong light. "Maybe I ought to," she said slowly. Then she shook the thought away. "Right now let's concentrate on you. You want to look like a lady by the third. Well, you come back tomorrow and me and the girls will give you the full treatment. That'll give your skin a couple of days to calm down— it may be a little red for a day or two."

Leaving the First Resort by the back stair so she wouldn't see any customers, Zan felt considerably better. She had

Lottie on her side, and Uncle Fred had promised to help her speak more elegantly. He had praised her for never using *ain't* and chuckled at her explanation that her mother would have died of shame if any of her children had sunk so low.

She wondered if it was too late to call on Miss Carson. Though her own interest in fancy clothes was minimal, Samantha Spencer used Jane to sew for her, and she had duds that were even fancier than Miss Lottie's. Maybe she ought to stop by the You Sew and Sew, just to see what Miss Carson had ready to go.

Zan's stomach rumbled and she remembered that she hadn't yet had supper. Somehow seeing Miss Lottie had been more important than going home. Her mother would assume she would be staying to supper at the Double B. Now, however, the memory of the cookies and cheese she'd eaten with Uncle Fred and his guests only served to make her hungrier.

Walking up the street, Zan didn't see any lights in the windows of the seamstress's bright green shop. The hotel, however, was sending out welcoming beams from the back windows. Surely Faith wouldn't mind handing out a meal on the cuff to her own sister.

She stood up on tiptoe to peek in the kitchen window. After all, Faith and her husband hadn't been married very long and if there was a romantic evening going on, she wouldn't bust in. But the scene that met her eyes was quietly domestic.

The family sat around the kitchen table, a lamp shedding warm, steady light over them. Faith's hands were busy with mending, though she smiled as she listened to Kincaid reading aloud from *Harper's*. Little Amanda stood near her father's chair, her head resting on his shoulder.

Zan dropped down, tears stinging her eyes. She could so easily imagine this as her family—Edward reading something out from one of his books, their children, red-haired and bright, taking time from their play to listen, and herself . . .

225

though she doubted she'd be sewing. Going over the accounts would be more likely. Maybe Uncle Fred would be there, too, bouncing the youngest baby on his knee.

"Who's there?" Faith called from the back door.

"Just me. Zan."

"Zan? What on earth are you, doing here?"

"I was in town anyway; thought I'd stop by and see if there was any supper going."

Kincaid appeared behind his wife. "Who is it, Faith? Oh, it's you. Come on in."

As Faith bustled around, laying out cold chicken and potatoes, Kincaid leaned close to Zan and whispered, "Those seeds and bulbs have come in. When can you . . . ?"

"I don't know. Next week? I've got something else to do before the third."

Faith poured a glass of milk for her sister. "What's this I hear about Fred Winchester giving some kind of fancy party on the third of July?"

"You know about that already?"

"Why, sure. Mrs. Parker and Mrs. Hastings stopped by on the way back from the Double B. They said they wanted to let everyone know they hadn't been abducted."

Kincaid chuckled. "As if anyone would dare."

"It would take a mighty desperate desperado to lay a finger on either of 'em," Zan agreed. "But, yes, Uncle Fred is having some kind of a shindig, at the mill, with any luck."

"Well, it's to be hoped, Zan Lind, that you don't go and make a fool of yourself like you did with that horse race. And you looked so nice that day, too, all dressed up."

Amanda piped up, "All the kids thought it was awful brave of you, Aunt Zan."

"Thank you, honey. But Faith is right."

"I was never so humiliated in all my born days. To think

that my sister . . . why Father didn't put a stop to it . . . What did you say?"

"I said you are right." She sipped meekly from her glass, watching Faith adjust to this new concept.

"I am?"

"Yes, you are. If I had the brains God gave a goose, I would have found someone else to ride when Joseph couldn't."

"But you nearly won," Kincaid pointing out.

"It wasn't worth it. I've got to stop acting like a wild Indian. You ought to know, Kincaid, that men prefer a quiet, peaceful sort of girl."

"Men?" Faith asked, sitting down heavily in a vacant chair. She stared at Zan as if her younger sister had suddenly started speaking in Choctaw.

"Come on, Amanda," Kincaid said. "It's about your bed-time, isn't it?"

"Not for half an hour," she protested.

"Well, I'll finish reading this story to you, first." He picked up the magazine from the table.

"Oh," the little girl said, nodding wisely. "They want to talk about lady's stuff, huh?" United in contempt, for a few more years at least, Kincaid and his daughter slipped out of the kitchen.

Faith fixed her sister with a probing glance. "It's Otto Krensler, isn't it? He's a fine, upstanding boy, though not likely to set the prairie afire. Does Father know? He'll be so pleased."

Zan swallowed a bite of chicken. "No, it's not Otto. Believe that. It's—"

"Couldn't be Joseph Taylor. I know he thinks you're pretty, but he also told me you were almost as good as a man, and I don't think a beau would talk that way."

"Are you going to run through every bachelor in town? It's not Joseph, or Zeke Gallagher for that matter."

"So he's a widower? Let me see . . . Alexander Evans? It's about time he married again. I know he's been lonely since Samantha got married and—"

Zan put her hand over her sister's to silence her. "It's Edward Winchester. I'm in love with His Lordship."

CHAPTER
17

There was real satisfaction in flabbergasting Faith twice in ten minutes. "That's . . . that's impossible," she said, not politely, but maybe with some truth. "He'd never . . . he's so stuck on himself he'd never give you a second look."

"Hey," Zan said with a shrug, "I didn't say he was in love with me; I said I was in love with him. There's a great big difference there, you know."

"Oh, good. Then you've got nothing to worry about."

"Nothing?"

"There's not much point in eating your heart out over somebody who doesn't care for you. It ought to be easy to put him out of your head. And Otto's a real nice boy. Or you could wait for Quintus Widstrand, like Father wants you to."

Zan shook her head. "If somebody had told you a couple of months ago to just forget about Kincaid, would you have been able to do it? Without a pang?"

Faith's silence was answer enough.

"Me, either. And maybe you're right. Maybe Edward won't ever care for me, but I've got to try and make him see that I'm the right one for him."

"But he's used to fine ladies and their la-di-da ways. You're . . ." Faith spread her hands, at a loss for words.

"I'm working on it."

"Working on what? His farm?"

"Nope. Deportment and manners. How to be la-di-da. I'm going to be a lady by the third if it kills me. And it just might." Zan outlined her plan.

"Lottie! You told Lottie about this before me, your own flesh and blood!"

"I figure Lottie will be the most help."

"A common prosti . . . She can't teach you how to be a lady. How can she teach you what she doesn't know?"

"Oh, Lottie knows a sight more than you might think."

"For instance?" Faith said, her eyes narrow.

"She knows how to talk to men and make 'em like her. I don't have the least notion how to do that."

"Of course you do. You talk to men all the time, and they like you. They even listen to you."

"I mean about something besides what kind of manure works best on wheat. And what the combines and Congress have been doing lately to ruin farmers. I need to know how to talk lightly to 'em. Miss Lottie knows how to do that. And she knows how to dress and how to walk. And how to flirt."

"No respectable woman wants to know how to flirt."

"Seems to me you did all right in that area, once upon a time. How many fellers did you have on the string?"

Faith colored. With some effort she said, "That wasn't flirting. That was . . . being nice. No boy ever thought for one minute that I was a loose woman or tried to kiss me or anything. I had never been kissed before Kincaid."

"That's not what I've heard."

"Well, if I ever was before, I've forgotten all about it. You forget that kind of thing when you meet the right man."

"The only man who's ever kissed me . . ." Zan began. She closed her mouth and gave her sister a half smile. Faith could be very sweet, but she also told their mother everything and always had. Better to keep what had happened between Edward and herself *between* Edward and herself.

Faith leaned forward, intent on Zan's half-spoken thought. "Who's kissed you? Don't tell me . . . ! What have you been up to at the Double B?"

"I won't tell you 'cause there's nothing to tell. I spend most of my time working or listening to Uncle Fred spout Shakespeare. You know, he's got pages and pages of that stuff learned off by heart."

"Don't try to change the subject. Say, is it true that Miss Minnie and Miss Maisie are after Mr. Winchester? I could have sworn Miss Minnie blushed when his name was mentioned."

"If she did, it was from pure vexation." Having already taken Faith so far into her confidence, Zan decided to tell the rest of the story. "They were all but ready to grab that letter back from his hand the second he'd opened it."

"So that's why you want to be a lady," her sister said, nodding in comprehension. "It'll never work. Especially not with Miss Luscious Lottie as your instructor."

"She does know a powerful lot about what tickles a man's fancy."

"Too much. You need someone with the right amount of reserve, and style. I can promise you that he'll be more interested if you play hard-to-get. Men just love that don't-touch-me air."

"That what you did?"

"Absolutely!" If Faith recalled a night of unwed passion in a ramshackle hotel, she gave no sign of it.

"All the same, I don't want to hurt her feelings. And she has offered to help me out and nobody else has. I reckon Miss

Carson will listen to Lottie when it comes time to fix up a dress for me."

"There isn't time to make a whole dress."

"I know, but maybe Miss Carson has something she can make over to fit."

The next day Zan found it difficult to face Edward. Not only had he seen, and handled, parts of her body that no one ever had, but he'd seen her eager and passionate. He had to be thinking of her that way when he saw her. Zan knew she was thinking about it, being unable to get those moments in the hayloft out of her head.

She stammered and stumbled through her greeting. Edward, however, was grave and civil. His eyes did not travel over her, but sought the distance past her shoulder. "What more needs to be done in the fields today?"

"Best thing to do now is nothing. Let the plants get a good hold before we get after the weeds."

"Very well. I shall continue to work on the barn; it requires much attention."

"You do like hard work."

"As do you."

Zan knew she'd sunk pretty low when three small words (and not even the *right* three) could make her blush and hang her head in confused elation. "If you want me to earn my pay, I could clean out the barn, or root around in your garden patch. I noticed Uncle Fred's having some trouble with his back."

"Sciatica."

"You're welcome."

He chuckled and walked away, shaking his head. Zan stared after him, her heart tumbling inside her body at the sight of a single erratic strand of his hair standing up at the back of his head. She had to clench her fists, for her fingers tingled with the desire to smooth it down.

Later that afternoon, as she walked into town, Zan repeated out loud Uncle Fred's recommendations for improving her voice. He'd given her a sonnet from his favorite author to memorize and to practice, cautioning her to remember always to speak slowly, allowing each sound to develop fully from the chest. She tried to match her own voice to her memories of Edward's, imitating the velvety smoothness of his voice. Try as she might, however, even to her own ears she sounded as elegant as a squawking chicken.

Pushing open the bright door to the seamstress's shop, she tried out her new low, soft tone. "Hello? Is anybody here?"

Raised voices came from the back, behind the curtain that separated the workroom from the selling floor. Zan walked past the assortment of white blouses, the uncut fabrics, and the lovely, frivolous hats to peek in. Her eyes popped open in surprise.

Both Faith and Miss Lottie were in the back room. Each woman gestured with more or less disapproval at a simple blue dress on a dress form. Miss Carson stood between them, her pretty mouth prickly with pins, nodding as each made her point.

"Hello?" Zan said again. "What's going on?"

All three women looked at her. Faith asked, "Are you coming down with a cold? You sound funny."

"Good," Miss Lottie said. "Now you're here, you can try on this glad rag, and she'll see that I'm right."

"You are not right," Faith countered. "That neckline doesn't need to be altered even a quarter inch. We want her to look like a lady born and bred, not a—"

"Whore?" Miss Lottie smiled. "I been called worse. But believe me, it'd take a lot more than showing a little chest to make her look like a whore. Take a good look at her face and you'll see what I mean."

Zan flushed under the three ladies' steady scrutiny. It would have been pleasanter to face Miss Minnie and Miss Maisie visibly wondering if she were pregnant. "I'll go and put it on, if you want me to. Uh, where?"

Miss Carson swept aside a second curtain and pushed the dress form into the little dark space. Zan could still hear every word her sister and Miss Lottie said. It sounded as if their arguing had gone on for some time with neither one willing to budge an inch on their point of view.

"It's really good of you all to help me," she said, loudly enough to break in before the level of acrimony could rise again. "I don't know how I'd manage on my own."

She came out after a few minutes of struggle. The dress fell a little short of her ankles, and her wrists stuck awkwardly out of the too-brief sleeves. She found it difficult to draw a full breath, as the high bodice had been made for a slighter figure than her own.

Half laughing, she said, "I feel like too much sausage in too little skin."

Then, however, she looked into the big cheval mirror and couldn't glance away. The blue material had a soft sheen to it, the ruffles at the neck mellowing the strong line of her jaw. She raised a hand to see if the figure in the mirror did the same. Only then could she be certain it really was herself she saw reflected.

"What do you think?" Zan asked when nobody said anything.

Miss Lottie took a couple of hairpins out of her own tumbled tresses. Catching up Zan's braid, she twisted it into a flat bun and skewered it. After taking a step back, she said, "Well . . ."

"It'll have to be let out." Faith squinted at her sister. "Way out. Either that, or you're going to have to stop eating everything set in front of you."

"There's no time for a reducing diet," Miss Lottie said. "Is there enough material in the seams?"

Miss Carson nodded and knelt down at Zan's feet. Taking out a little tool from where it was stuck, daggerlike, in her belt, she began to rip open the hem seam. With a quick glance up at Zan's face, Miss Carson gave her a fast wink. Zan smiled, knowing her clothes at least were in safe, sure hands.

"Maybe if a couple of ruffles were added to the sleeves," Faith said doubtfully.

"It would work to hide her hands." Miss Lottie turned Zan's hand over. "Look at these calluses! Rough as a cowboy's. At least her nails aren't too bumpy with ridges. They'll be all right with a little buffing up."

Zan drew breath to speak, and one of the tiny buttons flew off her bodice as loudly as gunshot in the small room. Faith and Lottie both ducked. Zan put her hand to the open spot on the placket. "Maybe I should bind 'em down a little?"

"No!" The two ladies glanced at each other, the merest hint of a smile emerging on both pairs of lips.

"It'll be all right once Jane's done with it." Faith let her smile grow. "I always told you, Zan, that you could be very pretty if you took the time to fancy yourself up a little."

"After all," Miss Lottie added, "it doesn't take long to make yourself presentable. Every girl needs to make an effort to show herself off to good advantage."

As wagonloads of farm families began to arrive on the third, Zan saw what her sister and Miss Lottie had meant. Never had she seen so many bright, scrubbed faces, so much exotic and downright dangerous hairdressing, and such frills and furbelows. And that was just the boys!

Every girl was starched and ironed within an inch of her life. The rustling as they disembarked from the wagons sounded like the passage of a thousand birds overhead. Many of the flounced skirts covered heavy boots and many pairs of gloves hid hands as rough and red as her own. Yet what each girl could do to improve herself had been done with determination.

Zan smiled and waved to the people she knew, yet did not stop long to visit. The final fitting of the blue dress had been yesterday and she must hurry to collect it. Miss Lottie and Faith waited for her back at the hotel, with a hot curling iron and a glut of last-minute advice.

Distracted for a moment by the sight of two wagons narrowly missing a crash, she did not look where she was going. Warm hands, whose touch roused all her yearnings, fended her off while a dearly familiar voice chuckled, "You don't have to knock me down, Zan. I was intending to ask you for the first dance for tonight regardless."

"You were?"

Edward nodded, his gray eyes still twinkling. "If you can bear with my clumsiness. Even at home I was never known for my grace in the ballroom."

"I don't dance much better than a trained dog myself," she admitted and then paused, her thoughts busy with the advice she'd heard from her eager teachers.

"Make promises with your eyes that you deny with what you say," Miss Lottie had said, fluttering her eyelashes to demonstrate the technique.

"A lady never permits a gentleman to think her preference is set," Uncle Fred warned.

"You got to keep 'em guessing," Faith had told her, nodding wisely. *"If they think they know where they're at, they stop being interested in you. A girl's got to make a man dizzy so he'll stick around."*

All week Zan had been trying hard to act just as usual around Edward. She'd kept her hard-won airs and graces a secret, planning to surprise him with her perfection in all ladylike arts during this special evening to come. But maybe it wasn't too soon to practice what she'd learned.

"I don't know if I can," she said, dropping her lashes onto her cheeks.

"Ah, well . . . Perhaps another time, then."

"Perhaps." Damn! she thought.

Edward stepped back so his shadow no longer fell on her. "I won't keep you."

"Thank you. I've got to get cleaned . . . I mean, I'd better think about changing for this evening."

He watched her hurry along the boardwalk toward the blazing storefront that housed the dressmaker's. If he hadn't known her so well, he would have thought she seemed frightened of him. With an impatient jerk of his shoulders, he continued down the street, his face so forbidding that at least two farm girls swore they'd never marry red-haired men with their terrible tempers.

Edward told himself he was glad Zan had come to her senses at last. He'd noticed all week how quiet she'd been whenever they were together, and he approved the change. Obviously he had forced her to face something unpleasant about herself and the resulting introspection had shaken her confidence. Sometimes the old spark flashed in her eyes when they spoke, but it never lasted more than a moment.

For approximately the hundredth time that week he reminded himself that it was just as well that Zan had given up her ridiculous infatuation with him. He'd already been tempted into taking advantage of her innocence and had spent many hours bitterly berating himself for his weakness. A man should have strength enough to resist his baser nature, especially when it whispered that all he had ever wanted waited for him in the arms of a Kansas farm girl.

The ladies of the town, led by Mrs. Taylor, had cleaned and decorated the inside of the mill. Some of the crepe paper and bunting would be taken down to be used again tomorrow to dress up the booths and games at the Fourth of July picnic. But for now, they served to hide the essentially functional nature of the building. The smooth threshing floor made a perfect dance floor, lit by a hundred paper lanterns strung on the beams.

Along one wall stood a long table of sawhorses and planks, though the construction was nearly invisible beneath the load of cakes, cookies, and pies it bore. The ladies, both of the town and visitors, hovered by this table, striving to display each goodie to the best advantage and chattering as though they hadn't met in weeks.

At one end of the table Uncle Fred stood by one of two brimming punch bowls, peering into the mixture as if uncertain of what swam in the depths. Carefully he pushed a lighted lantern along the table to a safe distance.

"One of your special brews, Uncle?" Edward asked.

"Something quite new, my boy. And I'm rather leary of it. In deference to the will of the community, this concoction has no alcohol in it. Yet."

"Yet?"

"Low be it spoken, but I have had word that the virgin condition of this brew will not long remain unglorified by the touch of the blissful Hippocrene. Already mysterious flasks have passed from hand to hand. Not a word to the ladies, but I believe that 'treasons, stratagems, and spoils' are plotted."

"How much of the alcohol did you pay for yourself?"

Uncle Fred waggled his eyebrows. "I am the host," he said modestly.

Edward smiled and shook his head. Then, idly, he glanced across the room to the entrance. Uncle Fred said something and laughed. Whatever the joke was, Edward didn't hear it, though he gave his uncle a second polite smile. All his attention fixed upon Zan, standing hesitating in the doorway. He began to walk toward her, drawn by powerful incredulity.

Could this be Zan? Her wild hair had been tamed by a broad ribbon, pulling it smoothly back from her forehead, only to explode in gleaming ringlets that caressed her exposed white shoulders. Her dress, buttoned snugly to her remarkably fine figure, turned her height into an advantage with its straight, unadorned skirt. But her fine feathers alone did not draw every eye her way. Zan's face shown with eagerness and expectancy, transfiguring her into a beauty. To Edward, she seemed the embodiment of youth and joy. He began to walk more quickly, determined to reach her before any other man could come to her side.

He saw her look about her as though searching for someone amidst the crowd of her friends and neighbors. The pang that pierced him at the thought of her seeking for anyone save himself was almost too much to bear with an assumption of calm. Then their eyes met, holding steadily despite the distance between them.

It seemed everyone in the mill paused, not speaking, hardly breathing, as a sweet connection came into being. Certainly the sounds of the revelry faded from Edward's thoughts. Zan seemed surrounded by a bright light, and he could not look away. They moved forward at the same instant.

A sudden influx of young people and an eruption from the two fiddlers and drummer broke the silent suspense in which all but themselves seemed wrapped. Zan was swept away by friends who greeted her mirthfully.

"Hey, no hanging around by the door. Come with me. You got to meet my cousin Zeb," said one apple-cheeked girl, linking arms with Zan.

"Nice to see you, Lena," Zan said. She glanced back at Edward, standing so sternly in the middle of the floor. As folks came out to dance, he turned away. Wondering if she'd only imagined the fervor that had flared in his eyes, she reminded herself that all her advisers had said that making a man wait only increased his eagerness. All the same, she had to struggle to be polite to Lena and her many cousins.

Onto the rough dais constructed at one end of the mill, gaily festooned with red, white, and blue bunting, Mr. Ramsay scrambled up to the cheers of the dancers. He said something to the bull fiddler who turned to his brothers to pass on the great man's request. Mr. Ramsay took a long swig from a jug, his Adam's apple leaping around beneath the fringe of his black beard. With a grin around at the waiting folks, he inflated his lungs and called, "Honor your partner!"

Zan danced with Zeb, with Ernie, with Larry, Harry, and Moe. Even Otto stood up with her, showing surprising grace during "Turkey in the Straw." Though he blushed and tried to leave right after their dance, the farm girls wouldn't let him go, once Zan spread the word that here was a boy who *wouldn't* come down on your toes at every step.

The only dance in which Zan was not sashaying down the line, she spent sitting next to Joseph Taylor. Keeping his injured foot up on a soapbox, he enjoyed the sympathies of half a dozen pretty girls. They competed in bringing him the choicest pickings from the refreshment table, which he accepted with a fine sad air of martyrdom. Zan felt amused, but unneeded.

"Might an old duffer dare ask the belle of the ball for the favor of a dance?" Uncle Fred asked, bowing somewhat stiffly, though with a charming smile.

She turned to him readily, holding out her hand. He alone knew how it trembled. In a low voice she said, "He hasn't even noticed me!"

"Now, now," the older man said, fumbling for his hand-kerchief. "You can't cry here."

"Cry?" She put up her hand to her cheek. "I'm just sweating. This dress is hotter than dungarees in August ever were.

And all our hard work is gone for nothing!"

"I wouldn't say that. You may not have noticed, but that nephew of mine hasn't taken his eyes off you once. If he keeps on scowling that way, he'll never get his brows unknotted again!"

"What?" She turned her head from side to side. "Where?"

"Don't look! You mustn't seem eager. Come, let's dance."

Zan longed to ask more questions, but the band had struck up "Golden Slippers." She'd always liked Mr. Ramsay, for he was a jolly and sociable man, but this evening he seemed to be trying to get her goat. The steps he called were too quick and complicated to allow any breath for speech. She had to be content to search the room when she could, while turning under Uncle Fred's arm or making an allemande left or right with some of the others.

Breathless, she made her final curtsy and turned. Edward stood there, not a foot away. Without a word he took her hand. His fingers were warmer than her own and his eyes held hers. "I believe the next dance is mine, Miss Lind."

"Is it? I mean . . . I should be pleased, Mr. Winchester."

Mr. Ramsay and the band had stopped for a moment, to wipe their streaming faces and sip again from thick stoneware jugs. Panting dancers skipped off to refresh themselves and repair torn flounces and split trousers before the music started again. Zan tried to fill the lull with the sort of idle chatter that Fred had told her ladies used. She strove to pitch her voice low and to remember to round off her vowels.

"Isn't a fine night? I trust you are enjoying yourself, Mr. Winchester," she said, fanning herself with her hand.

"Not very much."

"Perhaps it's not what you're used to. The parties in England must be very fine affairs. I imagine you have been to a very great many of them."

"Why are you talking in that funny voice?"

"What funny voice?" She put her hand to her throat.

"Look . . . do you want to dance or not?"

Zan couldn't stand it. She had worked so hard to make herself into a lady—fine clothes, new manners, a gentle tone that made her throat ache—and he was behaving worse than ever. She met his eyes fully. "No. Frankly, I don't want to dance."

"What do you want to do?"

"I want . . . ." Zan glanced about her. She could see Uncle Fred, Miss Carson, and Faith watching her more or less openly. Her parents were somewhere among the crowd. They were all willing her to behave, to land Edward like a fish after a long struggle armed only with best bait. But she didn't want to land him. She wanted to love him, and be loved in return.

"I want to get out of here," Zan said. "I want to go to the Double B."

"All right. Let's go." His face and voice were grim, not at all like a lover's. However, when she took his arm, she could feel the tension in his body. Her heart began to beat quickly, almost painfully.

She walked with her head high, affecting not to notice as Faith moved to cut them off from the exit. Her sister called her name, and Zan gave her a half smile and a wave but kept on walking. She didn't even stop to collect her bonnet and cape from Faith and Kincaid's buggy. The only reality she acknowledged was the hard muscle and strong bone of Edward's arm linked with her own.

Faith halted, her mouth open in shock and surprise. Zan knew that as soon as Faith recovered, she'd be off to search for their parents. With any luck, she'd be a long time looking.

Outside, the breeze set all the trees to waving like feathered fans. There was little moonlight, but the Milky Way shone down with the fires of a million diamond suns. Edward showed her to a hired buggy and helped her up.

She asked, "How will Uncle Fred get home?"

"He plans to stay in town at the hotel."

"Good."

They spoke little more on the way home. Zan kept her hand pressed against her stays, hoping to quiet the trembling that shook her within whenever Edward looked her way. Something wild seemed to have taken over her spirit. It wasn't fear than made her shake, but an awareness of what was to come.

When he lifted her down from the buggy, she felt his strength and her own weakness. Though she touched ground at once, she clung to his hands. Under the light of the blazing stars, he kissed her, his mouth gentle, but he held her hard against his chest.

"I'll put the horse up," he said when he let her go.

"Maybe you shouldn't."

"Why not?"

"If my folks come looking for us . . . well, you might need to get away in a hurry."

"I think I can manage your parents if they come."

"Even my father?"

"Go inside, Zan, and wait for me."

He was smiling as he chirruped to the hired horse and led him into the barn. Zan went up the porch steps, excitement coursing through her blood. Opening the door, she felt as if she were coming home at last. A lighted lantern stood on the gleaming table, in expectation of a late arrival.

As though she'd done it a hundred times, she walked down the hall to Edward's room. Standing by his dresser, she began to pull the pins from the elaborate hairdressing Lottie and Faith had fashioned for her. She lay the pins in a little china dish that stood on the marble top, just as if it had been put there for her to use in that way. Her fingers went to the two buttons on her collar but she paused before undoing them, knowing he stood in the doorway watching her.

"Promise me you'll never cut your hair."

"I've got to, sometimes, or I'll be like that girl in a tower whose lover . . ." She felt the floorboards jounce under her feet as he crossed the room. "Whose lover had to climb her hair to court her."

His hand ran lightly over the crimped waves of her hair, the silken strands tangling in his callused fingers. "So glorious a ladder," he murmured, a catch in his throat.

She stood passively beneath his touch, suddenly unsure of herself. She'd come this far while shamelessly hoping that *something* would happen—something wonderful. Now, it seemed that all she could see was the bed. Fear flooded her.

Edward touched her cheek, and she shivered, jerking her gaze up to meet his. "Don't be frightened," he said. "Nothing is going to happen that you don't want. Shall we go into the other room? Would you be more comfortable there?"

"It's not the room . . ."

"Me? Zan, you know I'd never do . . . well, I can't say that, can I?" He took a step away from her and smiled ruefully. "Not after what happened in the hayloft. That was very wrong of me. I'm ashamed to say I haven't very much self-control where you are concerned."

"You haven't?"

"You should be shocked, my dear, not pleased."

Under the healing warmth of his smile, Zan's fears dropped away. Giving him a sideways glance, she shook back her head, hearing the rustle and whisper of her hair falling over the soft fabric of her dress. She raised one hand to smooth the hair at her temple. His eyes darkened as his gaze slipped down to her upthrust figure.

"Zan, what are you trying to do to me?"

His thick voice held no amusement now. Zan liked the way he sounded. She turned to face him fully. "If you don't know, I must not be doing it right. Miss Lottie says—"

"Miss Lottie?"

"Never mind." Hesitantly, as if afraid of being burned, she touched his hand. It twisted under hers and caught it. Holding on firmly, he drew her closer.

"What about Miss Lottie?"

"Nothing, only . . . don't you want to kiss me?"

His lips tightened. "Don't you know not to take lessons in love from a whore? Be yourself!"

"All right, then . . . I will!"

Boldly she pressed her lips to his. Her free arm she threw around his neck, dragging his head down. Brazenly she kissed him with the full passion of her love, her mouth moving recklessly across his stunned face.

Then his arms closed about her, and Zan could hardly breathe so tightly did he hold her. They swayed together like trees caught in a sudden storm. The tempest raged out of control, driving them before it.

Zan wrenched his tie loose, flicking free his collar and eagerly unbuttoning his shirt. The crisp hair across his chest teased her fingers. His strangled sigh went right to her knees. If he hadn't had his hands flat against her bustle, she would have fallen. She nipped at his throat and shoulders, unembarrassedly eager. Only all of him would satisfy her now.

Edward realized he'd caught a tiger by the tail. The knowledge thrilled him. How like her, he thought, plunging his hands into the soft, vital masses of her hair. She is always like this, so ready, so audacious . . . He tilted her face and lost himself in the warm magic of her mouth.

CHAPTER
18

Edward put his hands on Zan's shoulders and held her off. Half the buttons down her front were open, both on her dress and on her white underclothes. Had he done that? His gaze dropped to the softly swelling rise of her pale breasts.

"Let's slow down," he said, striving to catch his breath.

"Let's not. . . ."

Zan noticed where his gaze lingered. Her hands on her hips, she swayed slightly side to side, showing off. "I'm impatient," she murmured.

Walking around to the side of the bed, she hitched up her skirt slightly and knelt with one knee on the white counterpane. "So impatient . . ."

Her full lips smiled at him with a humor her passion-darkened eyes belied. Beneath the open placket, her breasts rose and fell to a rhythm of breath as quick as his own.

Edward realized he couldn't refuse what she offered. Nor did he want to. This hesitation was but the last gasp of a drowning man. In a moment he knew he'd be well content to disappear beneath the waves of love she gave so generously. But he couldn't do it under false pretenses. His soul

PASSING FANCY

demanded honesty, even if it brought pain with it.

Deliberately he covered the few steps that separated them. Once again he put his hand on her shoulder, careful to touch only the cloth of her dress. One touch of her silken skin and he wouldn't have enough mind left to speak coherently.

"Oh, Zan," he said helplessly, unsure of how to speak honestly without her misunderstanding.

Her eyes filled with tears. "I know. It's all right."

"What do you know?"

One tear ran down her smooth cheek, and she scorned to wipe it away. "I know you don't love me. It doesn't matter."

Closing her eyes, she turned her face and brushed her lips against his hand. With her fingers curled around his wrist, she tugged gently and drew his hand to the opening of her dress. The soft tip there hardened at his touch. Zan sighed, a mingling of pleasure and sorrow.

Edward couldn't bear it. Suddenly as lightning striking out of a clear summer's sky, his reserve fractured. He felt naked and cold. Zan could save him. He couldn't drown in her love; it would support him and carry him safely to shore.

He wanted to tell her she was wrong—he did love her. He loved her with his whole being for he had never been whole until that moment. Right then, however, it seemed more important to kiss her, to kiss her a thousand times, to take away her tears with a silent promise that there'd be never be any more.

Leaning low, Edward possessed her mouth. At once she responded, rising against him with a glad sob. A fire began to burn inside him, and now he couldn't make himself go slowly. Impetuously he kissed her cheeks, her eyes, returning always to her open lips. Tasting her neck, he relished the shivers that went through her and nipped lightly at her shoulder.

Zan felt new strength ripening inside her. Edward hadn't

247

been repulsed by her weakness. She pushed at the restraining cloth of his shirt and coat. Without breaking the kiss they shared, he shrugged out of his clothes. The heat of his body scorched her hands, yet she touched him again and again, her fingers learning the structure of his muscles.

"You're beautiful," she whispered, not finding the words incongruous.

"No, you are. The most beautiful . . ."

Looking into his eyes, Zan saw that he meant what he said. For the first time in her life, she could believe in her own beauty, feeling no need to compare herself to her sister or anyone else. A warmth filled her that had nothing to do with his hands and lips stroking over her quivering skin. She could only thank him with kisses.

Soon the pale blue dress dropped off the bed onto the floor. Edward paused, stymied by the intricate buttonings and lacings of her lacy white petticoats and combinations. Zan laughed at his puzzled face.

"It's not that complicated."

"No? But it's damnably frustrating."

She pushed on his shoulder and sat up, lifting up her hair. Half turning her back, she said, "Untie the laces and I'll be able to slip out of everything."

"This isn't something men should have to manage. You need little fingers." He snapped the lace in two. "It was knotted," he explained. Then his mouth went dry as Zan stood up, and the lace-embellished linen slid down.

She stood before him clad only in pale white stockings and her shoes. One stocking wrinkled as it fell away from her thigh. Zan smoothed it, her eyes never leaving his. He saw in her blue-gray eyes a cloud of self-doubt. There was only one answer.

The feel of her unclothed body against all of his—the heat and the fragrance that was hers alone—drove him quietly insane. He didn't even remember taking his trousers and boots off. The bedroom, the farm, the knowledge that Mr. Lind was undoubtedly drawing nearer by the second, all retreated to a level of supreme unimportance. He was clasped in Zan's supple arms, finding joy.

Zan offered herself to him willingly, making every effort to give back the pleasure she took from him. Soon, however, she could only grasp his shoulders as quake after quake of desire shook her. He seemed to know how to expose each secret of her body, as his lips closed around the taut peak of her breast. He spanned her waist with his hands, calling excitement into being with the subtlest motion.

Remembering the hayloft, she couldn't savor the delights of his ingenious mouth, though excitement flooded her as he teased and tasted. "Hurry," she sighed. Restlessly tossing her head on the pillow, she reached down and tried to force his hand lower.

"Oh, please, there again," she said when he didn't instantly take her advice.

He raised his head to look at her face. He gave a low chuckle, a sound which surprised her so much under these circumstances that she opened her eyes. "Everything's going to happen just right," he promised. "But you'll enjoy yourself much more if we don't rush things."

"But . . ." What was the use of talking?

Using all her strength, she heaved upward. Taken unawares, Edward couldn't resist. In an instant, he was on his back, crushing the rumpled, heated sheet beneath him. Zan threw her leg over his hips, holding him down.

With a wicked smile she let her gaze drift over his body, followed by her gliding fingertips. The hair on his chest tickled her fingers, and he sucked in his breath as her nails lightly raked his stomach. Then she reached behind her to touch the smoother hair that flourished on his thighs.

The impatience she complained of began to sizzle in his blood. "Do you have any idea of what you're doing to me?"

Zan nodded, her smile fading. She couldn't control the slight tremor that shook her as she daringly brushed over his fervent sex. The softness of his skin there surprised her, even as the hardness that lived beneath it drove her to the brink of desire. With both knees on the bed, she leaned forward to capture his lips. As she did so, his arms came around her and held her strongly in place.

"Wait . . . wait." Edward was almost pleading with her. "You haven't even . . . Let me . . ." He combed down through her tight curls, and his fingers worked magic between her flared thighs.

When she recovered some of her senses, she laughed. "Let me see. I'm now supposed to feel deep shame and gratitude, am I right?" She wiggled her backside provocatively, relishing his groan like a prize.

Edward clasped her hips. "Hold still," he ground out between clenched teeth. "Or I won't be able to control myself."

She kissed him again and whispered, "Who wants you to?"

Audaciously she raised herself up slightly. Rocking back and forth, she felt his body's response. Like wind and rain at a window, his manhood demanded entrance. Like any other force of nature, it would not be denied.

Griping his shoulders, wanting more than anything to give him her love fully, Zan slowly sank downward. Against her will, her body tensed, denying him. "Damn!" she said, trying again.

"Zan . . . stop." Gently he lay her down beside him. "You can't rush these things. Let me show you."

Tremulously she learned all that he could teach her. Yet even as he taught her, she knew he was learning, too. The sweat that glistened on his body, the half-voiced moans he gave, the vibrations that racked him, told her that she was fulfilling his desires even as he brought her secret yearnings to fruition.

"Oh, Zan," he sighed as she opened heavy eyelids. "You're so beautiful . . . I don't think I can wait anymore."

Grindingly slow, he lowered himself over her. Zan ran her hands over his slick back, feeling so very ready. "It's right," she said in a throaty whisper.

"Yes, it will be all right. Raise up, just a . . . that's it. I'll try not to hurt you."

What pain could live in the midst of so much pleasure? Zan clung to him, laughing for pure joy even as she reached the pinnacle of love. And when his control slipped for the final time, the happiness she felt overmastered her. To think that she had satisfied him! That thought, even more than the sensations he aroused, pushed her into reaching another paroxysm.

Afterward, as they lay like two shipwrecked souls, she told him her thought.

"I'm not really that difficult, am I?" he asked, lifting up on his elbows to kiss her flushed face.

"I think I finally know how to handle you." To prove her point, she wiggled beneath him. Edward caught his breath.

"Didn't anyone ever tell you not to play with fire? Besides, it takes a while for a man to recoup himself after love-making."

"Really?" she asked, playfully running the flat of one hand down his back. Reaching the muscle of his rear, she squeezed the tiniest amount. "How long, exactly?"

"How long? I'm not . . ." He raised his eyebrows as he felt a renewed stirring. "Perhaps not so long as all that."

"Hardly any time at all, it seems," Zan said, once more moving eagerly beneath him.

Lydia Browne

And later, lying beside him, listening to him breathing deeply in sleep, she could pretend that he was hers for always. She could not regret giving up her virginity to him, even though she knew he would soon leave her to return to England and the girl who had once thrown him over. Zan hoped Edward would find happiness with her.

As for herself, she had no hope of ever being happier than she was at that moment. Marriage, never more than a remote chance for her, had now become impossible. No other man would want her; she could never want another man.

Realizing that she would dream of Edward for the rest of her life, she fought to stay awake. There would be plenty of time for sleeping later. Now she felt driven to treasure the few moments which were all she had. This hour would be the foundation of all her later dreams, sad though the lonesome waking would be.

Against her will, however, her tired body demanded that she close her eyes. Zan resisted as long as she could. Finally her head sank into the pillow they shared.

"Zan?" Edward whispered. Her only answer was a faintly voiced sigh. He rolled on his side, facing her, admiring her as she slept. From her lustrous hair, tousled now in wild abandon, to her long second toes, he thought her perfect.

"Zan," he said again. "I want to tell you something. I have long felt . . ."

A frown crossed Zan's forehead as a dog's bark penetrated her dream. She danced, as light as dandelion down, all alone in a large room. Mirrors on all the walls reflected her every motion, and the black floor shone as brilliantly as the mirrors. Even as she danced, Zan thought how difficult it must be to keep the floor so clean. A barking dog had no place in such a room. She tried to dance over to the windows to close them to muffle the sound. But the windows never came any closer no matter how much she struggled to reach them.

She awoke fully when Edward left the bed. Propping herself on her elbows, she yawned and asked, "Is something wrong?"

"The dog's barking. Someone's coming."

"My father?"

"I don't know. You should put your dress back on." He'd already drawn on his trousers and was buttoning up his white shirt.

"And you had better light on out of here, Edward. For a couple of days, anyway. This scandal will blow over after a while. You know Harmony. They'll find something else to chew on in a bit."

"I see no reason to run away, Zan."

"Then you can't be looking at me." She tugged the sheet over her bare shoulders.

"Not too mention the fact that I would be a foul coward to 'light out' and leave you behind to face the scandal. A gentleman would never do such a thing."

She wished he'd said "a man in love" rather than a gentleman. If he was determined to do the noble thing, it would be nice if he could do it for her sake, rather than on a point of general principle.

"I'll go out and meet your father," Edward said, stamping his feet down into his boots. "I'm sure we can discuss this reasonably."

Zan scrambled to make herself decent. Edward didn't know how much force Mr. Lind could pack in one of his large hands. Not that her father had ever struck her, but she'd seen how hard he could bring down a hammer.

She ran through the house, still buttoning up the front of her dress. "Papa, don't . . ." she shouted.

Coming to a screeching stop, she saw before her the mild countenances and humble clothing of Reverend and Mrs. Johnson. Rachel Johnson said softly, "I was only just saying to Mr. Winchester, Zan, that we didn't realize we'd be so early. The others must still be at the dance."

"Others?" Zan and Edward said in the same breath.

"Yes. Your uncle did say he'd invited several others. Mrs. Parker, and Mrs. Hastings. Never one without the other. Your sister, Mr. Hutton, and, of course, your parents. I never thought we'd be the first."

"Uncle Fred invited all those folks here?"

"Did he happen to mention the occasion?"

Mrs. Johnson's perpetually worried eyes lightened. "Don't you know? If you don't, then you're the only ones in all of Harmony who don't."

"Rachel . . ." her husband warned in a low, amused voice.

Edward glanced at Zan, who lifted her shoulders in response. Smiling stiffly at the reverend and his wife, Edward said, "Please forgive me for keeping you standing here. Won't you come in? As my uncle was expecting you, I feel confident he has prepared some refreshment."

Zan sat with the Johnsons while Edward went into the kitchen. He seemed gone a very long time. She could feel her smile hardening like plaster as the moments ticked by. "I'll just go and see if I can help," she said, sidling from the room.

"The ladies from the boardinghouse are here!" she declared in a panicked whisper. "And they brought flowers!"

"Flowers?"

"The biggest bouquet I've ever seen."

"That was good of them. Why does it alarm you so?"

"I can think of only two reasons they'd bring flowers. They're either expecting a wedding or . . ."

"Or?"

At her speaking look, comprehension dawned in his eyes. "Don't be anxious." Mildly exasperated, he wrapped his arms about her waist and brought her across two slow steps into his side. "There won't be a funeral tonight."

"No, they'll bury you in the morning. You've never seen my Father riled. I've only seen him *really* mad once in my life, and take my word for it, once is enough. Oh, why didn't you ride out when you had the chance? Acting like a gentleman won't save you from being spread over your own fields."

"In the American parlance, I had other fish to fry. Most delicious fish." He squeezed her waist and put one hand up to smooth her hair back from her creased brow. His dimples very deep, he said, "Your hair is falling down again. You should pin it up, for our guests' sake, not for mine. I love to see it falling wild and free. Especially over me."

"This is no time to talk about hair . . ." The warmth in the sea depths of his eyes made Zan stop and look again. She knew herself to be too wise to believe in dreams come true. Yet, with that look, she could almost believe that Edward felt more for her than simple lust.

"I'd . . . I'd better get back out there. What have you got to give them?"

All the guests arrived before Fred, with the exception of Mr. and Mrs. Lind. Thinking about what her parents would say and do, Zan made a very poor hand of being hostess. The lightest and most innocent words had taken on a whole new meaning, with her knowledge of what went on between a man and a woman. Her face, she felt, was bright enough to light the room without further waste of candles or firewood.

Edward seemed entirely easy, even when Mrs. Hastings made a direct remark about persons who left parties early for obvious illicit reasons. He merely leaned forward, fixing her with a steely look, and asked, "To whom—precisely— are you referring?"

Self-assured, Mrs. Hastings drew up her bony frame to deliver a scathing reply. It never passed her lips. Just then, the door opened and Uncle Fred said over his shoulder to someone in the yard, "It's all right. They're here."

He entered, smiling and nodding genially at the assortment of guests he'd called together. "Now don't be alarmed, anyone. You'll soon return to the party. 'Come unto these yellow sands, and then take hands. Curtsied when you have and kissed the wild waves whist, foot it featly here and there.' "

He snapped his fingers and giddily tore off a few light dance steps. Zan had little attention to spare for his antics, however. She stared at her shoes, too abashed to meet her parents' eyes for more than an instant. Though unable to regret what had happened between Edward and herself, she had imagination enough to look at her actions the way her parents would.

Mr. and Mrs. Lind stood in the doorway, their expressions as grave as in their wedding daguerreotype. Then Mrs. Lind saw the reverend and her eyes lightened. "It will be all right now," she said to her husband, patting his broad arm. "No one will worry about what they've done if they get married the same day."

"Married!" Zan reared back as though she'd seen a snake in her path.

Reverend Johnson said in some confusion, "That's why we're here. Mr. Winchester asked that I come prepared to perform a marriage ceremony."

For a moment hope leaped up in Zan's heart like a bright flame against the night sky. Then she realized the reverend meant the older Mr. Winchester, not the younger. She turned to Uncle Fred.

"So," she said, her eyes hard. "You've finally decided which of 'em you'll take. I bet it's Miss Maisie."

"What!" Mrs. Hastings sat bolt upright. "You want to . . . You never said anything!"

"The young lady's mistaken," Fred said quickly. He looked

to Zan like a buffalo who hears the howling of hunting wolves coming his way. She hated to be the one to hurl him into the snapping jaws of matrimony, but better he be sacrificed than Edward feel in any way forced to marry her. Trapping him that way had never been her plan. She refused to accept Edward as his uncle's gift to her, no matter how kindly meant.

"Stands to reason she's wrong," Miss Minnie said. "Girl's addlepated from love. Told her so when she came to us for help. Turn her into a lady so she can catch her man. . . ."

Faith added her two cents. "She would have done very well if she hadn't listened to Miss Lottie. That woman would corrupt a saint! My little sister—"

"Now, Faith," Kincaid said, trying to calm her.

Everyone began talking at once. Zan had seen less confusion in the hen-yard with a weasel's scent blowing breast-high. She did not dare look at Edward. What must he be thinking?

He tapped her shoulder, his forefinger hard and demanding. Fearfully she turned to face him. His jaw set, his gray eyes showed no trace of sympathy. "Does the entire community know that you set out to seduce me this evening? Or did you only tell the people in this room?"

"They all helped me when I asked them to. I only wanted to please you by acting like a lady—for once."

"I am sorry to inform you, Miss Lind, that ladies do not usually act as you have this evening. Nor do they announce to the world that they intend to snare the man of their choice into matrimony. Snipe hunts are nothing compared to it!"

He cast a glance around the room. Not even the ladies from the boardinghouse could meet his eyes. Reverend Johnson muttered, "I thought it was agreed between you. It never occurred to me . . ."

Uncle Fred stepped forward. "You mustn't blame Zan, my

boy. She didn't know I'd asked the Reverend here to perform the rite. The assumption was mine that, once you understood your own heart, naturally you'd wish to marry her without delay."

"You are too kind, Uncle," Edward said with great civility. Icicles would have found his tone too cold for comfort. "But in future I would prefer that you leave my life to my own designing. And pardon me if I choose not to request your counsel as to my marital plans. Nor, indeed, to ask for the recommendations of the persons gathered here tonight."

He started toward the door, his head high. But Mr. Lind stood in his way. He put his large, blunt-fingered hand, dark from long contention with the stubborn earth, in the center of Edward's chest. Edward glanced down at it with less alarm than astonishment.

Mr. Lind said, "Just a minute, here. You talk mighty proud, but there's still Zan. What do you mean to do about her?"

"Yes!" Faith crossed the room to put her arm about her sister. "You can't just walk out after . . . after . . . well, after what you did! A gentleman . . ."

Zan shook off Faith's caring but binding arm. "It's all right, Father," she said, walking up to the two men she loved most in all the world.

Mr. Lind's bright blue eyes transfixed her. "You want to marry him, I will see to it you do."

"But I don't want to marry him."

Edward and Mr. Lind said, "What?" in the same breath. Almost immediately the others echoed them. Only Mrs. Lind was silent. Zan did not see any disgust or reproach in her mother's look. On the contrary, a gleam of pride shone in the eyes that were no less blue at that moment than her husband's.

Taking strength from that look, Zan said, "What I did was not to trap you, or make you feel you have to marry me or

258

even to make you feel you *want* to marry me. It was . . ."

"Because you don't want to marry Quintus?" her father asked with a glum shake of his big head. "It would have been good to have my old friend's son in my family, but I wouldn't have made you do it. I thought . . . if you liked each other when you are meeting, why not?"

Zan patted her father's arm. "Quintus has nothing to do with it. There are a lot of nice girls in Harmony. He's sure to find one who suits him better than I ever would. Maybe Mr. Grasse's daughter would marry him. Even a stranger's got to be better company than her old man."

Uncle Fred said, "This Quintus fellow aside, why did you want so much to please my nephew? I certainly thought you were hoping he'd decide he loved you too well ever to go back to England."

"That's what I thought," Faith said.

"The gossip I heard seemed awfully clear," Mrs. Johnson put in, with an apologetic glance at her husband.

Looking around at her friends, Zan smiled sadly. "I don't think I'll ever get married, even if a feller could be found who'd want me after this gets out. I've never been like other girls. I didn't dream about a husband, a house and . . . children of my own."

Tears drowned her sight for a moment. Despite her tomboy ways, she'd always liked babies. She liked the way their tiny bodies lay so compactly and trustingly in even a stranger's arms while their brilliant eyes took in every detail of her face. Zan knew now that she was destined never to have any, but would be a stranger to babies all her life.

Swallowing down the peach pit that had appeared in her throat, Zan said, "My dreams were always of owning my own corner of land and of making it green and worthy. I went to work for Edward and Uncle Fred to earn the money I needed to make my dreams happen."

She stole a glance at Edward, who stood as stiffly as a picket fence post with a face that showed no more feeling than the post. His eyes were so tightly closed, it was as if he were trying to block out more than the sight of her. As if shutting out one sense would remove her from the knowledge of all his others.

Softly Zan added, "I never expected to fall in love."

Edward's eyes remained closed.

"In love?" Mrs. Parker asked. "Are you in love with *him*?"

A flicker passed over Edward's unemotional face at the woman's skepticism. In spite of herself Zan laughed. "Of course I am. Did you think I was just a bad girl?"

"Well, you have been spending an awful lot of time with that dreadful Miss Lottie. It's only natural to think that her wicked ways rubbed off on you. You've always been such a quiet, steady girl . . . utterly reliable, I would have said before this."

"Shows how much you know," her sister muttered, jabbing Mrs. Parker in the midriff with one of her angular elbows.

Zan stole another glance at Edward's cold, sealed face. "Well, anyway," she continued, with an inward conviction that she could talk to doomsday and Edward would remain unconvinced and—what was worse—indifferent. Their bodies might meet and enjoy the encounter, but their souls could never meet now.

"So I just want to make it as plain as I can that I never had any intention of . . . of . . . oh, what's the use?"

Abruptly she jerked around to stand toe to toe with him. Grabbing him by the arms, she gave him as strong a shake as she could. Though her muscles were built by hard work, she hardly budged Edward. For an instant he opened one eye. Zan addressed herself to that single hint that he might be listening.

"What am I doing? I've never begged for anything in my

life! If your gal in England is going to make you happy, go on and get her. What are you bothering with me for? Why did you ever come to Kansas if everything you want is back home? Just money? There must be better and easier ways of making it."

"It . . . wasn't money," he said slowly. "I thought it was at first, but now I see . . ." The words faltered. Zan held her breath, but he said nothing further.

"So go on," she repeated, hoping an outburst would work a second time. He was so close to making up his mind to stay, so very close she could feel it. "Go on back to your *lady* and spend the rest of your life in a cold city and a cold bed."

"Zan!" Faith said in a choked voice.

"I'll get along okay." She couldn't help adding, "But I think you're an awful fool to let me get away."

Edward stared at her. Slowly, as though it came painfully, the first presage of his soul-dazzling smile began to appear. Zan waited, an uncontrollable trembling fluttering her stomach. If he could only see past his hard, galling pride . . .

"*Well!*" Mrs. Hastings's flat, nasal voice cut across the silence that swelled between Zan and Edward like a promising bud. His smile died. "If this is how you Winchester men treat women, trifling with their affections and then . . . then . . ."

"Tossing them aside like a soiled glove," Mrs. Parker said helpfully.

"Yes, tossing her aside like a soiled glove, then I wouldn't let my sister marry you, Fred Winchester, if you were the last single man in Kansas!"

"Neither would I," Mrs. Parker added, buttoning her gloves with decision.

They exchanged a glance that said even they didn't believe their agreement. Nodding at their neighbors, they swept out past the Winchesters and the Linds as though to brush either group with the hems of their dresses would be degradation. Zan had no hope that the full tale of her wicked ways would be kept from the rest of the town.

With the same thought obviously in her head, Faith trotted out after the women. "Miss Minnie, Miss Maisie! Wait, I want to . . . please . . ."

Kincaid shrugged and followed his wife, turning on the doorstep to say, "Uh, good night, everyone. Had a really good time, Fred, until . . . uh, good night."

The Reverend stepped forward, his long-fingered hands twisting nervously. "If I can be of assistance, Mr. Winchester . . . Perhaps prayer would help you see the right path."

Edward's smile was a twisted, deformed caricature of itself. "I rather doubt—" he began.

"Oh, no, Mr. Johnson," Zan broke in bitterly. The moment when they might find a common ground was past. Suddenly the air in Edward's home gagged her. "His Lordship is much too stuck-up to ask God for anything, even for the things he already has."

Meeting her mother's eyes, she asked, "Couldn't we go home now, please?"

"Whenever you like." She reached out and Zan walked into the welcoming curve of Mrs. Lind's arm. "And you are wrong, Mr. Winchester. But you are a man and so will not admit it. No, husband. We want no men now. Come, Zan."

Without glancing back at Edward, though she very much wanted to, Zan let herself be taken from the room. Her limbs were heavy and tired as she stepped up into her parents' wagon. Seven-year-old Gary, a chocolate ring about his mouth, was fast asleep.

"I'm sorry, Mother."

"Sorry? And for why?"

"Edward and I . . . what we did . . . I suppose it's disgraceful?"

"I trust you, Zan." Mrs. Lind chirruped to the horses. When they started, they all but jerked her down from the flat board seat.

"Let me, Mother," Zan said, taking the reins. She laced the reins through her fingers without thinking about it. The muscles in her arms controlled the horse perfectly. Yet beside her tiny mother, she felt as if Mrs. Lind had more strength than she would ever possess.

"I don't see how you can trust me now. I made nothing but mistakes tonight. I've been making mistakes all along. I should have waited for Quintus."

"Is 'I' all you can say?" She tucked in the corners of her mouth in disapproval as Zan glanced at her without understanding. "You say 'I did this' and 'I should have done that.' You should be thinking of Edward. I like him. Your father will like him, after they fight."

"Fight!"

"Oh, yes. Your father is most likely taking off his coat right now. If he tears it, he had better not come home."

Zan pulled on the reins. "We have to go back!"

"No, let them alone. Sometimes men think better with their fists." Mrs. Lind patted her daughter's hands. "Drive on."

"But I can't let Father hurt him. And besides, I don't want him if he has to be beaten into marrying me. I only want him if he wants me. And he doesn't."

"Men are not like you and I. They are stubborn and need to be convinced that they should be married. If it were left to them, no child would know his father's name." Mrs. Lind nodded with conviction. "He will marry you, and for love. It is very silly to say he doesn't love you."

"No, Mother, I'm sure he doesn't." The thought alone was enough to break her heart. That the thought was true shattered it. She felt the bits drop from within her breast like jagged pieces of ice, rending her soul.

CHAPTER
19

Mrs. Lind had no sooner stepped down from the wagon than she said, "Hurry now, Zan. Take Gary to his room and then out of your dress. I'll draw you a bath."

"A bath? I had one before the party. Besides, I just want to go up and have a lie down." And a good cry, she added mentally, her shoulders slumping.

"No, you must have a bath. Too bad there isn't time to wash your hair, too. You want to be sweet and fresh when Mr. Winchester arrives."

Mrs. Lind tapped up the stairs and into her house. Wearily Zan lifted her sleeping brother into her arms and followed. Leaning backward against Gary's weight, she said, "Mother, Edward isn't coming. He made it pretty plain he never wants to see me again. He thinks I'm trying to trap him."

Turning up the lamp, Mrs. Lind drew the long hatpin from the nest of feathers that was her Sunday hat. "Do as I ask you, please. Take Gary up to bed. Then out of your dress and into the tub."

"Mother, did you hear . . . ?"

Blue eyes met gray. Zan still saw pride in her mother's

glance, though mingled now with aggravation. "You cannot meet your future husband while so upset. A man wants a calm woman to spend his life with, someone neat and practical. There is nothing like a cool bath to calm you. This way you will be ready to say 'Yes, Edward,' when he comes."

"How do you know he'll come here and ask me . . . that."

Mrs. Lind pressed her fingers to her forehead and shook her head. "Of course he will. He can't fight it. Love is much too strong a thing."

Zan hefted her brother, resettling him. "You really think—"

"What's going on?" Gary asked sleepily.

"Nothing, *min barn*. Sleep." Mrs. Lind pointed toward the ceiling, nodding at Zan.

Zan carried her brother from the room. On the doorstep she paused. "I was a fool, Mother. If I wanted to learn how to be a lady, I could have saved everyone a lot of trouble by coming to you first."

Mrs. Lind smiled as softly and wisely as the divinity of all mothers. "Certainly you should have. What did you think?"

But as the minutes pooled into hours, even her mother's optimism wasn't enough to sustain her hopes. Each sound drove her to peer out the door, into the yard, dimly lit by the stars. The dim forms of the trees and buildings fooled her eyes into thinking she saw motion. Always, however, she turned back, disappointed and despairing.

A turn of the door handle brought her out from her chair. Ben and Sarah jerked around and stared to see her spring upright. "Hey," Ben said, giving her half a smile. "You're home."

"That's right. What on earth happened to you two?"

Ben wiped blood away from under his nose, rubbing his hand afterward on his torn pants. "Nothing."

"Nothing," Sarah echoed. She tugged her ripped sleeve up over her exposed shoulder. "Uh, I kind of fell down."

"Fell down? On top of who?" The two children smiled at that, Ben's mouth lopsided and swollen. "Who were you fighting with, and why?"

They glanced warily at each other. Sarah opened her mouth and was about to speak when Mrs. Lind came in from the kitchen. "Goodness gracious! Zan, draw more water! Two more baths tonight!"

As she went out to the well, the groans of her siblings in her ears, Zan thought she didn't really need to ask why they'd been fighting. Ben's surprise at seeing her at home told her the reason. Obviously the rumors of her shameful behavior had already begun to circulate among the small fry. It warmed her heart to realize that Ben and Sarah thought enough of her to defend her honor tooth and nail.

Yet she ached to think of their future. How could Sarah say no to some audacious boy and be taken seriously? Everyone would know that her older sister hadn't any morality and would assume Sarah was cut from the same cloth.

Working the water up, Zan kept her white Sunday dress out of the mud around the pump. If only she could have kept her name as spotless! She knew she must face facts. Even if she could brazen it out, and she knew in her heart she could, there was still her family to think of. She couldn't condemn them to a life of sneers and whispers. Better she should disappear, making it look as if they'd cast her out.

She could still hear Ben and Sarah complaining in the other room and her mother's soft answers. Quickly Zan slipped up the back stairs. Fumbling with the tie of her sash, she recalled breaking the strings for Edward earlier in the evening. It was all she could do to keep from falling apart.

Once more in the comfort of her dungarees, Zan sat down to scribble a note to her parents. She dared not think too deeply about what she wrote for fear her heart would break anew.

PASSING FANCY

I'm going West. Forget about me and try to get on with your lives. Love always, Zan. She scratched out the nickname and signed her name in full.

Putting what little money she had in her pocket, she took one last glance around the room where she'd spent a girlhood that would never come again. Biting her lip, she gave a pat to the coverlet her mother had made. She straightened the rug she and Faith had spent a whole winter working on.

When the room was as neat as she could make it, Zan dropped her small bundle of dress and shoes out the window, hearing it fall with a slight thump. Then she slipped out after it and scrambled down the trunk of the tree that grew against the side of the house.

Stooping low to be less conspicuous, Zan ran across the yard. The light in the front window seemed unutterably dear and terribly far off. She vowed to carry that light in her heart, for it would forever mean her family to her.

Though this evening had brought her a world of trouble and heartbreak, Zan couldn't regret giving Edward her love. All the dreams she'd known in her room, even the tender dreams she had kept secret even from herself, had come true in his arms for one solitary moment. It would be enough to last her a lifetime. It would have to be enough.

Trying to look upon leaving Harmony as a great adventure, Zan worked to put some spring into her step as she started down the drive. After all, she was free! She could go where she liked and do whatever pleased her. But where and what was that? And how was she to get there?

Zan paused, struck by the enormity of what she had to decide. Whatever she settled on now would determine the course of her life for a long time.

Her father kept most of her money locked in his desk for safekeeping. The fifteen dollars she had on her could be made to last a long time, if she was careful. It wouldn't buy her a

267

horse, but a person could travel a long way on the railway for even half that. However, with Mary manning the depot, Zan knew she'd be stopped before she could catch a westbound train. Therefore, the only thing to do was to walk to the next town up the line and catch a train from there.

With that much of her future decided, Zan started forward. But she felt a check on her right leg. "Gulbrun!"

The fawn-and-black dog looked up, his eyes glinting in the starlight. He held her pants leg in his teeth. When she tried to take a step, the dog dug in his forepaws and braced his powerful legs. He didn't growl, merely stood fast.

"I have to go," she said, almost losing her balance.

The brows twitched together over the uncomprehending brown eyes. Zan felt Gulbrun wanted to understand, but they could neither of them reach across the narrow but fathomless gap between dear friends separated by their species. Zan squatted down to pat the smooth square head and to fondle an appreciative ear.

"Dogs have got it easy," she said after a sigh. The dog's long tail thumped on the ground but he didn't let go. "As long as you stay off the furniture and don't chase the hens, nobody cares what you do. I wish I was a dog, or anything but a girl."

After another few minutes of petting, she tried to stand up. Gulbrun clamped down again on her pants leg. "You've got to let me go. Come on, Gulbrun."

She insinuated a finger between the pointed teeth at one side of his muzzle. "Let go. It's all right."

The dog opened his mouth. Dropping down on his belly, he stared as Zan walked away. His ears twitched up when she paused to look back. He rose up, in the way of powerfully built dogs, as though drawn up by the shoulders rather than pushed up from the legs.

Zan could feel his longing to come, too, to dash off after

her as though they were going hunting or on a jaunt into town. He'd follow her for the fun of it and for the love of her, no matter how long a journey it turned out to be. All she had to do was ask. She wanted to ask, for already she was lonely.

"No, Gulbrun. You stay. Stay till Father comes. Good dog." He dropped once more onto his belly. Zan could feel his eyes on her back as she continued down the lane.

Miserable, she let her feet carry her where they would. Trudging along, she wished she'd taken a few more moments to think before setting off. Tiredness throbbed in her bones with a dull ache. Perhaps she should go back, get a good night's rest, and then set off at first light.

Zan shook her head. Her decision was made; she wouldn't go through the struggle again. She'd walk as far as she could get tonight and then hole up somewhere till morning.

After about half an hour of walking in the dark, Zan made a new decision. It wasn't that she minded the dark. After all, she'd been getting up before the sun for years. But whether from being unaccustomed to dancing or the demands of the other exercises she'd met with this night, Zan felt strange pangs and twinges in her lower body. They slowed her down and made her walk sort of lopsided.

The farm she'd wanted so much to buy, the Beakman Place, was only a few more minutes walk up the main road and then a ways back on its own drive. When she'd first surveyed the place, she'd seen an old davenport in the parlor. No one would mind if she dossed down there for the night. After all, the place had almost been hers. Zan reminded herself that she no longer cared what other people thought.

All the same, she felt a little hesitant about trespassing. However, the thought of that davenport, becoming more and more luxurious a memory as she tramped on, broke down her scruples. The house was a dark hulk between the shade trees that grew on either end.

She pushed the hanging door farther open, shuddering a little as the hinges creaked. Closing her eyes, she waited until they adjusted to the dim light that made the windows only just distinguishable from the darkness within. Half-crouched, she waved her hands before her, fumbling like a blind woman.

She stumbled over the davenport, barking her knee. Glad to find it even at the cost of some pain, Zan patted the cushion, the once soft plush a luxury as threadbare as a century-old fashion. Picking up the bolster, her fingers slipped into a ragged hole, filled with shredded cloth. The mice that had made a nest there had vacated long ago.

The davenport smelled of dust but nothing worse. In her present state of mind, it seemed like a cheerful and comfortable place to sleep. The future might not hold many beds as pleasant.

She'd hardly stretched out when she realized she'd better go behind the barn before she dossed down. On her return, she thought she saw a gleam of light flickering between the boards of the barn wall. Stopping, she stared, trying tell if it was real or if her eyes were playing tricks. Strange red circles floated before her vision, and she blinked to clear it.

Something inside fell over with a muffled crash. Zan froze. A wild animal might have wandered into the huge barn, maybe a skunk or raccoon, maybe rabid. Another rattling fall and she jumped.

"Damn."

The monosyllable was sharp and unmistakably British in tone. Zan nearly laughed, from relief and joy. What was Edward doing here?

Sneaking quickly around the corner, she peered through the window. The lantern's glow came from between two horse boxes. It burned steadily, confirming her impression that the barn had been better built and kept than the house. It also showed her that the barn was empty.

A hand clutched her shoulder.

"Yi!" Zan yelped, nearly jumping out of her skin. Spinning around, she shouted, "Are you crazy?"

"You ought to know," Edward answered, his white teeth showing. Putting his hands on the wall to either side of her face, he leaned forward, pressing her backward. "You've driven me mad from the moment we met."

"What are you doing here?" she asked. Her voice came out soft and breathy, alien to her ears. She had meant to make demands, and to let him know in no uncertain way how much she resented his not claiming her for his own.

He brushed a kiss over her lips. Her traitorous knees began to tremble. The power he had over her body had not lessened when he'd broken her heart. Retreating, she found her back to the wall. Edward kissed her again, with more energy, his mouth warm and firm.

"Why . . . ?" she began. Then her arms slipped around his neck and she raised her face. Even though she knew he couldn't feel the promises they exchanged every time their lips met, she couldn't resist them. Lies so sweet deserved to be believed, she thought as he gathered her into his arms.

"There's . . . there's a sofa in the house," Zan whispered when he began to nibble on her neck.

"Really?" He didn't seem to be listening.

"You know . . . somewhere we can . . . lie down?"

His chuckle rumbled through them both. He rested his forehead against hers, so that all she could see were his eyes. "You are the most remarkable woman, Zan Lind. Such a maddening combination of desirability and disturbance. How you can manage to intrigue me and beleaguer me all in one moment . . ."

"At least you're not bored."

"No," he said, sobering. "Never that. And that is why . . ." He moved back to the length of his arms, fixing her with a serious gaze.

Suddenly nervous, Zan asked, "What are you doing here, anyway?"

"I was about to ask you that."

"Um, I figured I'd just come and look the place over. Haven't been down here in a while, and I'd still like to own it one of these long-come-shorts."

"And what is this?" He poked the bundle she'd dropped with the point of his boot. "Do you always carry a change of wardrobe when you investigate a property?"

"All right," Zan said, ducking from under his arm. Standing free, she tossed up her head. "I was running away. I thought it over and figure it's best if I just up and clear out of Harmony."

"Better for whom, may I inquire?"

"For everybody. My folks, my brothers and sisters, everybody. After all, you'll . . . never mind."

"I'm going back to England soon." The dead, matter-of-fact tone filled her with despair.

"That's right."

"Leaving you here alone to face the censure of your neighbors."

"Well, it's nothing to do with you. Is it?" Try as she might, she couldn't keep the last dying flicker of hope from her voice.

Zan had never seen Edward move with such striking speed. He grabbed her arms and jerked her against the hardness of his chest. His kiss scoured her, leaving her weak and breathless, clinging to him as though to a spar in the storm-tossed sea.

"Good God! What have you been thinking of?" he demanded roughly. No air of gentility clung to him now.

Not even their lovemaking had done so much to reveal him as a man.

He rasped, "You're in my blood and bones. Every moment I think of you. You come between me and my books, me and my sleep! I lie there every night thinking of you, remembering how you look plowing a field, sowing seeds, or just standing there, the wind tugging your hair free. Do you know when the sun is setting, you're like a statue formed from pure gold? I want to see all of you in the sunlight, the moonlight, lantern light, and candlelight. I want—"

Zan clutched her burning face. "Stop! Lord . . ." Her ears felt scorched.

"Stop? I've hardly begun." This kiss was gentler, but no less possessive. "You're mine," he whispered against her temple.

"But England . . . ?"

"We'll go there together."

Zan longed just to cling to him. If only she could silence the doubts that mocked her dreams. They were too loud and too insistent.

"I can't go," she murmured. He didn't answer. More loudly, she repeated it. "I can't go to England."

"Of course you can."

"No. I've got too much to do here. There are all those trees I've been meaning to plant."

His arms tightened about her. "If it's the trip, I promise it will be as comfortable as I can contrive it. The ships are like floating palaces with every amenity, and the journey is swift now that steam has replaced sail."

"It's not the trip. And it isn't really the trees."

"Then what?" He released her. She didn't need to see his face to feel his puzzlement and exasperation.

Trying to make it clear even to herself, Zan said slowly, "This is where I belong. I was wrong to try to leave it. I could never live over there. And as for being your lady-friend while you're married to what's-her-name—"

"My good girl! Where did you get such a preposterous idea? If that is the sort of thing Miss Lottie has been filling your head with, then I'm going to put my foot down on that association."

"You are going to marry that gal, aren't you?"

"Certainly not! I fell out of love with Nerissa months ago. I didn't know it, though, until you walked into my cornfield."

"Until I . . . ?"

"Good God, Zan, do you really not know that we're to be married?"

"We? Meaning you and me?"

"Of course. Don't be so obtuse." His smile lingered on his lips as he kissed her. Zan had to bend her own to match it. When he lifted his head, she was still smiling.

"You sure took your time, Your Lordship!"

"Don't—"

"But I like to. You are lordly, you know. I mean it in a good way. You've got ideas and book-learning. You won't ever make a farmer, though."

"I've been thinking about that. Come along." Edward took her hand and lead her into the barn. The lantern light glinted along the floor, striking gold from the bits of straw still littering the floor. Zan had inspected the barn before, when she'd looked into buying the farm. Beakman had built a barn far too large for his needs, being a man with big dreams. That he was selling to her showed the folly of building before a dream came true.

"I think you are quite right about my not ever being a more than mediocre farmer."

"Not that I think less of you for it. Some folks just have a natural knack for it; some don't."

"Don't worry, Zan. My feelings aren't hurt. I have no knack for farming, true, but I might have one for horse-breeding."

"Horse breeding?"

"I've been looking into the matter. There's a deal of room for improvement in America's bloodstock. I want to bring in fresh strains from England and Europe. Mate their fine qualities with the stamina and courage of the American breeds, and you'd have a horse that I believe would be unbeatable, both for work and speed."

He looked into her face as though willing her to see what he so obviously saw. The force of his vision was so strong that for a moment, dim and insubstantial, she could see the barn transformed into a stable. From each box looked out a narrow, sensitive face. She could hear the low whickerings and stamping of hooves, and almost smell the manure.

"You don't have to convince me," Zan said, slipping her hand into his. "It's what you were born to do."

"I think, you know, it may be."

"It'll be expensive to get started."

"That won't be a problem. My father may not approve of Kansas, but he most definitely approves of horses. He'll approve of you, too. That's why you have to come with me to England in the autumn. My family must meet my wife."

Zan smiled shyly. "Won't he think you're taking your breeding plan a little too far?"

Edward laughed and Zan joined him. It seemed a good beginning to laugh here in a place where their dreams would grow together. She didn't tell him, but she saw more than horses here. She saw children, all with brilliant red-gold hair and pleasingly aristocratic faces. The vision filled her with serene confidence.

"While we're over there for our honeymoon, I'll select some breeding stock. Suffolk has some excellent coach studs. We'll start with coach horses, light and swift, I think. There are plenty of good Shire breeders in America already, although we may go into that line later."

"Um, Edward . . . ?"

"But I feel there's a tremendous untapped demand for swift coach horses. You saw how fascinated everyone was with our race. And Mr. Taylor spent far too much for his animal, in my opinion."

"Edward?" She tapped him on the shoulder.

"Yes, my dear?"

"I wonder if we could talk more about this inside."

"Inside? The house?"

"The house, too." Zan blushed when comprehension dawned in his eyes.

About two hours later Mrs. Johnson poked her sleeping husband in the back ribs. "Abe? Abe!"

He grunted sleepily and rolled over. "Not now, Rachel."

"I heard someone knocking. You'd better get up. Old Mrs. Wisart might be going at last."

Abe Johnson would have been the first to admit that he wasn't very quick-witted in the middle of the night. Zan and Edward had to tell him three times that they wanted to be married right away.

"But what about your family, Zan? They should be here. And it will only take a few minutes for someone to go and bring them." He yawned widely enough to show all his back teeth. "Better yet, wait till morning."

"Not another hour," Edward said firmly. "We want to be married immediately."

"Ah, to stop the rumors," Reverend Johnson said, his brain finally stirring.

"What rumors?" Edward asked. "We want to be married

immediately because we are too much in love to wait."

"Is that how you feel, too, Zan?"

Zan stood within the curve of Edward's arm, feeling safe and very much loved. "I wish you'd hurry, Reverend. We've got seeds to plant tomorrow."

If you enjoyed this book, take advantage of this special offer.
Subscribe now and get a

FREE
Historical
Romance

No Obligation (a $4.50 value)

Each month the editors of True Value select the four *very best* novels from America's leading publishers of romantic fiction. Preview them in your home *Free* for 10 days. With the first four books you receive, we'll send you a FREE book as our introductory gift. No Obligation!

If for any reason you decide not to keep them, just return them and owe nothing. If you like them as much as we think you will, you'll pay just $4.00 each and save at *least* $.50 each off the cover price. (Your savings are *guaranteed* to be at least $2.00 each month.) There is NO postage and handling – or other hidden charges. There are no minimum number of books to buy and you may cancel at any time.

Send in the Coupon Below

To get your FREE historical romance fill out the coupon below and mail it today. As soon as we receive it we'll send you your FREE Book along with your first month's selections.

A TOWN CALLED
HARMONY

PASSING FANCY

Lydia Browne

DIAMOND BOOKS, NEW YORK

This book is a Diamond original edition,
and has never been previously published.

PASSING FANCY

A Diamond Book / published by arrangement with
the author

PRINTING HISTORY
Diamond edition / October 1994

All rights reserved.
Copyright © 1994 by Charter Communications, Inc.
This book may not be reproduced in whole or in part,
by mimeograph or any other means, without permission.
For information address: The Berkley Publishing Group,
200 Madison Avenue, New York, NY 10016.

ISBN: 0-7865-0046-8

Diamond Books are published by The Berkley Publishing Group,
200 Madison Avenue, New York, NY 10016.
DIAMOND and the "D" design
are trademarks belonging to Charter Communications, Inc.

PRINTED IN THE UNITED STATES OF AMERICA

10 9 8 7 6 5 4 3 2 1